I hope you feel
the love in
every page!

HELLO DOCTOR

KELSIE HOSS

kh

Editing by Tricia Harden of Emerald Eyes Editing.

Proofreading by Christina Herrera.

Cover design by Najla Qamber of Najla Qamber Designs.

Have questions? Email kelsie@kelsiehoss.com.

Readers can visit kelsiehoss.com/sensitive to learn about potentially triggering content.

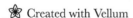 Created with Vellum

For the HALO Project in Oklahoma City. Thank you for changing our family's life.

CONTENTS

1

LIV

I tried to act like my life wasn't falling apart as I walked into the Cottonwood Falls doctor's office. I'd been going there to see Doctor Deb since I was a baby, and she'd treated me for everything from measles to HPV.

Unfortunately, I didn't know how long it would be until I saw her again because losing my job also meant my health insurance would run out this month. Lucky me.

Nurse Brenda smiled at me from her desk in the waiting area—it was really the living room of a four-bedroom house that was converted into a practice years ago, with antique drapery and hardwood floors that had seen more feet over the years than the boot shop in the next town over.

"How's it going, Liv?" she asked with a sympathetic look.

Perks of living in Smalltown, USA? Everyone knows your business before you do.

"I'm glad to be out of there," I admitted. "I loved working at the feed yard, but it was time to go." More like

I couldn't handle the new, pigheaded manager a second longer. He acted more like an animal than the cattle we were caring for, and I couldn't deal with it anymore. "The only thing that sucks is losing company housing. I'm staying with my parents while I look for something new."

"I bet your parents love having you around." Brenda smiled, reaching into her desk for a clipboard and paperwork. "Any idea what you're doing next?"

"Not a clue." I took the board from her, glancing at the form. "I figured I should get my yearly exam in before I don't have insurance anymore."

"Smart." Brenda winked, making her flawless skin crease. She had to be in her fifties at this point, but I swore we looked the same age. "Go ahead and fill that out, and then I'll bring you back to the room."

I headed to the empty waiting area, sitting in a cushy chair and filling out the form, including my endometriosis and PCOS diagnosis like I did every time, then brought the board back. Brenda took it, walking with me to one of three exam rooms. I could hear murmurs coming from the other office. Deb was busy with another patient.

After taking my vitals, Brenda told me to undress and get comfortable on the table for my pap. "Shouldn't be much longer."

"Thanks." I smiled and waited until the door was shut to undress. With all my clothes off, I put the sheet over myself and lay back on the table, scrolling through a job board on my phone. But the longer I looked, the sadder I felt.

Every open position that matched my skills and paid enough to support myself was more than an hour away from Cottonwood Falls. I closed my eyes and put my arm over my face, fighting back tears.

Most people hated the small town they grew up in and couldn't wait to get away, but for all its flaws and quirks, I loved living here. My brother and sister-in-law lived right in town. My other brother lived ten minutes outside of the city limits. And my oldest brother, who just got married to a single mom, giving me three new nieces and nephews, was just a couple hours away in Dallas. Not to mention I had dinner every Wednesday with my parents.

I knew who did my hair every other month. Where I could go for a good burger and fries. Who to call if I needed a plumber or an electrician. And my two best friends lived here. I didn't want to leave.

I *really* didn't want to leave.

But it was starting to look like I didn't have another choice.

A knock sounded on the door, and I hurriedly wiped my eyes so Doctor Deb wouldn't see me crying and ask me too many questions.

But instead of Deb, the most handsome man I'd ever laid eyes on walked into the room wearing a white doctor's coat. I almost fell off the table.

This certainly wasn't Doctor Deb.

It was Doctor Fletcher Madigan.

The boy I grew up crushing on.

The one who only ever acted like I was his friend's dorky kid sister.

The one who got married to some beautiful model type from Dallas and moved away.

The one... about to give me a pelvic exam.

2

FLETCHER

Liv scrambled up on the table, moving to a sitting position with the sheet wrapped carefully around her. Even under the shapeless fabric, I could easily tell how much she had changed since I last saw her. Instead of a tomboy clad in jeans and cowboy boots, she was clearly a woman in every sense of the word.

But her wide blue eyes and brunette hair were the same, along with those blushing cheeks. "Oh my god, *Fletcher?*"

"Olivia Griffen, aren't you a sight for sore eyes," I said with a grin.

"No one's called me Olivia in years," she replied, batting a hand at me. She had one of those smiles that made me want to smile right back. "I didn't know you were working here—I was expecting Doctor Deb?"

I glanced over my shoulder in the direction of the reception area. In the last few days, I'd learned Brenda was a great nurse with an incredible bedside manner. The patients loved her. Her computer skills and professionalism, however? Well, those could use some help. "I told Brenda to warn the patients about me being here. You're the second surprised one today."

"I'm more surprised the rumor mill didn't tell me before Brenda could." Liv's eyebrows drew together. "Why didn't I hear that you were filling in for Deb? Where is she by the way?"

"I'm not just filling in. I'm back in town."

"You're kidding," she said, shock clear on her face. "What brought you back from the big city? I thought you and your wife loved it there."

I leaned up against the sink counter, crossing my legs, and told her the real answer. Not the one that made me look good. "Regina and I split up a year ago, and Maya has been struggling ever since." Liv's sympathetic look kept me going. "I thought maybe it would be good for her to be in a small town where she won't slip through the cracks. And when I asked Doctor Deb if I could join the practice, she said she would love to have some help." I shrugged. "I was supposed to finish unpacking this week and start next Monday, but she came down with shingles."

Liv's sympathetic look turned to worry. "Shingles? Is she okay?"

I nodded. "She should recover, but it's not fun—she doesn't have your mom to rub calamine lotion all over her and duct tape oven mitts to her hands."

Liv chuckled, probably remembering that time all us kids got the pox. My dad was newly widowed and had no idea what to do with five sick boys and a farm to run. Deirdre had been a godsend, a second mom to my siblings and me.

I smiled at the memory and picked up the chart Brenda left for me. "So what brings you in today?"

Her features quickly fell. "I have a well-woman exam scheduled."

Sensing her concern, I said, "We can reschedule it for when Doctor Deb comes back in a few weeks, if you'd be more comfortable."

"I have to do it today," she said with a frown. "It's the last day my insurance will cover it."

I nodded, going to the cabinet and readying the supplies, and then finished looking over her chart. "I see you're on the pill. Is it helping with your endometriosis?"

Shrugging, she said, "I mean, my periods are..." She eyed me then. "It's weird talking to you about this stuff. I still remember that time my brother threatened to put a used tampon in your boot and you nearly fainted. I hope you've gotten better with blood since then."

The tips of my ears got hot as I ran my hand over my face. "Well that wasn't fair because I didn't have any sisters. But I assure you, I'm much more mature than I was back then. In this office, you're just another patient and I'm just another doctor."

She nodded resolutely and took a breath that moved her shoulders. "Okay, so my period sucks. It's so painful every month, and before I quit my job, I had to use almost all my sick days and vacation days just to lie in bed with a heating pad and wait it out."

I frowned. Doctor Deb really let her endure that much pain? "What kind of treatment plans have you and Deb discussed?"

"At my last exam, we talked about removing my ovaries, but keeping my uterus so I could get pregnant through IVF. But I'm so young and not married. It seemed like a hard decision to make, even if the odds of me conceiving naturally are low... so I've been stalling."

My chest ached for Liv. I respected Deb and all she'd done for this community, but some things were too old-school. "You know, some women have laparoscopic surgery to help remove the extra scar tissue. They've had luck reducing period pain, and some women successfully get pregnant afterward."

Liv's eyes widened. "Seriously?"

I nodded. "I'll write you a referral to a specialist in Dallas. It might take a bit to get in, but I think it's a promising option for you."

"I could hug you," she said. Then her cheeks flushed. "If I wasn't naked." But just as quickly as her joy came, it was replaced with disappointment. "I can't do the surgery."

"Why not?" I asked. "Are you worried about anesthesia?"

She shook her head. "I don't have any insurance since I quit my job. And I have no idea when I'll find something else.... There aren't a lot of options around here."

An idea flashed through my mind. It was crazy, but... it just might work. But first, we needed to finish this exam.

3

LIV

Lying on an exam table was not the way I'd dreamed of Fletcher and me hitting second base. And trust me; I'd done plenty of imagining. I stifled all my embarrassment—and most of my inappropriate thoughts—as his large hands cupped and kneaded my full breasts.

This close, I could smell the fresh scent of his cologne, see the short, dark brown stubble along his strong jawline. Fletch had always been good-looking, even as a teenager, but now he'd grown into his height, going from a lanky teen to filling out his dress clothes and white coat like no one's business. And does a breast exam always feel like this...?

Whoops.

Thinking inappropriate thoughts again.

But still... I wondered what he thought of me. Back in high school, before all my hormonal issues, I'd been a lot smaller than I was now. Not that I'd never been thin in my life, but I'd gained almost a hundred pounds since graduation. A lot of which he had seen up close and personal in the last half hour.

He stepped back, removing his warm hands from my skin and nodded. He looked completely unaffected by the exam, while my nipples were still hard and aching for his touch. "Everything seems normal, but Brenda will call you with the results of your pap. Should be ready by the end of the week, if not early next week."

"Great," I said with an awkward smile.

Silence hung between us. We used to know each other so well. Spent almost every weekend together and saw each other at school. To be fair, he'd hung around to see my older brother Rhett, usually keeping him out of too much trouble, but it had been years since we'd seen each other or even talked.

I wondered if he was still the same person I'd known back then, the one who always told Rhett to let me tag along. The one who took me to prom when my former date moved away unannounced.

I'd never had so much fun.

But after that night, he'd never called.

I was just Rhett's kid sister all over again.

"Well, thanks for the exam," I said finally. "I'll go square up with Brenda."

"Actually..." He glanced at his watch. "Can you meet me at the diner in an hour for lunch? There's something I want to talk to you about."

My stomach fluttered nervously, and heat hit my cheeks. "Oh-um-yeah-sure," I chirped so quickly it would be a miracle if he understood me. *God, could I stop acting like I was sixteen years old, please? That would be great.*

"Great." His smile made my heart beat faster. Thank

god the stethoscope was around his neck instead of on my chest because he'd be able to hear even more clearly how much my high school crush affected me.

I turned to leave the office, and he said, "Hey, wait up."

I stopped in the hallway, my overly theatrical heart waiting for him to admit his undying love for me because I definitely *felt* his lack of a wedding ring. (His hands were on my breasts, after all.)

Instead, he held his hand on the cherry-wood door-frame and said, "Don't tell Rhett I'm back yet. I haven't had a chance to call him."

Yet again, it was about my brother. I tried to hide my disappointment with a smile. "Sure, but don't wait too long. The rumor mill might beat you to it," I replied, ducking my head and walking away so he could see another patient.

In the waiting room, Brenda grinned up at me. "Your copay is thirty dollars, my dear."

My dear? My coochie was out, and a man who was not Doctor Deb walked in. *My dear* my unshaven ass. I might be hanging onto this grudge against her for a little while for not warning me about Fletcher.

I got out my card and let her swipe it, signing the receipt and getting the heck out of Dodge.

With still an hour until lunchtime, I got in my truck, pulled up to the diner's parking lot and then texted my friends group messenger thread. Henrietta was my sister in law who quickly became one of my best friends, and Della had been my bestie since she moved to town in seventh grade. She especially knew all about my massive crush on the new doctor in town.

Liv: FLETCHER MADIGAN IS BACK IN TOWN. I REPEAT, FLETCHER MADIGAN IS BACK IN TOWN.

Liv: AND HE JUST SAW MY VAGINA.

Liv: AND I DIDN'T EVEN WAX.

Della: YOU HAD SEX WITH FLETCHER?!

Henrietta: I DON'T KNOW WHO FLETCHER IS OR WHY YOU HAD SEX WITH HIM OR WHY EVERYONE IS YELLING.

I shook my head at the phone, smiling.

Liv: We didn't have sex. HE GAVE ME A PAP SMEAR AT THE CLINIC. I am *mortified.* All this time, I thought if I was ever going to see him again, it was going to be with long flowing hair and a dress and Spanx. Not jobless and hairy.

Della: On the bright side... it's probably a good thing you two didn't have sex considering HE'S MARRIED.

Henrietta: Wait... Fletcher's a doctor?

Since it would take too long to text, I sent her a voice message explaining the massive and embarrassing crush I'd had on my brother's best friend in high school and how he all but forgot about me since going to college.

Henrietta: I just googled him and found his pic on a hospital website. Hot damn. What did they put in the water here that makes all the men sexy gods?

Liv: First of all, you're married to my brother. Ew. LOL Second of all. I don't know but I'm so embarrassed. WHAT DO I DO?

Della: Just avoid him forever. You can do that, right?

I rolled my eyes at my friend, even though she couldn't see me.

Liv: Maybe, except I agreed to have lunch with him.

Della: Alternate idea. Go and have sex with him in the parking lot. *smiling cat emoji*

Hen: *Face palm emoji*

Liv: You're no help.

Hen: Why are you having lunch? Just to catch up?

Della: He's going to admit he's in love with you. Obviously. I saw the way he looked at you at prom.

I sent an eyeroll emoji. Della had this crazy theory that Fletch wouldn't date me back in high school because he was afraid of Rhett. As if. Rhett never would have done anything to hurt him.

Liv: I will keep you posted.

Hen: *Popcorn emoji*

I smiled and set my phone down in my lap.

I'd find out what Fletcher wanted soon enough.

4

FLETCHER

I said goodbye to Brenda, who was shutting down the clinic so we could take our lunch break, and then walked to the diner. It was about a quarter of a mile away, but with the May sun coming down, the blast of air conditioning in the restaurant was more than welcome.

I saw an open booth toward the back, but I had to say hi to Bora, the florist; Dan, the retired preacher; and Steve, the farmer who did more sitting around and talking than he ever did farming.

By the time I made it back to the open table, I wanted to bury my head in the sand. Living for so long in the city where no one knew my name made me forget how intense Cottonwood Falls could be. Everyone was family. And just like family, some of them didn't know when to stop talking.

"Fletcher Madigan," said a sweet older voice.

I glanced up to see Agatha holding a pad and pen in her hand. I'd seen her every Friday night after games and on half my dates in high school. Someone I was actually happy to see.

"You still work here?" I grinned.

She folded her arms across her chest, giving me a cheeky smile. "Lucky you and Rhett never burned the place down with all the trouble you got into."

"Hey," I laughed. "You probably have me to thank for the lack of fires."

She chuckled, batting my arm. "It's good to see you all grown up and handsome! Your dad said you might be coming back to town."

Dad ate lunch here a few times a week, which was a good way for him to socialize since he mostly worked alone on the small family farm. Of course he'd tell Agatha I was coming back.

"You'll have to meet my daughter," I said. "I'm planning to bring her here Sunday while everyone's in church."

"I'll see you both then," Agatha said with a crinkle-eyed smile.

She took my drink order, and while I waited for Liv, a text came through my phone.

Dad: Any luck?

I cringed and replied.

Fletcher: I hope so.

"Hi there," came a friendly voice.

I looked up, feeling relieved to see Liv's warm smile. "Glad you could make it," I replied. "I don't know if you still like vanilla Dr. Pepper, but I got you one just in case."

Her smile widened. "I do. Thank you so much."

I nodded, sliding the drink and an unopened straw her way.

"So what did you want to talk about?" she asked before sipping the drink. The way she looked up at me gave me flashbacks to dancing with her at my senior prom, country music playing and couples spinning around us. But things were different now.

"Look, I'm not one to beat around the bush," I said. "You're out of a job, and I'm desperate for some help."

She wrinkled her eyebrows together. "The clinic's hiring?"

"No, but I am," I said.

Now that line between her eyebrows was deep like it always got when Rhett tried to tell her to stay back and let the boys play. "For what?"

"I need a nanny," I said finally. "For Maya." I got out my phone and showed her the lock screen of my eight-year-old daughter.

Liv held the phone, smiling at the picture. "She's beautiful, Fletch."

"She is," I agreed. Maya was just as lovely as her mother, with long, wavy caramel hair, dark green eyes that bordered on hazel, and a smile that could wrap you around her finger in two seconds flat. "But she's also... a lot."

Liv chuckled. "We were all a lot at that age. Remember when you and Rhett blew up Dad's old truck that Fourth of July?" She made the sign of the cross. "May Clarice rest in peace."

"More like in pieces," I retorted with a laugh. "But the problem with my strong-willed child is that I haven't been able to keep a nanny for more than a month or two since Regina left us. I hoped it would be better here—you know how we all look after our own in Cottonwood Falls —but I've already had three nannies quit."

Liv's eyes bugged out. "Three? I thought you've only been here a week?"

"I have." I raked my fingers through my hair. It had grown longer on top, and I was in desperate need of a trip to Ms. Rhonda's salon. "The first nanny didn't make it past lunchtime. The second told me she quit after two days, and the third only lasted a day. It's like Maya has made it her personal mission to run them all away."

Liv's eyes widened. "Who were the nannies?"

I counted off on my fingers. "Laura Roland, Patty Walsh, and Frances Finch."

Her mouth fell open. "Patty quit? She had eight kids!"

"She's the one who quit before lunch," I said. "And that's *after* I offered to double her pay."

She cringed and sucked in a breath through clenched teeth. "Let me see that picture again?"

I turned the phone screen, showing her the photo.

"Where are the claws and green skin?" Liv asked.

I chuckled, despite the tension in my shoulders. "She's not a monster, but she is a handful. She's very good at finding your buttons and poking them. She's a picky eater. And she can hold her breath until she passes out."

Liv chewed her bottom lip, giving me a sympathetic look. "Sounds like her mom's leaving was really hard on her."

My heart warmed to Liv instantly. I already knew she was a good person, but the fact that she wasn't judging me for my parenting or condemning Maya... it was a breath of fresh air. "It was hard. Especially because Regina blamed Maya."

Liv covered her mouth. "She didn't."

I nodded sadly. "It wasn't really Maya's fault; it was mine, but that's a story for another day..."

She looked like she wanted to say more, but instead took a sip of her soda. After a pause, Liv shook her head. "That poor baby. And every nanny leaving is just another reminder..."

I wiped at my eyes, not wanting everyone in the diner to see me cry. "Maya is the only thing I've ever gotten right, and I feel like I'm failing her. But I can't afford not to work and stay home with her."

"Of course," Liv said, gazing at the laminate tabletop with ads printed from ten years ago. Oils Automotive had long since changed to my youngest brother, Hayes's, body shop. "So you need a nanny?"

"I do, and I think you'd be perfect for the job." Before she could second-guess, I added, "I bought the Fernandez property outside of town, and it has a guest cottage behind the main house, which you can live in free of charge. I'll also offer you one and a half times what your salary was at the feedlot, even when Maya is in school. You don't have to clean or do laundry if you don't want to. I swear all you have to do is keep her alive and fed."

"Jeez, can you set the bar any lower?" she asked, only halfway joking.

"I'd love to put it on the moon, but the thing is, I'm desperate. All my brothers have jobs, and my dad's agreed to watch her, but I can tell he's about had it. He needs to be a grandpa to her, not another dad."

She chewed her lip, and I felt like I was standing on the edge of a cliff just waiting for her to pull me back or shove me off. Maybe I shouldn't have told her all that stuff about Maya, but Liv was a friend. I couldn't just trick her into a job and then have her be another person who quit on Maya.

"Of course the job would include insurance," I added. "And if you wanted to try that surgery we talked about earlier, I would cover the deductible and give you ample recovery time."

Liv's eyes widened. "You're kidding, right?"

I shook my head. "I need someone for Maya. Someone good, like you."

"Good like me?" Liv brushed her fingers over my arm. "You're the godsend, Fletcher. This morning I was thinking I'd have to move away from Cottonwood Falls."

I shook my head at her. "This town wouldn't be the same without you." And selfishly, I wanted her to stay to help me. I was out of options.

"Okay," she said. "I'll do it. When do you want me to start?"

"Tomorrow?"

With a grin, she stretched her hand across the table. "You've got yourself a deal."

5

LIV

My mom looked incredulous when I got home and told her I had a job and was moving out tonight. I swore her curly hair got frizzier the more I told her about the situation—a sure sign that she was overwhelmed.

She sat on the bed as I began piling clothes into an open suitcase. "Are you sure you want to do this?"

I nodded. "Mom, I've been dealing with a pigheaded, narcissistic blowhard for the last year. I've been miserable, but I've done it. How hard could one eight-year-old little girl be?"

She chuckled. "You'd be surprised. Sometimes in the classroom, I feel like pulling out all my hair."

"But you manage," I said. "And so will I."

She seemed unsure as she went to my closet and began pulling out hangers. "What that poor girl has been through... it might do you some good to look up the effects of childhood trauma."

"That's the kind of support and advice I need," I said. "Thank you."

She smiled, but I could still see the concern in her eyes. "Are you sure you don't want to wait a week or so to move in? You know, feel it out?"

"It has to be all or nothing," I said resolutely. "I need Maya to know that I'm not going to be just another nanny she can push around and run off." And I needed to remind myself not to quit when things got hard. Any job was hard at the beginning. "Plus, I already creeped the house on Zillow, and it's super nice." I stuck my tongue out playfully. "Can't keep living with my parents forever."

Mom shook her head at me and then got up, helping fold my shirts before putting them in the suitcase. "If you ever need help with her, you bring her over, okay? And I'm sure Tyler and Henrietta would be more than willing to have you over too."

"I plan on it," I replied. "You taking us all over town when you were a stay-at-home mom made some of my best memories." Us kids did everything with her, from visiting friends in town to helping Dad out around our family farm. I hoped I could make good memories with Maya doing the same thing. At the very least, we'd get through the summer before school started back full-time. Because I had to make this work. I didn't want to move away from the only home and friends I'd ever known.

"You know who you should call?" Mom said, wagging her finger. "Farrah. She's so good with those three kids."

I smiled, thinking of my new sister-in-law and her three children. They were some of the most good-hearted kids I'd ever met. "I definitely will. I wish I could sit around and watch her for a week or so to see how she does it all *and* deals with Gage."

Mom chuckled as she zipped my full suitcase. "Do

you want me to come over with you and help you unpack tonight?"

I shook my head. "I'm sure Fletcher can help me."

It took us a couple hours to pack up my room, and by the time we were done, Dad was back from working to help us load it all up. Unlike Mom, he was thrilled about my new situation.

"It's about time Fletcher moved back home. Kids need to be around their family," Dad said in the driveway, shielding his eyes from the evening sun.

I nodded. "It was like perfect timing. I quit my job and here he is needing someone."

Mom seemed thoughtful. Maybe even hopeful. "Sometimes fate has its hand in these things."

Shaking his head at her, Dad said, "And sometimes it's just dumb luck."

"Either way, I'm glad," I said. "I better get over there, though. I told Fletch I'd be there at seven."

Dad nodded. "We'll see you Wednesday for dinner. And this weekend if you want to hang out."

My smile grew. "Someone's going to miss me."

He rolled his eyes and gave me a quick hug before saying, "Get out of here, kid."

I hugged my mom, then got in my truck, ready for a new adventure.

FLETCHER'S HOME had to be one of the most stunning builds in the county. It was a beautiful farmhouse set on a hill a mile away from the blacktop. As I drove over the dirt path, I took in the green pastures and cattle dotting

the hillsides. I parked in front of the separate shop building, seeing the main house and an adorable cottage out
back.

In the backyard, I could see a trampoline, a swing set,
and a covered picnic area. Maya and I would have so
much fun out here this summer.

I turned off my truck and got out, tucking my phone
in my back pocket. As I walked to the house, I noticed the
row of flowers lining the sidewalk and smiled. Picture
perfect.

I didn't have to ring the bell, because as soon as I
reached the porch, the front door opened, and Fletcher
stepped outside, smiling at me. "Have I mentioned how
amazing you are?" he asked.

My stomach somersaulted. I would definitely have to
cool these nerves around him. He wasn't my brother's
older, hot best friend anymore, and I wasn't the dweeby
girl tagging along in braces. I was a grown woman. Time
to act like it.

"You're the amazing one," I replied, gesturing around
me. "I mean, look at this place. Dream job in a dream
location."

"It is nice," he agreed. "I never could have afforded
anything like this in the city."

I reached out, punching his arm lightly. "Look at you,
all grown up, talking about real estate prices."

Shaking his head at me, he said, "Come inside.
Maya's watching TV."

We walked through a gorgeous entry area and into a
big living room with built-in shelves lining a stunning
stone fireplace. A little girl sat on the couch, her knees

tucked to her chin, as a children's program played on the TV.

"Maya," Fletcher said.

She ignored him.

He gave me an embarrassed look. "Maya."

Again, she kept her gaze on the TV.

Pulling up an app on his phone, he tapped a button and the TV screen went black.

"HEY!" she whined, looking at him.

Fletcher gestured at me, a strain to his voice. "This is Liv. Rhett's little sister. She's going to be your new nanny."

I smiled warmly at her and waved, but Maya gave me a massive stink eye.

"She looks old," Maya sneered.

My lips parted in a shocked smile, but I quickly recovered, trying to act like the comment was no big deal. "I know, thirty seemed like a million years old when I was a kid too."

Seeming thrown off that I wasn't upset, Maya said, "Can I watch TV now?"

Fletcher let out a quiet sigh. "Sure." He flicked it back on and said to me, "I'll give you a tour."

While he walked me back to the bedrooms, he said, "Sorry about that. She doesn't like meeting new people."

I batted my hand at him. "I'm sure she thinks I'm just another nanny who's going to disappear after a day or two."

The guilty look on his face told me I was exactly right.

We stopped at a bedroom door showing the most beautiful girl's room I'd ever seen. It had a canopy bed, a hammock full of stuffed animals, a bookshelf lined with hardcover titles, and a little swing anchored to the ceiling.

"Oh my gosh, Fletch, this room is amazing," I said, looking around. "Everything a little girl could want."

With a bashful smile, he said, "I wanted her to feel at home here."

"What about your room?" I asked, turning toward the other doors in the hallway. "Do you have a twisty slide hidden in there or something?"

"Oh, you don't have to..." His voice trailed off as I stepped into what looked like the master bedroom.

Except it was completely the opposite of Maya's room. There were boxes stacked along the wall, a simple bed in the middle of the room, a dresser and... that's it. No color. No photos. No art or decorations or *warmth*.

I turned and gave Fletcher a confused look. "You know you live here too, right?"

He frowned slightly before saying, "The guesthouse is much nicer. Let me show you."

6

FLETCHER

The back of my neck felt hot as I walked Liv across the lawn to the guesthouse. She'd been here for all of two minutes and had already seen straight through me. After all I'd done, I didn't deserve to make myself a priority right now.

She interrupted my thoughts, saying, "I bet you're excited to spend the summer out here."

I smiled, looking around at the yard. It was one of the things that made me want to buy this place as opposed to something in town. I thought having swings and a trampoline to play on would help us spend more time together. But all Maya wanted to do lately was watch TV or ask me for a million and one snacks while I unpacked. "I hope we make it through the summer," I admitted. "Maybe next year Maya will be more settled and able to enjoy it better."

Liv made a noncommittal sound I didn't question.

We reached the cottage, and I pushed the door open, flicking the lights on. It was a modest studio-style house with a bed in one corner, a living area in another corner, then the kitchen and dining room on the opposite side with a small bathroom in the back. The decorations were understated, and the shiplap ceiling with dark wood beams gave it character.

"It's not huge," I said, "but you're welcome to spend most of your time in the main house, even if you're technically off the clock."

Liv put her hand on my shoulder, stalling my words. The heat from her touch caught me off guard. "This is adorable. Way cuter than the company apartment I had with the feedlot." She walked ahead of me, gazing around at space. I hoped money I invested here on furniture and decorations helped Liv want to stay.

"Can you imagine if we had a place like this when we were kids?" she asked. "We would have played out here all day."

I smirked. "And drank all night when we were teens."

"Fair," she replied with a chuckle. "Maybe you'll lock it up when Maya's older."

I hadn't even thought that far ahead, but she was right. Having an eight-year-old was one thing... I was terrified of being a dad to a teenage girl, especially if Regina stayed as checked out as she was now.

"I guess I'll start bringing my stuff inside, if that's okay," Liv offered.

"I'll help you."

We made quick work of unloading her bags, getting them all inside the guesthouse within half an hour. I offered to help her unpack, but she shook her head. "It will be better if I know where everything is."

I nodded, feeling like I should say something, but not

knowing what. She may have been the girl I crushed on in high school, but now we were two adults who hadn't spoken in years.

"What time should I come over tomorrow morning?" she asked.

"I need to leave the house at seven thirty, so if you could come at seven so you and Maya can get settled in before I leave, that would be great."

She nodded with a smile. "I'm looking forward to it. I make the best Mickey Mouse pancakes."

"Maya will love that," I said. "And thank you, really. You're doing us both a big favor here."

"Fletch?" Liv put her hand on my shoulder, the warm sensation quickly spreading.

"Yeah?"

She met my eyes, hers all blue and open. "You don't need to thank me so much. You and Maya deserve someone you can depend on."

I shook my head at this ray of sunshine. She was like a life raft, rescuing Maya and me from the waters. I just hoped it could last. "I'll see you in the morning."

She smiled, echoing my words. "I'll see you in the morning."

I turned and left Liv in the cottage, and for some reason, I felt better knowing that Maya and I weren't alone out here. Probably because it was hard to be a single parent. Even though my dad and brothers were around, they had their own lives going on. It would be nice to have someone here as dedicated to caring for Maya as I was.

I got inside and was about to start getting Maya ready

for bed when my phone went off with a call. The name on the screen? *Rhett.*

"Shit," I muttered to myself. I'd completely forgotten to call him and let him know I was back in town. Luckily, Maya was too focused on the TV to hear the cuss word slip.

"Hey, bud," I answered.

"Don't 'hey bud' me! You're back in town and you don't call to let your best friend know about it? And now my *sister's* working for you? My mom knew you were back in town before me! What gives?"

Okay, he was mad. But also joking a little bit? Maybe? It was hard to tell with him sometimes.

I scrubbed my hand over my face and went to the fridge for a beer. I definitely needed one. "Yeah, I've been meaning to call you. I've just been so busy trying to find a nanny for Maya and getting settled in at the practice. It was a dick move. I'm sorry."

"It was a dick move," Rhett said. "But at least I got out of carrying your couch this time."

I laughed. "If you want to come over this weekend, there are plenty of boxes left."

"Boxes? My favorite subject." There was a smirk in his voice that had me shaking my head. We were such opposites—him, the fun-loving, girl-crazy one. Me, the responsible one trying to keep us both out of trouble, for the most part.

"I'll bring a case of beer," he continued. "Between you, me, and Liv, we should be able to get it finished up."

I smiled at the idea. It had been a long time since I had enough space in my life for friends. Regina and Maya had required so much. "Just bring the beer, but don't worry about unpacking. We'll grill some food and catch up."

"Sounds good. And be good to my sister, you hear?"

"Wouldn't dream of anything else," I said honestly.

We hung up, and I went to the living room to turn off the TV and get Maya ready for bed. I squared my shoulders, bracing myself for another round of World War III.

MY STOMACH WAS ALREADY a ball of nerves when my alarm went off too early in the morning. I did some deep breathing to calm down and then rolled out of bed and drank the cup of water on my nightstand. (Some things you learned in med school just stuck.) Then I got on my Peloton and did a quick workout before going to wake up Maya.

She was old enough now that she usually did a pretty good job of getting herself dressed and combing her hair, but I still had to help out with braids or a ponytail, depending on her mood.

I finished on the bike, then got in the shower, hurrying to get ready so I'd be ready before Liv came over. Still, this sense of dread persisted. The last thing I wanted was a call at the office telling me this was yet another failure. Brenda had already vetoed keeping Maya busy in the waiting room, even if it was just for summer break. And the idea of bouncing her between my dad and my brothers just so I'd be covered...

I toweled myself off, praying this would work. *Please let it work.*

After dressing, I went to check on Maya in her room. She was gone, and I caught a whiff of something. Bacon?

Shit! Was Maya trying to cook again?

I sprinted toward the kitchen, only to see Liv standing by the stovetop, one hand on the pan's handle, another on her hip as she spoke to my daughter.

"You may not speak to me like that, Miss Maya."

"Why? You're not my mom!" Maya yelled.

"I'm not, but I do get to decide how I am treated," Liv said firmly. "And I do not let people call me fat in a mean way. You may call me Liv, Olivia, Livvy, or Miss Griffen."

"How about Miss Piggy?" Maya fired back.

Anger flared in my chest. "Maya Marie Madigan," I snapped. "You go to your room right now, and you do not come out until you are ready to treat Liv with respect."

Maya opened her mouth to argue, but I pointed in the direction of her room. "*Now.*"

Maya stomped past me, and then the door slammed, rattling the house.

I flinched at the sound and faced Liv again, hoping she wouldn't take Maya's comments to heart. "I am so sorry, Liv. That was out of line."

But instead of looking hurt, Liv glared at me. "I had it handled, Fletcher!"

I raised my eyebrows, feeling like I was a little kid being scolded. "What do you mean? I'm supposed to stand by and watch my daughter talk to you like that without saying a word?"

"If I am going to be in charge of Maya, I need her to listen to me without you having to come in and be the heavy. It's going to be hard for a little while, but you need to take a step back and let me handle it."

I went to the island, sitting at the counter and rubbing my face in my hands. It was barely seven o'clock, and I was already messing up as a dad. "You're right; I'm sorry. I'm just nervous about today. I want things to work for you and Maya."

Liv smiled gently at me. "You made it through med school. You can do this too."

7

LIV

I sent Fletcher on his way to work with a breakfast sandwich and a travel mug of coffee before plating up food for Maya and me. It hadn't been easy to hear Maya tell me I was fat and ugly, but she was a little girl. I couldn't let an eight-year-old ruin my day.

When Fletcher's truck had disappeared down the dirt road I could see through the front window, I walked back to Maya's room and tapped on the door. "Maya?"

"What do you want?" Maya snapped.

It was like hearing her door slam all over again. "Can I come in and talk to you?" I asked gently. "Please?"

After a moment, she uttered an irritated, "*Fine.*"

I turned the door handle and looked in the room to see stuffed animals and clothes scattered all over the floor like she'd thrown them in her tantrum. She sat cross-legged on her bed, arms folded angrily over her chest. My first instinct was to make her pick up every last item, but instead, I knelt on the floor in front of her, getting below eye level.

Some of the websites I'd read online when I couldn't sleep last night said being lower than the child helped them feel comfortable and safe. I gave her a gentle smile and said, "Hey, I'm not mad at you about earlier. Sometimes it takes a little time to learn how to treat each other."

She gave me a confused look. "You're not mad?"

I shook my head. "But I do have some breakfast on the counter, and I really don't want it to get cold. Why don't we go eat, and then we can come clean this up together?"

With a short little nod, she got up and followed me to the kitchen. I sat in front of my plate, and she sat in front of hers. I was so excited for her to see the pancake I'd made with little ears and a chocolate chip smile. But instead of being happy about the food, she said, "Ew, this bacon looks nasty."

"That's okay, you can eat the eggs," I said.

Her lip curled up like she'd smelled something sour. "I don't like scrambled eggs. I like dippy eggs."

"That's fine," I said, taking a sip of coffee. "I'll know that for tomorrow. But today, you can eat what I made for you."

Giving me a glare, she shoved the plate off the counter, sending it clattering to the floor.

My lips parted, and I swore I saw red. If I'd done that as a kid, my parents would have reamed my butt. But I knew spanking wasn't right, especially after all the research I'd done last night.

So instead of blowing up, I got off my seat, took my coffee, and walked outside, trying to calm myself down.

With the door closed, I took an angry sip, maybe seeing why the other nannies quit.

The back door opened, and Maya peeked her head out. I turned to see her smiling. "Are you leaving?" she asked. "Grandpa can watch me when you go."

That's when I realized—she was testing me. Trying to see how much I would take.

I let out a laugh, probably looking like a crazy person standing there cackling with my coffee at half past seven in the morning.

Maya's face screwed up. "You're weird."

"I am. Now get in the truck."

"What?" she asked.

"Get. In. The. Truck."

Her dad had set up her booster seat the night before, so I went inside, shoved an extra outfit for her and a swimsuit in a plastic sack and went out to my pickup. She was still standing outside it.

"Climb in," I said, playing up my southern accent. "We ain't got all day."

With a huff, she opened the back door and got in. I checked to make sure she was buckled in before taking off down the dirt road.

⚘

WE GOT APPROXIMATELY two miles away from the house when I realized I had absolutely no idea where we were going. I just knew I needed to get her out of her element and do something new. Because I was not sitting around the house all day being terrorized by an eight-year-old.

At least Maya was being quiet for a moment so I could gather my thoughts and contemplate what there was to do in town. We could go to the park, but she might be a little old to enjoy that on her own. We could go to the baseball field once I got a ball and some bats—maybe that would help take out her aggression. Or end horribly, horribly wrong.

Then I remembered my brother Tyler and his wife, Henrietta, were building raised garden beds at the boutique apartments they owned for seniors. A couple extra hands would be good, and Maya could benefit from some hard work.

I called Henrietta to double-check that it was okay, and she eagerly said yes. She loved kids, and I knew she missed her nieces and nephews back in California. And Tyler was as patient as people come, way more so than me. This could be good.

"Where are we going?" Maya whined for the millionth time from the back seat.

"I'm putting you to work," I chirped. "You'll be moving dirt and compost into garden beds."

Maya looked so horrified in the rearview mirror, I had to hold back a laugh. "I'm not doing that," she said.

"Well then, you're sitting around and watching while I do it," I said. "But you won't get any ice cream after."

She seemed to consider it. But at least she didn't argue any more. "Am I getting paid for this?" she asked after a minute.

"Sure. If you're good help today, I'll give you ten dollars."

"Fifteen," she replied.

I had to laugh. "You're a good negotiator. Sure. If you work extra hard, I'll give you fifteen and a milkshake."

She smiled smugly. But I was the happy one.

I'd learned something new: Maya Madigan was motivated, at least a little bit, by money.

8

FLETCHER

I had trouble focusing all morning at work after the terrible morning at home. I kept waiting for a call from Liv to tell me that she couldn't deal with Maya anymore and worried about what I'd do if it didn't work out.

But it was past one now, and Liv still hadn't called. In between patients, I stepped into the backyard, which Doctor Deb had designed to be a meditation garden of sorts with blooming wildflowers, and paced along the gravel trail as I dialed Liv's number.

After a few rings, she picked up, and I could hear wind come through the phone. But no screaming. "Everything okay?" I asked. "How's it going."

"Your daughter's crazy with a shovel," Liv said, giggling. "Back up, Shia LeBeouf!"

"What does that mean?" Maya called in the background.

I laughed at the oddity of it. "What? Why does she have a shovel?"

"I put her to work at Tyler and Henrietta's apartment building... I hope that's okay."

"It's totally fine as long as she's safe," I said. "She is safe, right?"

Liv chuckled. "It was a little touch and go this morning, but she's perfectly fine now. Want us to swing by the clinic when we get done here? We can grab a shake for you from the diner or something."

I grinned, overjoyed at the news. "That would be great. I completely forgot to pack a lunch and we had a walk-in at noon, so I didn't have time to eat."

"Great," she said. "Do you want to talk to Maya?"

"Please," I said.

There were a few mumbled words, and then my daughter's voice came through the phone. "Hi, Daddy."

"Hey, honeybee. How are you doing?"

"Good. Henrietta let me make a mud pie!"

I grinned. "And you and Liv are getting along?"

Maya grunted a little bit.

At least it wasn't a no.

"I'll see you in a few hours, okay? Have Liv call me if you want to talk about anything," I said.

She didn't say goodbye, just gave the phone back to Liv.

"Hello?" Liv said.

"Hey, thank you again. I mean it; call me if you need anything."

"I will," Liv promised, and then the line went silent.

The back door to the practice opened, and Brenda called, "There's a kid here with a broken arm, Fletch. It looks bad."

My heart quickened, and I got the focus I always needed in an emergency. Time to get to work.

☙

AROUND FIVE O'CLOCK, Liv and Maya came into the office, and since my last appointment didn't show up, I brought them to the picnic table in the backyard and we sat around the table with our milkshakes and fries.

Maya was in a different outfit than I left her in this morning, and there was a streak of mud at her hairline, but other than that, she was all in one piece, and so was Liv.

I had never felt so relieved.

"Maya," I said, "can you go find some flowers to set out on the table at home? I think I saw some marigolds in the far corner over there."

Maya got up from the table and ran to the corner of the lot, giving me some space to talk to Liv. "How was she today?"

"This morning was rough," Liv said. "She dumped her breakfast on the floor and trashed her room, so she needs to clean those up when we get back, but she did good today. She was shyer around Tyler and Henrietta, but then she warmed up and we had some fun."

My lips spread into a smile. "You're a miracle worker, Liv."

She shook her head, worry in her eyes. "There was one other thing."

My chest constricted. "What do you mean?"

Liv bit her lip, glancing to Maya, who was coming our

way with a handful of yellow flowers. I took them from her saying, "Those look great, Maya."

She smiled proudly.

"Do you think we should get some white ones to go with it?" Liv asked.

Maya nodded and went back in search of more flowers.

It had only been one day, and Liv was already getting on with Maya better than my last six nannies. But the way Liv looked, I could tell something was wrong.

"What is it?" I asked.

"I gave Maya fifteen dollars for working so hard today, and she said something that worried me."

"What was it?"

Liv bit her lip, looking over at my little girl and then back to me with wide blue eyes. "She said maybe if she made enough money, her mom would come back."

It was like a punch to the gut. Even a year after her mom left, Maya was still holding out hope. Even with the lack of calls and visits. I felt like the shittiest dad in the world because I had chosen Maya's mom, even worse knowing she left because of me.

"Thanks for letting me know," I finally said.

Liv nodded. "I'm sorry for giving her money. I didn't know that's why she'd want it."

I shook my head. "How could you have known?" I looked up at our new nanny, a woman who'd only been here for a day but had already seen so much. "I'm failing her, Liv."

Liv reached across the table, putting her hand on my arm. The warmth of it almost brought tears to my eyes, and I looked down, blinking quickly, before pulling my arm away. "Come on, Maya," I called. "Let's head home."

Liv looked confused. "Do you want me to meet you at the house?"

I shook my head. "You have the evenings to do as you please."

Her nod was jerky. "Okay. I'll see you tomorrow morning."

Without another word, I took my daughter and left.

9

LIV

I couldn't get Maya's words and Fletcher's sudden cold-
ness out of my mind as I drove over to Della's house. For
some reason, I didn't feel like I was welcome at the house
right now, but I knew that was silly. It was my place now
too. I just needed some time to decompress after the
world's longest day.

So I spread out on the floor in Della's living room,
staring at the ceiling as she cooked supper for me.

"I've never understood why you insist on lying on the
floor," she muttered as she handed me a Cayman Jack
margarita.

I took it from her, groaning. "I've already told you; the
ground is always there for me."

She chuckled, sitting next to me cross-legged and then
taking a long swig from her own drink. "Newton would
agree with you."

I stared at the popcorn ceiling and then the fan,
following one blade as it spun around. "I thought I did

good with Maya today. Not perfect, but good. So why do I feel so bad?"

"Because it's not the kind of job you can clock out of," Della said, tucking a strand of curly hair behind her ear. Even though she always wore her red hair up in a bun, curls were constantly breaking free.

"What do you mean?" I asked, rolling my head to the side to look at her.

"It's not like my job where the paperwork is sitting on my desk waiting for tomorrow. Maya's still hurting whether or not you're on the clock."

I looked back up at the ceiling. "You should have seen his face."

"When you told him about Maya?"

I shook my head. "When I touched his arm." I blinked back the memory. "He looked so disgusted that I was touching him, and he pulled his arm away so fast. I know it's pathetic to say, but it makes me wonder if he was that grossed out when he was giving me the exam, but he had to touch me for that."

Della shoved my thigh with her foot. "Stop it right now. That man has issues that have nothing to do with you."

I let out a sigh and sat up, drinking from my margarita. "Why do they make these taste so damn good?"

She chuckled, making her lips spread thin and her big cheeks squint her eyes. "So you'll drink them. Duh. Come on, dinner's ready."

We ate our food together, and she told me about her day of work at the insurance office. We giggled way too much about the guy who filed a claim on his car because his neighbor's goats climbed all over the hood and left dents.

She offered to let me stay over after I finished helping her with dishes, but I shook my head. "I need to go all in on this job and make it work. Can't do that if I don't go back."

She gave me a thoughtful look, and this close, I could see the dozens of freckles dusting her cheeks and nose. "You still like him, don't you?"

"Thanks for dinner." I gave her a hug and purposely avoided the question. "Love you."

She waved goodbye, and I drove back to the house, hoping I could make this job work. Trying to ignore the fact that Fletcher's silent dismissal hurt more than anything his daughter had said out loud.

FOR THE NEXT FEW DAYS, Maya tested me to my wit's end, "accidentally" spitting chewing gum in my hair, dumping a toad in my boot, and refusing to eat at least one out of three meals I made a day. But at the end of every day, I looked her in her pretty little hazel eyes, smiled, and said, "I'll see you in the morning."

Because no matter how tough she acted, I couldn't stop hearing her say, "Maybe I'll make enough money for Mommy to come back."

I wasn't going to be another person to walk out on her. But Friday at five, I retreated to my cottage, declined an invitation to go out with Hen and Della, and turned on the TV to veg out on the couch.

Watching that girl and keeping my cool took every bit of energy I had.

Half an hour into *Yellowstone*, a knock sounded on the door. I glanced up, seeing Fletcher through the window. He smiled, holding up a bottle of wine and two glasses.

Grinning, I got up and walked to the door, opening it.

His eyes widened. "Um, your face is green."

My mouth fell open. "Oh my gosh, I forgot I had a facemask on." So freaking embarrassing. "I didn't know you were coming over."

"I thought we both deserved a drink," he said.

"True," I agreed. "Why don't you pour us a glass and I'll go wash my face so you're not drinking with a green-skinned monster."

He chuckled, and I hurried to the bathroom, wondering how much more I could embarrass myself. At this rate, he'd only see me as Rhett's dorky sister forever.

I washed the mask off my face, swiped a little mascara through my lashes and squared my shoulders, trying to remind myself that Fletcher wasn't an old crush—he was my boss, coming with a peace offering.

When I walked out to the living area, Fletcher was already on the couch, sipping a glass of red wine. He hadn't seen me yet, so I watched him for a moment. He had such great bone structure—a square jaw, high cheekbones, a perfectly pointed nose that was chiseled and just slightly rugged. Dark stubble dusted his jaw, and his pink lips were tantalizing as they pursed over the rim. Not to mention he wore a dark blue T-shirt and gray sweats instead of his usual dress clothes, showing his strong arms and legs.

He was art, the best possible kind.

"Hey," I said before my jaw could come unhinged and fall on the floor.

He smiled over at me, and my heart melted, forgetting the way he'd pulled away from me, how distant he had seemed this week. No, to my heart, I was sixteen years old again, and he was the cutest boy I'd ever seen. Forbidden and way too cool to notice someone like me.

"This is a good show," he said, gesturing his glass toward the TV.

"It's my favorite," I agreed. I sat on the opposite side of the couch, tucking my feet under me and getting comfortable. He handed me a glass of red, and I took it, saying, "Thanks."

He held out his glass, and I clinked mine to his.

"The first week." He sipped, looking at me cautiously. "How are you feeling?"

"Exhausted," I admitted. "How do you do this all the time?"

He shook his head a little and shrugged with a small smile on his face. "Parenting is... the hardest thing I've ever done. About ninety percent of the time, I'm worried I'm failing miserably. But then there are these moments that make everything okay again."

"Really?"

He nodded. "Kids have this way of keeping you humble. I'll be so mad at Maya one minute, and the next, she'll ask for an extra hug before bed or tell me I'm the best dad in the world, and all is right again."

"I get that," I said. "After she put gum in my hair, she offered to braid it so I looked like Elsa."

His jaw dropped. "She put *gum* in your hair?"

"Whoops." I cringed. "I didn't mean to tell you that."

He shook his head, rubbing his lips together. "And yet your things are still here. Does that mean you'll stick around for another week?"

His brown eyes were on me, just a shade or two darker than Maya's hazel. I used to be mesmerized by all the flecks of green I saw there. The way his eyes always smiled even when his lips were level.

Hell, I was still mesmerized.

"Me and my short piece of hair are staying," I said. I reached up, finding the two-inch section of hair at the crown of my head that was now shorter than all the rest.

He rubbed his free hand over his face. "I can't believe she did that."

"You know, I talked to my sister-in-law this week—the one who married Gage. She said, 'all behavior is communication.' Maya's just communicating really loudly how hurt she is."

His eyes shined as he nodded. "I want her to start communicating that she's going to be okay."

I put my hand on his forearm, wishing I could take away his pain along with Maya's. "She'll get there."

This time, he didn't move away.

He only glanced at the spot where we connected, and I nervously pulled my hand back.

"Sorry," I whispered, taking a drink to hide my embarrassment.

"Don't be." His eyes stayed on mine for a moment before he looked away. "I'm planning on having Rhett over tomorrow night, but I wanted to run it by you too."

"Oh, do you need me to watch Maya?" I asked, already giving myself a mental pep talk to work an extra day this week.

He shook his head. "It's your home too. You have a say in who comes over."

The thoughtfulness of it took me off guard. "That's nice of you. It's totally fine with me. Do you want me to shop for food or drinks or anything?"

"I've got it."

I chewed my bottom lip, in awe of this man. I was exhausted after five days when he worked full time *and* cared for his daughter at night. When was the last time he'd had a proper break? A night off?

"Why don't I take Maya after supper with Rhett?" I offered. "We can watch a movie over here and put on monster skin and braid each other's hair. It could be fun." Emphasis on *could*.

He seemed tempted, but quickly shook his head. "It's too much, Liv."

"Let me do this for you," I said. "For all you've done for me."

He set his glass down and gave me a hug. God, he smelled good. And his arms wrapped around me, strong but soft at the same time? I swear it felt like heaven. "You're the best, Liv."

And just like that, I'd fallen all over again. And he'd never even asked me to.

10

FLETCHER

While I grilled steaks and jalapeño poppers, Liv and Maya decided that we should make the evening's get-together a "pool party."

I didn't have a pool—had no desire for one as a doctor who'd seen too many accidents with at-home pools—but we did have a Slip 'N Slide and a splash pad in a storage tote in the garage.

The girls dug them out and set them up in the back-yard, a little bit away from the picnic area, while I was grilling. Liv told Maya to change into her swimsuit, and then Liv disappeared into her house for a few moments.

I stood at the grill, tending to the food and sipping from a beer as I took in my surroundings. I'd always meant to come back to Cottonwood Falls after med school. Having grown up here, I knew there was nowhere better to raise a family. But Regina would never leave the city.

We'd had a decently sized house with a maid and a nanny and a landscaper and... never enough money, no matter how much I made at the hospital. I'd been on a hamster wheel. And after Regina left, I didn't want to stay on it anymore.

Now, with the fresh country air mixed with the smell of grilling meat and vegetables, I felt refreshed in a way I never had in Dallas. From here, I had a panoramic view of the countryside, waving green grass, dimming blue sky, and puffy clouds in the air. It was picture perfect—the exact kind of place I'd always dreamed of Maya growing up.

The problem with dreams is that they almost never turn out exactly like you pictured them. I always thought Maya would have a mom, siblings. But our life seemed so small. Just her and me against the world.

The door to the house opened, and Maya came running out in her cute pink swimsuit. "Where's Liv?" she asked, jogging up to me.

I pointed toward the guesthouse. "Why don't you turn on the hose, test it out?"

Maya seemed happy with that idea and ran to the spigot. Within a few moments, water sprayed out of the Slip 'N Slide and splash pad. She danced through the spray, giggling. It warmed my heart, seeing her act playful like a girl her age should. Maybe this moment was a sign of things to come.

I heard the door to the guest cottage open, and my eyes connected with Liv. More specifically, the way she looked in her swimsuit.

I was supposed to be focusing on the food.

I was supposed to be watching my daughter.

But god, if I couldn't keep my eyes off her body in the one-piece swimsuit and cut-off denim shorts that hugged her thick thighs and showed off her ample chest. I swallowed, hard.

Get your eyes off the nanny, I said to myself. *Get your eyes off Rhett's sister.*

He'd made it clear, all those years ago, that I was not to go anywhere near his little sister. Now I had multiple reasons to stay away: I wasn't good enough for her. She was my employee.

I stared hard at the grill as Liv called to Maya, "Should I try the Slip 'N Slide?"

Dear god, the woman was teasing me.

"Do it, Livvy!" Maya cheered.

Livvy?

Now I had to look. Maya didn't give anyone nicknames. But now she was grinning at Liv as the woman shimmied out of her denim shorts. I bit down on my knuckle, hard, glad there was a grill between me and the girls. *Get it together, Fletch.*

Liv's curves bounced as she bounded toward the Slip 'N Slide and launched herself down the yellow vinyl, her ass jiggling seductively the entire way.

If I bit on my knuckle any harder, I swear I'd taste blood.

I physically turned my body away from the girls and looked at the countryside. *Grass. Sky. Flowers. Clouds.*

Liv's jiggling ass.

The roar of a diesel engine shocked me out of my trance.

Rhett was here.

Within minutes, he was walking my way, carrying a case of beer and wearing his trademark shit-eating grin. "My long-lost friend! I thought you'd abandoned me," he drawled, ever one to make an entrance. "Holy shit, you have a Slip 'N Slide!"

I chuckled, feeling lighter already. In the city, with a wife and kid, Rhett seemed so different from me living his wild single life. But now I realized I was the one who was different, shutting down all the fun parts of my life to live the way I thought I should. "It's great to see you," I said earnestly. "And watch your mouth." I waved my spatula toward the girls. "There are ladies around." Never mind the thoughts that were going through my head(s) earlier.

Rhett ran forward and picked up Maya, spinning her around.

She squealed, pounding on his back. "UNCLE RHETT!"

Liv gave me a questioning look. I only shrugged.

Rhett and I may have visited only a couple times a year since Maya was born, but he sure did make an impression.

"It's so good to see you, kiddo!" Rhett said, setting her down. "How old are you now? Don't tell me." He scratched his chin. "Sixteen?"

Maya giggled, shaking her head.

"Ugh, nineteen?"

She laughed. "NO!"

"I remember. Twenty-one." He sent me a wink.

"I'm eight and you know it," Maya said.

Rhett chuckled. "That's right." His voice grew stern. "Now, I heard you've been giving my sister some trouble."

Maya fidgeted uncomfortably, and the tips of my ears heated. What all had been said to Rhett about my daughter's behavior? Were they both judging me for my failures as a father?

Rhett extended his fist for her to bump. "Keep it up."

Maya tapped her knuckles to his, and Liv shoved his shoulder. "Grow up," she told her brother playfully. Then she went to get a towel, wrapping it around her shoulders, but the fabric did nothing to cover up her tantalizing cleavage. A cleavage I'd felt before.

I closed my eyes. *You're a fucking doctor, you pervert.*

"Need any help on the grill?" Rhett asked.

I opened my eyes, realizing he was beside me.

"I'm good," I said. "But I will take another beer." Or three.

He reached into the cooler and got one out for me before opening the box of beer he brought and shoving a few down in the ice. "I can't believe you're back in town," he said. "Feels like my birthday wish came true."

I raised an eyebrow at him. "You wasted a birthday wish on me? I figured you'd be wishing for strippers to come out of your cake."

He smirked. "Don't need to wish for something that's already happening."

Chuckling, I shook my head at him. "I like being home, except for the fact that everyone and their mother is trying to hook me up with any single woman in town."

Rhett drank from his beer. "That's a problem?"

I rolled my eyes. "Catch me up, Rhett. What's new?"

He leaned back against one of the support poles of the picnic area, folding his arms over his chest. "Still working at the ranch during the week, riding bulls on the weekends. Eating with the family on Wednesday nights. Same ol', same ol'."

"No girlfriend?" I asked, surprised Rhett hadn't found

at least one person to hang around longer than a weekend or two.

"I have a new one every Friday night." He winked.

I shook my head. "How do you do it? There's only a couple thousand people in this town."

"It's simple math," Rhett said, holding up his fingers around his beer bottle.

I rolled my eyes at him. "Here we go."

"Say half the people are men. That leaves a thousand. Another quarter, olds and underage."

"Olds?" I laughed, already hurting in my stomach. God, I hadn't laughed like this in a while.

"Right. Olds. That leaves five hundred women. If I sleep with a different one every week, I'm set for five years, give or take, then I can go back through the rotation. And that's not even including neighboring towns."

"And they say math isn't useful in real life," I said with a laugh.

11

LIV

I felt Fletcher's eyes on me all throughout dinner, and I couldn't help but feel shy about the attention. I was a big girl, and part of me wondered if he judged me for that. He was a doctor, after all, and even though Doctor Deb was nice, I still got the spiel about losing weight every year at my exam.

But Rhett kept us all laughing, even Maya, and by the time we finished eating, she was in a great mood. She even seemed excited to have a sleepover at my place.

We packed a bag for her, even though I was right next door, and included several of her favorite stuffed animals, plus a walkie talkie in case she wanted to talk to her dad.

Even though she and Fletcher butted heads, it was sweet seeing how much they loved each other. Fletcher would do anything for her. And Maya? She acted like he hung the moon.

When we came back outside, Fletcher and Rhett were sitting around the fire pit, telling stories and laughing with each other. For the week I'd been around Fletcher, he'd seemed so serious, so heavy. But now, he had a ghost of his fun younger self on his face. And it was refreshing to see.

I put my arm around Maya's little shoulders and said, "The sleepover is about to commence. No boys allowed."

"Yeah," Maya agreed, folding her arms over her chest. "No boys."

Rhett stuck out his tongue. "That's good because girls have cooooties."

"We do not!" Maya protested.

"Yeah, girls rule, boys drool," I teased.

Fletcher smiled at his daughter, so much warmth in his eyes. "You two have fun and don't stay up too late."

"We will," I promised.

Maya started walking toward my place, but I looked back at Rhett and Fletcher, giving them a wink.

Thank you, Fletcher mouthed.

You're welcome, I replied.

Inside the guesthouse, Maya got on the fold-out couch, bouncing up and down. "What do we do first?"

I set her bag down by the couch and said, "Haven't you had a slumber party before?"

With a sad look in her eyes, Maya shook her head. "No."

My heart broke for her. "Your parents didn't allow it?"

"I was never invited."

Gosh, this poor girl. We were getting her around some other kids starting on Monday. But for now, I said, "That's okay, because you are with a slumber party *professional.* There are three things we always do. We braid hair, we eat tons of snacks, and we watch movies! Which one do you want to watch?"

She tapped her chin thoughtfully. "I don't know."

"What about *The Parent Trap?*" I asked.

"Never heard of it."

My jaw dropped open. "I am having a word with your father about that. But for now, your education begins."

I clicked through to the show, and while we watched Lindsay Lohan cause mayhem, I carefully put little braids all over Maya's head with tiny rubber bands I'd had since I was about twelve.

I wondered if this was what it would feel like to have a daughter of my own—like every day was a sleepover. And then the aching thoughts came. I was thirty years old... Would I ever find a man to fall in love with and make a family? If I could have children, would my own daughter be as spunky and full of life as Maya?

When the movie finished, Maya was practically bouncing up and down. "Do you think we can prank Dad like that? It would be so funny."

I giggled, thinking of Fletcher sliding over the floor, covered in shaving cream. "It would be hilarious. We have to start small though."

"Like what?" she asked.

"Asks the girl who put a toad in my shoe," I teased, tickling her side.

She giggled evilly.

"Hmm." I tapped my chin. "What if we sneak into the house and put salt in his sugar shaker? When he mixes it in his coffee, he'll be like..." I screwed my face up like I'd just tasted something bad.

She clapped her hands together. "Let's do it!"

I went to the front door, looking out the window, and saw Rhett and Fletcher were still at the fire. "They're still talking. Want to do face masks while we wait?"

She nodded eagerly, and for the next hour or so, we had fun painting our faces green, wearing cucumber slices over our eyes and painting our toenails. I was already getting tired and felt relieved when I heard Rhett's engine fire up and drive away.

"Mission Saltshaker, begin," I said. I wasn't sure whether or not Fletcher left with Rhett, so we had to be careful, like he was still home.

I put on all black and let Maya wear one of my black T-shirts. It hung off her like a dress, but it worked. Then we used mascara to put black streaks on our cheeks. We both had to fight off giggles as we crouched-ran to the main house and crawled into the kitchen.

Maya said, "The salt's up there."

I stood up for a half second, wondering how on earth I'd explain this to Fletcher if he walked in, and then got the salt and the sugar dispensers, then crouched back down.

Maya giggled as I undid the sugar shaker and let her pour a stream of salt inside, spilling some over the edge. While she screwed on the cap, I swept the scattered salt under the cabinet, making a mental note to sweep it up on Monday.

Fighting back laughter, we crouch-ran back to my place and fell onto my bed, laughing.

Maya rolled her head to me, grinning wide. "Sleepovers are the best."

I reached out, cupping her cheek. "I totally agree."

12

FLETCHER

I'd hung out with Rhett all of a few hours, and he'd already convinced me to go driving around back roads like we used to. Maybe it was because I'd been the responsible doctor dad for so long, I wanted to remember the part of myself that could have fun too.

And it was nice, flying down the dirt roads with the windows down, my best friend at my side. Not judging me based on how much money I made or how many hours I worked, but appreciating who I was.

"You know, this girl I've been talking to has a pretty cute friend," Rhett said with a wink.

I held up my fingers in an X. "No way in hell."

"Blonde... Curvy... Tits you just want to sink your face into." He quickly shook his head back and forth.

God, my ears felt hot already. "The answer stands."

"Why?" he asked, glancing over at me.

I shook my head, not wanting to admit how terrible my foray into dating had been after the divorce. "A few months after Regina left us, this nurse at the hospital asked me out."

Rhett dropped his head back and readjusted his ball cap. "Nurses are so fuckin' hot."

"This one was," I admitted with a smirk. "And we had some fun around the hospital, outside of the hospital, in the car on the way to the hospital..."

"Then what the hell are you doing here?" Rhett asked.

The memory of it felt fresh as the air outside. "After seeing each other for a couple months, I took her home to meet Maya..." I let out a sigh. "And it didn't go so well."

"With Maya? She's an angel."

"Just like you were an angel growing up," I said. "More like hell on wheels."

"What happened?"

I looked out the window, noticing the stars dotting the sky. I barely ever saw the stars in Dallas. "Maya finger-painted her white dress with spaghetti sauce, and Sherry, the nurse, told me she could keep seeing me, but she was never going to see Maya again."

Rhett let out a low whistle. "So you broke it off."

"I had to. How could I have a relationship with someone who doesn't like the most important person in my life?"

"Yep." He tapped the steering wheel with his fingers. "This is exactly why I always bag it before I tap it. Chicks be like 'no Rhett, I'm on the pill, you don't have to wear one.' Fuck no."

I chuckled as he continued talking.

"I figure between ninety-nine percent effectiveness of

the pill and eighty percent effectiveness of a condom, there's a hundred percent chance I won't fuck up some kid's life."

"There's that math again," I teased.

He smiled slightly and tilted his head. "You're a great dad, Fletch. I could never do what you do. And Maya's a good kid. Don't let anyone tell you otherwise just because she's strong-willed."

"Thanks, man," I said. "I'm lucky as hell that Liv was looking for a job when she was."

"It's been rough on her," Rhett said.

My eyebrows drew together. Was Liv complaining to him about nannying for me? Was that how he heard about Maya being difficult? "What do you mean?"

He shook his head angrily, looking like he could spit. "That fucking feedlot. Liv's been assistant manager there for the last six years, and you know what they did when the manager spot came open? Gave it to some dumbass out of Fort Worth who doesn't know his head from his ass."

I groaned for Liv. She always held her own on the farm growing up, probably more so than half of us guys.

"And this idiot," Rhett continued. "He treated her like she was there to do paperwork and clean the office and get coffee."

"She didn't report him for being sexist?" I asked.

Rhett shook his head. "She tried, but the person over his head accused her of being jealous of his promotion. So one day Liv had enough."

"She put in her two weeks?" I asked.

"You could say that." He chuckled. "She took the

tractor and loaded the guy's pickup with cow shit, then left her note on top." He held out his hand like describing a banner. "'You're a piece of shit. I quit.'"

I laughed so hard at the image of this guy walking out to his truck piled high with shit, just to find her note. I was fucking crying. "Good for her. Guess I better not piss her off."

"Better not," Rhett agreed with a grin. "She knows I'd go to battle for her, but she can definitely hold her own."

"Good thing Maya's learning from her," I said.

Rhett nodded. "She'll be a great nanny 'til she settles down with kids of her own."

For a moment, I couldn't speak. But I wasn't sure why.

RHETT DROPPED me back at my place sometime around midnight last night, and I woke up to my alarm, deciding to go for a run instead of a stationary bike ride, since all the lights were still off in the guesthouse.

I put on my digital watch that would track my distance and heartrate, then put in my ear buds and started jogging down the gravel road. There were hills by my house, and the morning sun was already heating up, so I had a pretty good sweat going just half a mile in. A few trucks drove by, and I waved at each one.

In the country, things were organized in square-shaped sections, and each section was four miles around. So I jogged around one section, then got back to the house, doing stretches in the front yard to cool down.

When I reached the front door, I could hear upbeat music blaring from inside. I smiled to myself. Maya and Liv must be awake.

I pushed the door open, but they didn't notice me. Maya sat on the island, a mixing bowl between her legs and flour brushed on her forehead. Liv stood with her back to me, her hands on her knees and her hips swinging to the beat while Maya giggled at her.

I leaned against the wall, grinning way too big at the two of them.

Liv punched her fists in the air, spinning with her long brown hair whipping around her, and then froze at the sight of me.

Her eyes went wide and her lips parted, and she covered her mouth like she wished she could disappear into the floor.

"DADDY!" Maya put her bowl aside and jumped down from the island, running and hugging me.

She hit me with such force I almost fell backward. I wrapped my arms around her and picked her up. "What did I do to get such a warm welcome?"

The volume on the music lowered as Maya said, "I had so much fun with Livvy! And we made coffee for you!" She giggled, and then Liv chuckled as well.

"What?" I asked with a nervous laugh. "Did you pee in it or something?"

"No!" Maya laughed. "Gross."

I shook my head at them and went to pour myself a cup. I took a cautious sip, but it tasted like regular coffee, so I doctored it up like usual with milk and sugar.

When I took another sip, it tasted so bad I had to spit it in the sink.

When I looked up, Maya and Liv were rolling on the floor in stitches.

13

LIV

Right before Fletcher walked out the door for work, he said, "I left something for you in the bathroom."

I raised my eyebrows. "Aren't you a little old to prank me by leaving a turd in the bathroom?"

His face instantly went red, making me laugh. "Damn it, just go look."

Maya covered her mouth, pointing at her dad. "YOU SAID THE D-WORD!"

"And don't you repeat it," he said, coming to kiss the top of her head. "Love you, bye."

"Bye," she said, and I echoed the word too. After the door shut, I said, "Wonder what he left."

"Let's go see." She got off her chair, following me to the guest bathroom. On the counter was a jar of peanut butter with a folded piece of paper on top.

IN CASE you have any more gum "accidents."

Fletcher

I CHUCKLED AT THE NOTE, and Maya said, "Why did he leave food in the bathroom? That's so weird."

Not wanting to give her any ideas, I said, "Sometimes boys are just weird."

While Maya ate her breakfast, I called the city pool and signed her up for swim lessons, starting this afternoon Fletcher said he and Regina had taken her to infant swim rescue lessons, but that had been it. He was all for Maya getting out and meeting new kids.

As we drove into town, I asked, "What did you and Dad do yesterday while I was at my parents'?"

"We went to Grampy's, and my uncles took me horseback riding!"

"That sounds fun," I said. "Do you like riding horses?" That was something we could do at my family's farm too.

"Yeah, but I always ride behind Uncle Hayes and hang on because I don't want to fall off."

I glanced over my shoulder at her. "You know, my dad always said you're not a cowgirl until you fall off a horse at least five times. I think I fell on purpose after that."

She laughed. "Was he right? Were you a cowgirl after that?"

"I think so." I shrugged.

I pulled onto the highway, and within a few miles, red and blue lights shined in my rearview mirror. "*Shit.*"

"LIVVY!" Maya said.

"Shoot!" I corrected. "Shoot."

"Were you driving too fast?" Maya asked.

"I mean, a few miles over the speed limit, but that shouldn't be enough to get me pulled over." Besides, I did *not* want to use my first paycheck on a speeding ticket. I had some catching up to do.

I reached over into the glovebox, getting my registration and insurance, then pulled my driver's license out of my purse.

A tall, tan officer approached the car and bent over, all dark aviator glasses and chiseled jawline. I'd recognize that face anywhere.

"Uncle Knox!" Maya cried from her booster seat.

"Ma'am, do you know you have the cutest niece in the back seat?" Knox, Fletcher's little brother, grinned, pulling off his glasses.

"Knox!" I hit his arm. "You scared the crap out of me!" He'd been a couple years younger than me in school and was always the person behind a prank. The fact that he was a cop now was a mystery to us all.

He chuckled, opening the back door, and Maya launched into his arms, hugging him tight.

"I missed you yesterday," he said to her. "Sorry I had to work."

She put her hands on his shoulders, looking at him as he held her up. I got out of the car to talk with them both.

"I'm going to swim lessons," Maya told him.

"Swim lessons? That sounds fun. Think you can teach me?"

She laughed. "I don't know how yet!"

"Well, when you do, I'll have my floaties ready," he

said. He grinned at me. "Want a police escort to the swimming pool?"

I chuckled. "Don't think I could turn one down."

Maya said, "Can I ride with you?"

Knox gave me a questioning look, like he was asking permission.

"It's fine with me, if it's okay with you. I'll have to tell her dad, eight years old and she's already in the back of a cop car."

Knox laughed. "Riding around with you, she's bound to stir up trouble."

"You know I'm a good girl."

"Yes, you are," he agreed in a sultry voice that made my cheeks flush.

"Come on, Maya," he said.

He carried her back to his car, and they drove off, lights flashing. I fanned myself before taking a picture on my phone, then put my truck in gear and followed them to the city pool. When we got there, the other kids in the lesson thought Maya was so cool for riding with a cop, so they instantly had something to talk about.

I sat in one of the empty pool chairs and sent Fletcher a text, including the picture of Knox's car.

Liv: Look who gave Maya a ride to swim lessons.

A few minutes of scrolling social media later, my phone chimed with his reply.

Fletcher: I bet she loved that. How are lessons going?

Liv: She's doing great. Already made some new friends. They're practicing kicks now.

I sent him a picture of Maya hanging on to a floating board and kicking at the water.

Fletcher: Have I mentioned how thankful I am to have you as our nanny?

Liv: Maybe a time or two. But it never hurts to hear it.

Fletcher: Well, I am very thankful for you.

Liv: You did me a favor too. I'm starting to think nannying is the best job ever. Now that Maya's pranking you instead of me. ;)

Fletcher: I believe she had an accomplice.

Liv: Who ever would that be?

Fletcher: Cute.

Fletcher: Almost as cute as those dance moves.

My cheeks instantly flamed, remembering the dance party he walked in on. Gosh, I was such a nerd.

Liv: Sorry you had to witness that. You're probably scarred for life.

Fletcher: I didn't mind the view.

My eyes widened at his text.

Was Fletcher Madigan *flirting* with me?

Before I had a chance to reply, another text came through.

Fletcher: I have another patient coming in. Talk soon.

I took a screenshot of the conversation and sent it to my group chat with Henrietta and Della.

Della: OMG HE IS SO FLIRTING WITH YOU!!!

Henrietta: I say play the music and dance it up. ;)

Liv: He's my BOSS. You're supposed to keep me from making bad decisions.

Henrietta: LOL sometimes bad decisions can be the most fun.

Della: Which makes them good decisions.

Liv: Have a mentioned I love you two?

Della: A time or two.

Henrietta: Love you too.

⋎

WHEN SWIM LESSONS WRAPPED UP, Maya and I loaded into the truck and went back to the house for lunch. I pulled all the ingredients out of the fridge for cucumber sandwiches and when I was looking through the drawers for a spatula to spread the mayo, I found a heart shaped cookie cutter.

While Maya showered and changed, I made the sandwiches and cut hers into cute little hearts. Then I arranged two hearts on her plate for eyes, used a big strawberry for the nose, and a line of baby carrots for the smile.

I smiled at it and took a little picture, sending it to Fletcher.

Liv: Lunch time. :)

Before he could reply, Maya came out from her room, her wet hair hanging in waves down her back, leaving damp spots in her navy-blue shirt. "Where's my food?" she asked a bite to her voice.

I tried not to be offended because she was probably really hungry from all the swimming. "Right here," I answered, eagerly waiting for her to see the surprise.

She got on her chair and looked at the food, her lip curling up. "I'm not a baby."

"I know, I thought it looked like one of those emojis with the heart eyes."

Still frowning, she asked, "What's in this sandwich."

"It's one of my favorites," I said. "Cucumber with

mayo, cream cheese, and some seasoning. I think you'll love it."

She looked at it for a long second, then picked it up and dropped all the food in the trash. "I don't like cucumbers."

I clenched my jaw together. "What the heck, Maya? Are we really doing this again?"

"Doing what?" she snapped back.

"Doing the thing where you pretend you're not a great kid with a big heart who makes good choices and doesn't throw away food I worked really freaking hard on."

She put her hands on her hips. "Make it better next time."

"You make it yourself," I replied, stepping outside to cool off before I could go off on her. I thought we were making so much progress, but maybe I was kidding myself. Was our whole summer really going to be like this?

I got out my phone to call my mom and she answered after a few rings.

"What's up, honey?" she asked.

I let out a groan, filling her in on the whole thing.

"That poor girl," Mom said.

"Poor her?" I demanded. I looked into the house to see she was already watching TV with a bag of chips in her lap. "Poor me! I don't know how to do this!"

Mom let out a soft laugh, making me give an exasperated laugh too.

"Help me," I whined.

I could hear the smile in her voice as she said, "You got too close to her, and she's afraid you'll leave, so she pushed back. She's probably afraid and worried and really stinking angry at all that's happened. She needs to find a way to get her anger out. Throw something, hit something. Anything to move that rage out of her body."

I nodded. "I think I have an idea."

"That's my girl."

When I got off the phone with my mom, I called Hayes.

A short conversation later, I walked back into the house, grabbed the remote from the coffee table, and turned off the TV.

"Hey!" Maya said. "I was watching that!"

"Not anymore. Get in the truck."

She let out a loud groan, but I waited until she got up and followed her out to my pickup. When we were inside and buckled in, she asked, "Where are we going now?"

"You'll see," I said.

We drove the rest of the way to Cottonwood Falls and stopped at Hayes's Body Shop on the outskirts of town. It was a big tin building with a small shop of front and a massive lot of vehicles used for parts next door.

"What are we doing here," Maya asked.

"You'll find out in a little bit. Come on."

We got out of the truck and started walking toward the shop. Hayes came out of the garage, wiping his oil stained hands on a rag. "If it isn't my two favorite girls."

Maya went to him, giving him a side hug, despite all the grease on his clothes.

"Come with me," he said.

I followed behind him and Maya, and he walked us through the shop where a few mechanics were working on different vehicles. A big fan like the ones from the school gym circulated air through the space, but it was still a bit hotter than it was outside. Sweat was already beading down my neck.

When we reached the back corner, Hayes handed us both helmets, then goggles. After we put them on, he gave me a bigger sledgehammer and Maya a smaller one. "Come with me."

Maya had lots of questions, but Hayes stalled while he walked us to the car lot next door. Outside, he pointed at three rusted up vehicles. "You can use any of these. Okay?"

"Thanks," I said.

He gave me a small, sad smile before patting me on the back and walking away.

"Tell me what we're doing," Maya said, no more room for questions. She leaned against her small sledge-hammer on the ground.

I picked mine up, held it over my head, and then crashed it into the windshield of the closest car.

"Hey!" Maya said.

But I did it again, feeling my muscles work, the rebound of the hammer as it hit glass, hearing the shatter and crunch under metal.

"What are you doing?" she yelled.

I turned back to her, lifting up my glasses and

kneeling in front of her. Her eyes were wide as she stared at me.

"Maya, I get it," I said gently. "You're eight years old and your mom and dad split up. Your dad works a lot. Your mom doesn't call as much as she should. And you're confused. You're angry."

Tears started forming in her eyes, telling me I was hitting the nail on the head.

"You have every right to be angry at what they did. You can be mad, pissed as hell that they didn't stay together like they promised and that your life isn't what you think it should be... But you're taking it out in all the wrong directions."

She tilted her head, and I reached up, brushed a piece of hair back over her shoulder.

"Parents aren't perfect," I said sadly. "They make mistakes. They break up sometimes. But you can't push away the people that are here. The people that love you. So let's be mad at these stupid cars and smash the hell out of them, okay?"

She sniffed then wiped at her eyes.

"You can do this," I said. "You can get all your anger out. Right here, right now. And if you ever get angry again, we can always come back. Hayes promised me we could."

"Really?" she asked.

I nodded. "I'm on your team, okay? You and me against this anger."

She nodded, her little lips pursing together. And then she picked up her hammer and swung it as hard as she could at the side mirror. The glass shattered, and the plastic broke off the car, hanging on only by a few wires.

Grinning, Maya jumped up and down. "Did you see that?"

"I sure did!" I said. "Now beat the shit out of it!"

She didn't even scold me for it. Just picked up her hammer and wailed away. She hit the car over and over again until her arms were shaking, and her breath came fast. And then she looked at the damaged car, her hammer dropping at her side.

"What is it?" I asked, looking at her. "Are you hurt?"

Tears streamed down her cheeks and she came to me, burying herself in my arms. "I'm sorry," she cried.

"Oh honey..." I held her close, brushing my hand over her hair. "It's okay. It's all going to be okay."

"Why doesn't my mommy love me?" she asked.

I held my breath. Some questions didn't have answers. But I was going to try.

FLETCHER

Brenda came into my office. "Hey, I have a call from Hayes on line one."

My eyebrows drew together. "Why's he calling me at work? Is everything okay?"

"I don't know, said you weren't answering your cell," she said.

I nodded, glad that the last hour of my day was saved for completing paperwork. I went into my office to take the call and shut the door before picking up.

"Hello?" I said, bracing myself for bad news.

"Hey," he said. It was quiet, like he was in the office or something. "I wasn't sure if I should call or not, but I thought you should know..."

My pulse picked up. "Know what? Hayes, spit it out."

"Liv brought Maya here and something seems off. They're out beating up old cars and I don't know... I feel like maybe something happened today and I thought I should tell you about it so you're ready when you get home. Didn't want you to be surprised or anything."

"I'll be there in five minutes," I said. "Thanks, Hayes."

"Of course," he said.

I told Brenda everything was okay, but I had to handle something and left the office, worry settling into my gut. It took a lot to worry Hayes and even though I knew Liv would take good care of Maya I worried something bad had happened today. I knew the good texts and that cute lunch were too good to be true. I was just waiting for the other shoe to fall.

The drive to Hayes's shop outside of town felt way too damn long, but eventually I rolled up into the gravel lot and left my truck running as I got out and jogged to the open garage door. Hayes was up front, working on a car.

"Where are they?" I asked.

"Out in the car lot," he replied. "Haven't heard any banging in a little bit."

I nodded, jogging around the side of the shop and seeing Liv and Maya several rows of cars back. I walked their way, but they didn't seem to notice me at all. They seemed to be deep in conversation, so I slowed, not wanting to distract them from what looked like an important talk.

I stopped beside an old car and lowered myself beside the rotted tire, just listening.

"Do you see this dollar?" Liv asked.

Maya was silent.

"How much is it worth?"

"A dollar," Maya said, like it was obvious.

"What could you buy with a dollar?"

"I dunno," Maya said quietly. "Maybe a candy bar. Some gum."

There was quiet for a moment, then the sound of crumpling paper.

"Why did you do that?" Maya asked, surprise clear in her voice.

Liv said, "What's it look like now?"

Maya let out a small huff. "Looks like a wrinkled-up dollar bill."

Then came the sound of tearing paper.

"What are you *doing*?" Maya asked.

"It's got some rips, now, huh?" Liv said.

"Um yeah, you ripped it," Maya replied.

"But look at it."

There was quiet, just the sound of a soft breeze playing through the short grass growing around all the cars.

"How much is it worth now?" Liv asked. "Could we take it to the store and buy a candy bar?"

After a moment, Maya said, "Yeah. We could."

"You're right," Liv said. "You know you're like this dollar?"

"I am?" Maya asked, her voice sounding small.

I squeezed my eyes shut. Was Liv telling my daughter she was damaged goods? I was about to get up, and confront her, but something held me back.

"You've gone through some hard times," Liv said. The paper crumpling sound came again. "Your parents divorced." She ripped the paper. "Your mom didn't call." She ripped it again. "A nanny quit." Another rip. "And another nanny quit, and then another. And it really freaking sucked."

I heard Maya sniffle, and my heart went out to her. I wanted to take her in my arms and protect her from all those things. But I couldn't. I hadn't.

"But no matter how many tears and crinkles this dollar has, it's still a dollar. It still has value. It is still worth spending and still worth taking care of. You've got some rips and wrinkles and some hurts, Maya Madigan, but you are still a little girl. And that means you are worth loving and taking care of, no matter what. Do you understand?"

A small cry broke loose from Maya's chest, and Liv said, "Come here, baby girl. I've got you. Always."

Tears rolled down my cheeks, and I pushed up from the car, walking back to Hayes's shop.

When he saw me, he asked, "Everything okay?"

My voice sounded rough as I said, "I think it will be."

But deep down, I wondered. Was I like that dollar? Or was I damaged beyond repair so no one, especially not Liv, could see the value in me?

Studying me and seeing a little too much, Hayes said, "Come on, let's grab a beer."

I glanced at the car he was working on. "I don't want to interrupt your work more than I already have."

"To me," he replied, drying his hands off on a rag, "it looks like work is interrupting family time."

He started back toward the office, and I followed him. He reached into a mini fridge in the corner and pulled out a couple beers, passing me one.

The liquid slid over my lips, tangy and cool then warming my insides. I took a breath and rolled the can in my hand. "I needed that."

"I know," Hayes replied.

"What do you think happened today?" I asked him.

"They didn't say, but Maya looked like she was in a mood and Liv was on a mission."

I chuckled. "That about covers the last couple weeks."

Hayes looked up at me. "You're lucky to have her, you know?"

"Liv's been a lifesaver," I agreed.

But Hayes shook his head. "Don't get me wrong, Liv is great. I was talking about Maya."

I looked up at him, needing to hear more. For the last several months, I'd felt like I was flailing, like I was being judged for Maya's behavior. Hayes's words... they were a life raft, and I hung on tight.

"When Mom died, I was just a little younger than Maya. I know I wasn't easy for Dad. I probably acted out the worst of all of us. And one day after I ripped up Deidre's flower beds for the hell of it, Dad took me out for a drive. I thought he was going to ream my ass. Tell me to shape up or he was shipping me off to military school."

"Sounds like something Dad would say," I agreed.

Hayes smirked. "I would have deserved it too. But he didn't do that. He stopped at the pond, got out of the truck, and started skipping rocks. When I went to join him, I stood a few feet off, and he said, 'Join me.'

"Of course, I was confused and angry and said something like, 'I didn't think you'd want to be around me.' But Dad got on his knees in front of me, and I swear he was tearing up when he said, 'I'm lucky to have you. On the good days, but especially the bad, because those are the days I can show you how much I love you, no matter what.'"

Now my eyes were stinging, and I cleared my throat. "I never knew about that."

"Seemed like it was between Dad and me, but now, I think it needs to be between you and Maya too."

A knock sounded on the office door, and we glanced over to see Liv and Maya coming in. With my heart full and aching, I reached for my daughter and pulled her to my side.

"Hey, sweetie, what do you say we go to Grandpa's pond and skip some rocks?"

After Fletcher left with Maya, I went over to Henrietta and Tyler's house for dinner. When we finished eating the steak and vegetables Tyler made on the grill, they offered for me to stay and play corn hole, but I needed to get back home.

Earlier, when Fletcher came to Hayes's shop, he'd seemed so conflicted. I hoped I hadn't overstepped in some way by taking Maya there, and I knew we needed to talk it out just to make sure we were on the same page.

When I got back to the house, I saw his truck in the driveway, so I parked beside it and steeled myself before going to the main house. When I reached the front door, I could hear country music playing through the speakers.

Looking through the big picture window, I saw Fletcher spinning Maya in a dance. She had a smile on her face, and he looked more at peace than since I started working for him and Maya.

Not wanting to interrupt the moment, I turned and

walked to my place, knowing we'd get a chance to talk in the morning.

Back at my place, I took my time in the bath, relaxing from an emotionally heavy day. Then I turned on some country music on my Alexa and went about making a bedtime snack. Remembering that Fletcher mentioned a popcorn machine, I opened the top cabinet and saw it toward the back.

Maybe if I reached high enough I could... My fingertips grazed the edge of it, and I reached harder, trying to get it without needing a step stool or anything. But then I felt a solid muscled body reach over me and get it.

I screamed, backing away to see Fletcher holding the popcorn making.

"What the hell!" I yelled, holding my hand over my chest and feeling very aware of my wet hair and long t-shirt nightgown.

Looking sheepish, Fletcher said, "Seemed like you were struggling, and the door was open..."

My eyebrows drew together. "The door was open?"

"I mean, after I opened it," he said.

I laughed. "Well, thank you for getting that down."

He set it on the counter, and I rummaged through the cabinets for the popcorn, trying to hide how much his hard body pressed to mine affected me. This man was sex on a stick, and he didn't even know it.

I poured the kernels into the back of the machine and once I had it on, I faced him again. "Did you just come to scare five years off my life? Or was there something else?"

Chuckling, he said, "The scare was only a side effect. I wanted to talk to you about earlier today."

I folded my arms across my chest, and I swore I saw

his eyes travel to my chest for a moment before glancing back up. My skin heated under his stare.

"What did you want to talk about?" I asked.

He seemed confused for a moment, like he'd forgotten the reason for coming over here. Then he said, "I just... I wanted to thank you for what you did for Maya earlier."

I rubbed my hand over my arm. "I was worried you'd be upset."

"Upset with you?" he reached out, brushing his thumb over my cheek. Goosebumps ran down my spine. "I had my first conversation with Maya tonight that felt like... I don't know. Like maybe things could get better between us. And that was a big part because of you."

Pressing my hand to my chest, I said, "Fletcher, that's amazing news. I'm so glad."

His lips lifted slightly. "Your popcorn's done."

"Oh." I turned, realizing the machine was whirring but nothing else was spitting into the bowl. I flicked the button to turn it off and then held out the bowl. "Do you want some?"

"Sure," he replied.

I got down a bowl and poured half out for him. Then I went to the couch, sitting on one end. He took it and followed me, both of us sitting on our own ends. For a moment, we ate the popcorn in silence.

"What are you thinking about?" I asked him.

His cheeks gained a little color. "I want to ask you something, but I don't want to get yelled at for eavesdropping."

I chuckled. "I knew you were listening to me and Maya at the shop."

"Well then... The dollar thing. Where did you hear that?"

I bit my lip, not sure how much I wanted to admit to Fletcher.

"You can tell me," he said gently.

So I took a deep breath. "When I went to college, I think the stress of moving away from home made my PCOS flare up. I gained way more than the freshman fifteen. None of my clothes were really fitting anymore, and I was really insecure about it. My first boyfriend in college wasn't a good guy. He said a lot of things about my body that made me feel like I'd never get better than him. It made me feel like I'd never be good enough for anyone."

He frowned, but before he could comfort me, I continued. "I went to counseling about it, and that was one of the things my therapist told me. I always keep cash in my wallet now to remind me that I have value, no matter what."

He reached his foot out, covering mine with his, and he smiled gently. "If you ever need reminded that you're beautiful, you can ask me too."

My heart warmed, tugged. Because I'd wanted so badly for him to feel that way about me. But I could tell there was more. "What is it, Fletch?"

He looked down. "Do you think... you think that applies to everyone? That they're worth something no matter how crumpled and ripped they are?"

I looked at him, wondering why this perfect, beautiful, caring man was even asking. "I think the secret is that no one's ever really crumpled and ripped up. They just have trouble seeing themselves any other way."

He was quiet for a moment, eating his popcorn. "I should probably get back to the house, in case Maya wakes up."

17

LIV

The next day, I walked to the house preparing myself for anything. But when I got there, Fletcher smiled at me, making my heart beat faster.

"Good morning," he said, his voice gentle, warm.

Maya said, "Morning. Can you do my hair in fishtail braids for swim lessons?"

I laughed. At least she got the good morning in there first. "Sure thing. And good morning."

It struck me that when I was living alone and working at the feed lot, I might not hear anyone's voice until I got to work. I liked waking up and hearing Fletcher and Maya's words before those of anyone else.

We ate breakfast together and then Fletcher went to work, and we got ready for swim lessons. Maya seemed to be in such a better mood, which was a breath of fresh air. Still, I decided we'd go to my mom's house after swim lessons.

Maya behaved so much better when we kept her busy.

I think having time to sit around and think about her mom just made her sadder.

So after lessons, we drove toward my parent's place. As the farmhouse came into view, Maya stared around. "It's so close to Grampy's house!"

I nodded. "Your daddy was my neighbor growing up."

"I wish I had a neighbor to play with," she said. "Dad says the closest house is a whole mile away."

I grinned. "We're about a mile from your Grampy's house, but we always rode our bikes back and forth through the pasture so we didn't have to ride on the road."

"Can we ride bikes sometime?" she asked.

I pulled in front of my parents' house and parked beside Mom's truck. "I don't have a bike anymore, but if you have one, I can take you to town and watch you ride around the trail?"

"I want you to ride with me!" She pouted.

My heart warmed, and I tried not to show how much her words mattered to me. She'd gone from pushing me away yesterday to inviting me to join her in something fun. I smiled back at her before facing the road again. "If I can find a bike, I'll ride with you." *Just need to find a seat big enough that it doesn't disappear in my ass crack.*

We got out of the truck and walked into the house. It smelled like cookies, and I smiled at Mom. She loved being a grandma to my brother Gage's stepchildren and was probably counting down the days until the rest of us would catch up and give her more kids to love on.

"Maya!" she said, smiling at the little girl sticking close to my side. "Oh, you look so much like your daddy."

Maya's face scrunched up. "I'm not a boy!"

Mom and 1 laughed together, and I put my arms around her shoulders. "You have his eyes. And his smile."

Maya pressed her lips together.

"You can't hide it!" I said, tickling her side.

She grinned then, lighting up the room with her toothy smile.

"What are we doing today?" I asked Mom as we followed her through to the kitchen.

"I want to get the attic cleaned out before school starts," she said. "But I made us some cookies to snack on before we get started!"

Maya clapped her hands together. "Are they chocolate chip?"

Mom nodded. "The best kind, right?"

We reached the kitchen, where Mom had milk and cookies already on the table. She gave each of us two cookies with a glass of milk, and we sat eating them while Mom told Maya about Cottonwood Falls Elementary School.

"Twenty kids in my class?" Maya said over a mouthful of cookies. "We had twelve at my last school."

"Was it a private school?" Mom asked.

Maya nodded.

Mom said, "I bet it was great. We also have a playground, and fourth graders get two recesses a day and gym class."

Maya's mouth fell open. "*Two* recesses? We only got one!"

Mom nodded with a smile. "Plus, our music teacher has really fun instruments the fourth graders can play."

By the time Mom finished telling Maya about the

Cottonwood Falls elementary school, she seemed a little more excited to go in the fall.

We finished our cookies, and then Mom said, "Before we go to the attic, I have something I wanted to show you."

"What is it?" I asked.

She waved her hand over her shoulder. "Follow me."

Maya and I trailed behind her to her bedroom, where a cream-colored dress lay on the bed. I stared at it, recognizing it from the photos. "Your wedding dress? I thought it was lost."

Mom grinned, shaking her head. "I found it in the attic yesterday when I started sorting things. I thought maybe you could try it on?"

I stared at the dress. "Are you sure? I don't even know if it's the right size."

"It's a twenty-two," Mom said. "Should be pretty close."

"Do it and you're cool, do it and you're cool," Maya chanted.

Mom and I caught each other's eyes, laughing.

"Okay, okay," I said, taking the dress and walking to the en suite bathroom. The satin fabric rippled through my hands, and something about holding my mom's wedding dress felt so sacred.

I was taken back in history, imagining the day she and my dad said "I do". She was twenty when they married, twelve years younger than I was now. What must have been going through her mind as she walked toward my dad at the front of the church?

As I slid the dress over my head, I pictured my mom getting ready with her friends. And then I turned and looked at myself in the mirror, speechless. It was like seeing an echo of my mom that day with off the shoulder sleeves, the pinched waist and the A-line skirt highlighting my curves. It was *gorgeous*.

"Need help?" Mom asked.

"I don't think so," I called back, reaching behind me to hoist the zipper.

With it all zipped up, I took a final look in the mirror, smiling at myself, and then walked into the room.

Maya's eyes were wide. "You look like a princess."

Mom nodded in agreement. "It's perfect on you."

I did a spin, making the skirt flare around me. "Maybe I can wear it on my wedding day?"

Mom looked so happy. "You want to get married someday? After you broke things off with Wayne a few years ago, I was wondering if you wanted to be the cool aunt forever."

"Why wouldn't I want to be married?" I asked, smoothing my dress in the mirror. "A man promising to be by my side forever, for better or worse, in front of everyone I love? It's sacred."

Mom smiled at me in the mirror. "Which means you have to wait for just the right one."

"Exactly," I said with a smile. "Wayne wasn't right for me, but maybe I'll meet 'the one' someday."

"You will," Mom said confidently.

Maya said, "You can wear the dress anyway."

I grinned at her, hugging her tight. "I like the way you think. Now we have to get to work in the attic. Let me take off this dress."

After I changed, the three of us walked back toward the stairs. At the top, there was a ladder built into the wall that led into a dusty attic. My brothers and I used to love going up there in the winter because it was the warmest place in the house and felt like a secret hideout. But now, in the late July heat, it was downright hot.

I climbed up first, moving the trap door and then standing on the wooden floor and pulling the string to light the room.

Dust motes swirled in the light from the lone bulb and a small window on the side. Boxes were stacked along the edges of the small space.

Maya crawled up after me and looked around. "It's like a haunted house!"

I held my hands up by my ears and said, "Boo!"

Mom tossed a box of trash bags up, and they made a loud thud on the floor, making Maya and me jump and then giggle. Then she passed up a box fan, which I immediately plugged in.

Mom came up, smiling, and said, "Maya, I think there's a box of Liv's old Barbie dolls over there. Maybe you can go through and see which ones you like."

I scowled. "None of them have feet."

Maya gave me a curious look while Mom laughed.

"Dad's goats used to chew on them," I explained.

"Serves you right for leaving them on the porch." Mom said.

I rolled my eyes, still a little sour about it. But Maya went to dig through the box while Mom and I picked separate boxes and began the process of deciding what to keep and what to toss or give away. There were some really cool gems up here, like an antique flour sifter Great Grandma Griffen used and some old dresses she sewed from flour sacks for my great aunts. And much to my surprise, there were, in fact, a few Barbies still intact.

As Mom was looking through a box, she said, "Oh my goodness. You two *have* to see this."

Maya and I got up from our spots on the dusty floor, going to my mom, who was holding up a black cardboard photo frame, the kind used for sports and prom photos. As soon as I got closer, I instantly recognized the picture.

Fletcher and I stood in the awkward prom pose, my back to his front. His hand rested on my forearm, my arms hanging by my side, and we both smiled cheesily at the camera. My strapless lilac dress had a wide black lace belt around the middle, and I wore a thick black statement necklace. Fletcher looked so handsome then, with a smooth face, dimples in his cheeks, and a heart-melting smile. Add the suit and bowtie with the lilac boutonniere, and he looked like every girl's teenage dream.

"That's you and my dad?" Maya asked.

I nodded, smiling over at her and putting my arm around her. "He took me to prom."

"Were you in love?"

I was, I didn't say. "No, we just went as friends."

Mom said, "You two had so much fun that night."

I nodded in agreement. "We did."

"Can I have the picture?" Maya asked.

Mom looked to me, and even though I loved the picture, it had just been sitting forgotten in the attic for ages. It would be good for Maya to have a picture of her dad when he was younger. "Sure you can," I said with a smile.

She took it and flounced to her pile of Barbies, setting the photo carefully beside it.

Mom nudged my arm, whispering, "You're so good with her, Liv."

Coming from my mom, who was the best with kids, it was a really big compliment. My cheeks warmed. "Thanks. I'm trying."

For the rest of the afternoon, we worked our way through the attic, getting rid of a few garbage bags and reorganizing a several boxes before calling it a day.

When we were done, Mom gave Maya a five-dollar bill for her piggy bank, and then we headed back to the house. Maya brought in one of her new dolls, and I got to work making supper for the three of us.

When I heard Fletcher's truck pulling into the driveway, a smile spread on my lips. Even if my crush was unwarranted, I liked being around him. He had this steady presence that was both calming and exciting at the same time. He had a sense of humor, but not quite as obnoxious as my brother's. And the way he loved his daughter? It made my heart melt.

When he walked through the door, Maya went to hug him. He rested his cheek on her head, and I could tell he was savoring the moment. When she let go, she said, "Come check out these dolls we found at Livvy's house."

He raised his eyebrows. "Did I miss something from when the Fernandezes were here?"

"My parents' house," I explained. "We cleared out the attic, and you're not going to believe what we found."

"What's that?" he asked, getting on the floor next to Maya.

"Our prom picture," I said with a smile.

His own smile was nostalgic. "That thing's a million years old by now."

"You might be old, but I'm not," I teased.

He chuckled, looking down at Maya's dolls. "If my dementia isn't acting up, I remember it being a pretty fun night."

"It might surprise you, but it was the best prom I went to in high school. You were just doing me a favor, but I remember it all, right down to the flowers in your boutonniere."

"Where's the picture?" he asked, getting up from the floor.

"I think Maya left it in the back seat of the truck."

"Honey," he said to her. "Can you go get it?"

She nodded, grabbing two dolls in her hands and running out the front door.

Fletcher stepped closer, looking at me over the island so intently my breath caught in my chest.

"Lilac."

My lips parted.

He remembered.

And then Maya came running back through the door.

18

FLETCHER

I walked to the front of the practice to tell Brenda I was going for lunch. She smiled and said, "I'll walk out with you." She always used her lunch break to walk around town. Even on hot summer days like today.

"How are things going with your cute new nanny?" she asked.

Heat instantly went to the tips of my ears. Could she see inside my head to know I'd been thinking about Liv in ways that I shouldn't be?

No, I decided. She was just making conversation. "Maya loves her," I said earnestly. "She's been doing swim lessons and going out to the Griffens' farm, riding horses. Hanging out with my dad. It's been a great summer for her so far."

Brenda nodded, pausing beside me on the sidewalk. "You seem a lot less distracted and worried. Maybe that frees up time for other things. Like dating?"

I nearly choked on my own spit. "Brenda, I'm sorry, but you're a colleague. I just don't see you like—"

She tossed her head back, laughing. "Not me, you silly goose! My daughter. She's a year older than you and went through a divorce about the same time you did. I think you two would have a lot in common."

"Oh." I raised my eyebrows. I remembered Brenda's daughter Morganne from school. She was cute enough. Quiet. And married her high school sweetheart. "She's divorced? Everyone thought she and Charlie would be together forever."

She lifted a corner of her lips in a sad half-smile. "Time changes things."

"It sure does," I agreed.

"Don't decide now," Brenda said. "But get back to me when you're ready to say yes." She winked and began walking off, waving over her shoulder.

I shook my head to myself as I walked toward the diner to meet my brothers Knox and Hayes for lunch. There were five of us kids, but Ford was away in Dallas, playing professional football, and Bryce was off at college.

When I got to the diner, Hayes and Knox were already at a booth toward the back, and on my way to join them, I said hi to Rhonda, the hairdresser; Bora, the florist; and Hazel, the woman who ran the local newspaper like a one-woman show.

When I got to the booth, Hayes winked at me. "Looks like you're fighting off the ladies."

I rolled my eyes at him, picking up a menu, even though it hadn't changed since high school. "No, but half my clients are giving me their daughters' or granddaughters' numbers. And Brenda's trying to get me to go out with her daughter too. How do you two handle being single in a small town?"

Hayes winked. "I don't mind it so much." Between him and Rhett, it was hard to tell who the bigger womanizer was.

Knox let out a sigh, stirring sugar into his coffee. "I'm not liking it so much. Actually... I was thinking about asking Liv on a date."

It was like all the air had been sucked from the room. Knox wanted to go out with Liv?

"I mean, if it's okay," he continued. "I promise I won't mess things up with her as your nanny."

Every word felt like sandpaper on my tongue as I said, "You don't need to get my permission."

He smiled to himself. "Good."

Hayes looked up at me and said, "You need to see Rhonda. Looking like a shaggy dog."

I rolled my eyes at him. "How's your business?"

We changed subjects, talking about Hayes's auto shop and the trouble he was having finding a good mechanic to come and help him out. Then we chatted about the new dispatcher working nights at the courthouse. And before I knew it, lunchtime was over, and I had to get back to work to make the next appointment. But I still couldn't get Knox's question out of my mind.

Or the fact that it bothered me so much that Liv might say yes.

THAT AFTERNOON, I realized I had a gap in patients and a meeting on my schedule instead of a patient visit. When I asked Brenda about it, she said, "That meeting's for us. Doctor Deb wants to speak with both of us in the kitchen."

"Oh," I said, surprised. "I thought she wasn't coming back in until next week?"

Brenda shrugged. "Maybe she wants to see how things have gone without her."

I raised my eyebrows. "You mean outside of the daily calls you two have while you're out walking?"

Brenda's cheeks warmed. "How did you know about that?"

I winked. "Small town."

She took my arm, walking us both back toward the kitchen. "I'll have you know, all my reports were positive, aside from the fact that you've disappointed half the moms and grandmas by turning down dates with their daughters." She gave me a pointed look.

I chuckled; glad she was taking it good-naturedly.

We reached the kitchen and Doctor Deb smiled up at us, wrinkles deepening on her skin. I didn't think I'd ever seen her outside of a lab coat, so it was strange seeing her in chinos and a silk buttoned shirt.

"You're looking great," I told her. The scabbing on her neck and chin was almost completely gone, leaving light scars that would hopefully fade soon. "Are you raring to get back to work?"

She folded her hands on the table. "That's what I wanted to talk to you both about."

The room seemed to grow heavy, and Brenda asked, "What's up, doc?"

Deb cracked a smile. "Buh dee, buh dee, buh dee."

I chuckled at their joke. "Is that all folks?"

With a sad smile, Deb said, "These past few weeks

have given me a lot of time to think, and I've realized it's time for me to retire. I've held back for so long, because I wanted to make sure this town was taken care of, but seeing what a good Job Fletcher's done this past month..." She shook her head. "It's my time to go."

"Deb..." Brenda said softly.

I put my hand on Brenda's shoulder to comfort her and said to Deb, "I was looking forward to working with my former pediatrician."

Deb cackled. "If that isn't a sign it's time to retire, I don't know what is."

Brenda wiped back a tear. "I've worked with you longer than I've been married."

Deb said, "Now our relationship will be even better— we can just enjoy each other's friendship."

Brenda smiled. "What happens next?"

I wanted to know the same thing.

Doctor Deb said, "I'll be selling the practice. Fletcher, I know you just got here, but I hope you'll think about purchasing it. If you don't want it and I need to sell to someone outside of town, they might not understand the way things work in Cottonwood Falls."

Her words caught me off guard. "Me, buy the practice?" I'd only finished my residency a few years prior. "I'm not sure I have the experience, and I have so much going on with Maya..."

Deb held up her hands to stall me. "You wouldn't be doing it on your own, Fletcher. I'm willing to consult, of course, and Brenda knows just as much about running a practice as I do. We wouldn't leave you high and dry."

I looked between the two women. "Can I have some time to think about it?"

Deb nodded. "I'll give you two months. How does that sound?"

"Great, I appreciate it," I said. "And the opportunity. I never even expected it."

Deb said, "You have something special, Fletcher."

"An MD?" I asked.

She smirked, then shook her head. "You understand the people of this town, and you care for them like your own. Just like a family, we aren't perfect, but we're here for each other."

The door chimed and Brenda said, "That must be our next patient." She gave Deb a quick hug and then walked back to the reception area.

Deb stood with me and shook my hand. "I know this came sooner than you expected it, but if there's something I've learned in sixty-eight years of life, it's that destiny rarely calls within business hours." She patted my back and walked toward the front door as I gathered myself for the next patient.

I was reeling for the rest of the day, trying to reconcile my responsibilities with this opportunity that wouldn't come around often. If a bigger hospital system bought the practice, I'd likely never get a chance to have my own practice in Cottonwood Falls.

But Maya needed so much from me right now. Could I really handle the extra pressure that would come with owning a business like this?

I hadn't come to an answer by the end of the day as we locked up and I went out to my truck. I used to dread going back home. When I was married to Regina, I would know another fight awaited. And then when

Regina left, I worried what the nannies would tell me about Maya's bad behavior throughout the day.

But with Liv, things were different.

The house always smelled amazing with whatever dinner she cooked. Maya ran to hug me. Liv's smile warmed me from the inside out.

It was what coming home should feel like.

Today was no different. Maya came and wrapped her little arms around my body, and I kissed the top of her head. "How was your day, honey?" I asked.

"I got invited to a sleepover!" She bounced up and down.

I looked from her to Liv. "Really?"

Liv nodded proudly as Maya explained, "A girl from swim class is having a birthday this weekend. Can I go? Please? Please?"

I chuckled. "Which girl is it?"

"Luna," Maya answered.

"Frieda Wilkins's kid," Liv explained.

Frieda's mom had been head of the PTA and always volunteered around town. According to Dad, Frieda was just the same. Maya would be well taken care of at their house. "That's okay with me," I said. "When is it?"

"Saturday night," Liv answered. "Which is perfect timing, because I have a date." She shimmied her shoulders.

My stomach dropped, and I had to turn and slip off my shoes just to hide my face from Liv. "With who?"

Maya was clapping her hands together. "With Uncle Knox! If they get married, Livvy will be Auntie Livvy!"

Liv chuckled, oblivious to the weight settling in my gut. "Don't get ahead of yourself, Maya. It's just dinner and dancing." She tucked Maya's long hair over her shoulder. "Your dad and I went on a date in high school, and we aren't married now."

Maya pouted while I tried to make sense of what I was feeling.

Jealousy?

No. White-hot fucking rage that I wouldn't be the one with Liv on my arm.

Shit. I was jealous of my brother for dating my nanny.

And I couldn't ask her out myself. Because the way Maya adored Liv? I wouldn't risk that relationship for the world. And I would need Liv to be here for Maya if I bought the practice.

Besides, if my past showed anything, it was that I'd fuck it up and Maya would have yet another woman leave her life.

I needed to stop being selfish and let Liv live her life. And maybe, I'd get to living mine.

Before I could talk myself out of it, I got out my phone and texted Brenda.

Fletcher: I'll go out with Morganne.

Della and Henrietta agreed to go shopping with me for my date with Knox. My entire wardrobe basically consisted of jeans, leggings, and T-shirts, none of which felt right for tonight.

He was taking me to Rutlage, a bigger town about half an hour away, so we could go out to eat without everyone in the town gossiping about us. And then we'd go to a dance hall. I loved going out to the bar with Della and Henrietta for a night of dancing and drinks, since we mostly just danced with friends we knew in town. But this was different, and my stomach was a ball of knots.

Maybe because I was still hung up on my boss I couldn't date or the fact that Knox was said boss's younger brother. I tried to push that thought out of my mind no matter how much it kept rushing back to the surface.

Even though there had been a couple heated moments between Fletcher and me, he was my boss and we needed to keep things professional for Maya's sake.

And my own, to be honest. I couldn't afford to lose this job, especially since I had so much fun hanging out with Maya every day.

Watching her wasn't like showing up at a job and clocking in. We did life together. And seeing her grow from the untrusting, angry child she was just a month ago to this blossoming little girl was the most rewarding thing I'd ever experienced.

I was falling in love with her more every day, and I couldn't bear the thought of parting ways with her because of a silly crush I had on her dad.

Della held up a black dress. "What about this? It's classic. And it'll show off the girls."

I glanced at the length. "Too short. My ass'll turn it into a T-shirt."

Henrietta chuckled. "You remind me of my friend Mara."

I remembered meeting Mara at Henrietta and Tyler's wedding. "The super-hot famous writer?" I winked. "I'll take the compliment."

"Good." She smiled back at me. "Maybe you could wear the dress over leggings?"

"I think I'd get too hot with all that fabric," I said. "Especially if the bar is crowded."

She nodded.

I flipped through the rack, knowing I was being difficult. "I hate clothes shopping," I muttered. "Even if it looks good on the hanger, it looks so different on me. And that's *if* it fits."

"I know," Henrietta said in agreement.

Della kept it positive for us. "You just need one good outfit. Not the whole store."

"Unless she goes on a second date with him," Henrietta grinned.

Della laughed. "True. Two good outfits, then he gets the jeans and boots."

They knew me too well. I held up a floral blouse with elbow-length sleeves. "What if I wore this with a pair of my jeans? I'd probably be more comfortable if I went in cowboy boots anyway."

"I think it's cute," Hen said.

Della nodded. "Go try it on. We'll be out here looking for second date fits."

I took the shirt to the dressing room and started changing when my phone went off in my purse.

It was a text from Fletcher with a picture of Maya standing with a few girls from swim practice. She held her fingers in bunny ears behind another girl's head, and her smile was so big I thought my heart might burst.

Fletcher: Just dropped Maya off at the sleepover. I barely got her to say goodbye to me.

I smiled down at the picture. Maya looked so happy.

Liv: She's going to have so much fun tonight. And get absolutely no sleep. Be ready for her to be cranky tomorrow.

Fletcher: Looking forward to it...

Fletcher: I swear she was a baby yesterday.

Liv: My dad says life's like a roll of toilet paper. The closer you get to the end, the faster it goes.

Fletcher: Your dad's right.

Liv: So what are you doing now? Crying about your baby girl being gone? Combing all your gray hair? Stuffing your pockets with Werther's?

Fletcher: Nah. Too busy putting STAY OFF THE LAWN signs out front.

Liv: If I wasn't going out tonight, I'd hang out and keep you distracted.

Fletcher: No need. I have a date tonight too.

The words felt like a punch to the stomach. All of a sudden, I was twenty years old again, seeing the announcement for his and Regina's wedding coming through the mail. They had looked so perfect together in the picture from their elopement. Her, thin, with perfectly glossy hair and stunning olive skin. Him, a young resident with a jaw that could cut stone and a smile that could melt ice.

And then there was me. A twenty-year-old with only an associate's degree, working at the local feedlot. Single as a Pringle with no prospects in sight just like my verbally abusive college boyfriend had predicted.

I wanted to hide my phone, ignore how upset I was about him going on a single date. But if I didn't reply, it would probably look suspicious. I didn't want him to know how much this bothered me.

Liv: Fun! Who are you taking out?

I stared at the phone, forgetting that I was in the dressing room for a reason other than texting him.

Fletcher: Morganne.

The word stared back at me. Of course he would date Brenda's perfectly petite daughter. It was just another reminder that Fletcher wasn't into big girls like me with wide hips and boob sweat and thighs that rubbed holes in jeans.

I needed to focus on *reality*. On this date with Knox, who clearly liked what I had to give.

So I texted Fletcher to have a good time and tried on the shirt. Because I wanted to look and feel good tonight, not like I'd never be enough.

$\mathcal{V}$

I LOOKED in the mirror moments before Knox was due to pick me up. The shirt had been a good option, and we even found a pair of khaki linen shorts with a paper bag waist so I didn't have to wear jeans. I paired it with sandals and curled my brunette hair so it fell below my shoulders in loose waves.

I didn't wear much makeup usually, but mascara and eyeliner made my eyes stand out and a swipe of dusty rose lipstick made me feel a little more confident. And that was good because Knox was objectively a catch.

He had a good job, looked great in his uniform, and we'd grown up together. I knew him. I didn't need to wonder what kind of guy he was or if he'd disappear on me after a couple weeks.

A knock sounded on my front door. I expected to feel nervous, but... I didn't.

I smiled at myself in the mirror, doing one last check that there wasn't anything in my teeth, and then went to the door.

But it wasn't Knox.

It was Fletcher.

All my nerves kicked up in my stomach as I saw him looking handsome as ever in trendy khaki pants with white sneakers, paired with a white button down that hugged his defined pecs.

Just when I thought he looked hot in his doctor outfit

with a stethoscope around his neck, he put this image in my head.

"What's up?" I said, feeling his eyes slide over my body.

Suddenly, I was very aware of my bare legs with all their curves and dimples. Heat rose up my neck, filling my cheeks, as his gaze slowly grazed back up to my eyes.

"I..." He cleared his throat, scratching at the back of his neck. "I just wanted to say... don't wait up for me. I might stay out tonight."

He could have punched me and it would have hurt less.

FLETCHER

Liv arched an eyebrow. "So it's okay if Knox stays the night?"

My gut turned over, and I thought I might be sick. Coming over here was a mistake.

Knox dating Liv was one thing... but sleeping with her?

And now I couldn't say no to him staying in the guest house with Liv because I'd be an even bigger hypocrite. So I said, "It's your place. You're free to do as you wish."

She looked like she wanted to say something, but after a moment, just smiled and nodded. "Have a good night, boss."

I shook my head at her, already in a sour mood. "Don't call me that."

She recoiled slightly, seeming hurt and confused. "Okay? Sorry, Fletcher. I didn't mean to upset you."

"Just don't do it again," I said, then I turned and walked away, feeling like the biggest piece of shit in the world. I'd gone over there to ask her not to go on the date with Knox. Tried messing up my own brother's relationship for some unrequited feelings I couldn't act on even if I wanted to.

So I'd made up some dumb comment to make it seem like I hadn't knocked on her door for the reason I was and then she hit me with that?

And my reaction, the visceral way my stomach ached at the thought of her with someone else... it just proved how far away from her I needed to stay. Even if she'd always be as close as my backyard.

I walked to my truck, shutting the door a little too hard, and then took off down the dirt road. Just a couple miles from the house, my brother drove by, smiling and waving at me through the windshield.

Liv's face as she asked me if he could stay the night flashed through my mind, and I almost drove into the ditch.

Shit, I needed to focus. *Focus.*

I could perform surgeries, give stitches to a wiggling child, tourniquet a bleeding wound, but I couldn't handle the thought of my nanny sleeping with my brother? They were both adults, and so was I. I just needed to focus on what was possible instead of what I couldn't have. And Morganne was available to me, at least for the evening.

I slowed at the main road in town and glanced at the text Morganne sent me earlier with directions to her house.

Morganne: The yellow house at the end of Oak St. One block past the bank.

I set my phone back in the cupholder and drove down Main Street, turning a block after the bank. As promised, her house sat on the corner, faded yellow siding, a big oak tree out front with a tire swing.

It looked like Mayberry.

And I knew I should be excited for a date with her, but I... wasn't.

I should turn around right now. Tell her how I was feeling and go home. But backing out at the last minute would just be cruel. Besides, we could go out to dinner together and not pursue a relationship, have a friendship.

I parked, rubbing my hands over my face, and let out a groan.

My head was all mixed up.

The front door opened, and a little girl peeked her head out. She had to be three or four, a few years younger than Maya. Someone came to pull her back, and I recognized Morganne. Light blond hair in waves, snatched waist, big blue eyes, and a wide smile.

It took all I had to smile back. What the fuck was wrong with me?

Shouldn't any red-blooded male be into this?

I was in a funk. That was it. Once we got on the date, I'd settle my mind and gain some perspective. I got out of the truck, walking toward her house.

With the little girl inside, Morganne stepped out and said, "Let me say goodbye to the kids and I'll be back out?"

I nodded, clasping my hands in front of me.

She went inside, and I heard voices before she came back out and with a joking laugh said, "Run, run! We're free!"

I chuckled, knowing the feeling. We got in my truck, and she buckled up, smiling over at me. "It's so good to see you, Fletcher. I feel like I need to do a double take; you're so grown up."

I laughed as I pulled out into the street. If only she could hear the thoughts going through my head. "Grown up" was the last thing she'd call me. "I could say the same about you. Brenda's always bragging about her grandbabies."

She smiled, nodded. "I swear, she's so nice to them it makes me jealous sometimes."

"I get it," I said. "My dad babies Maya like he never did with us boys. How old are your kids again?" I asked, falling into the conversation. It was easy to make small talk with other parents about their children.

"Miss Belle is three, almost four, and Henry just turned one."

"Wow, they're so young."

She nodded. "Chris and I struggled with fertility issues before the split."

"What happened?" I asked, curiosity getting the better of me. "I thought you two were a match made in heaven, honestly."

She let out a harsh laugh. "Me too. But the funny thing about falling for someone in high school is that so much changes as you grow up. People like to say it's okay if you grow together, but that's easier said than done. At the end of the day, the man I was married to wasn't the same man I fell in love with way back then." She glanced down at her hands, fidgeting. I wondered if she used to spin her wedding ring around her finger like I did.

"Divorce sucks," I said.

"Hear, hear," she agreed. "What happened with you and your wife?"

I shook my head. "We got married because Maya was on the way. I thought it was the right thing to do back then."

"And now?" she asked.

"Now..." I sighed. "Now, I wouldn't know a good idea if it bit me in the ass."

She laughed. "Honesty. I appreciate it."

We caught up about lighter subjects as we drove to the lone nice restaurant in the next town over where we wouldn't feel like we were in a fishbowl. She told me about her job working as a virtual assistant so she could be with her kids and work around their sleep schedule and visits with their dad. I talked about med school and how I decided to specialize in family medicine.

Our conversation was amicable.

Easy.

Maybe I just craved drama after everything that went on with Regina and this felt strange in comparison. I could get used to a relationship like this, over time.

When we got to the restaurant in Rutlage, I parked in a spot near the back and we walked inside together. But the second we got through the front door, I muttered, "You've got to be shitting me."

Liv and Knox were standing at the front podium, his hand on the small of her back, right above the swell of her ass.

I saw fucking red.

"Is that your brother and Liv?" Morganne whispered.

I nodded, my jaw tight.

She smiled. "Small world. Should we make it a double date?"

I should have said no.

Lord knows I should have said no.

But even eight years of school and a medical residency hadn't made me smart enough to do that.

Instead, some masochistic part of me nodded and said, "A double date sounds great."

"Liv, Knox?" came a woman's voice, and I turned to see Morganne walking in next to Fletcher.

No fucking way.

They looked like a model couple. Her in a cute light blue sundress and dainty little heels, him in khakis and a white shirt. Her blond hair fell perfectly in the waves I'd attempted, not a single strand out of place.

She smiled at us and came with her arms outstretched. "It's so good to see you, Liv."

Now I needed to hug the person capturing my boss's heart?

It sounded so pathetic when I thought of it that way, but it was true. God, what would happen if they got married? Would he fire me? Or would I have to watch her kids too with a front-row seat to their relationship? I didn't know which fate would be worse; all I could think of was seeing him happy with someone else.

I'd accepted the fact that Fletcher and I couldn't be

together. (At least I tried to.) But that didn't mean I needed to have his new relationship rubbed in my face.

I forced myself to hug her without throwing up, and behind me, Knox chuckled, giving his brother that weird half-hug/handshake thing that guys do.

Morganne giggled. "It's so funny we all got out of Cottonwood Falls to avoid the townies, and here we are. Should we stop fighting fate and eat together?"

I could feel Fletcher's eyes on me as I turned to Knox, silently begging him to turn her down.

Either he couldn't read me or didn't want to, because he grinned and said, "The more the merrier. We're going out dancing after this too if you want to join us."

"That sounds so fun!" Morganne said. "It's been forever since I've been on a dance floor, and I seem to recall Fletcher being an excellent swing dancer."

I fought a scowl. She must have paid enough attention to him in high school to remember. Now the present was right in my face, messing with my head and my date with a cute cop.

The host smiled between us and said "I have a table for four available. Right this way."

We followed her to a booth toward the back of the restaurant and sat down, Knox next to me and Fletcher across from me.

We must have been right under a fan, because I shivered. "It's chilly in here."

Knox put his arm around my shoulders, and I leaned into his warmth.

Fletcher's eyes held mine across the table for a moment before he physically turned his body away from me, facing Morganne.

"What's your favorite thing to get here?" he asked, flashing her a smile that melted my heart as much as hers.

She glanced at the menu left by the host. "It's been so long since I've been out. Single mom budget, you know."

"Not tonight," Fletcher said. "Whatever you want is on me."

Gag. I looked up at Knox. He was cute, with blond hair short on the sides and longer on top. He had bigger muscles than Fletcher, and one arm was covered in a tattoo sleeve. I wondered how many women had come on to him to get out of a speeding ticket and ended up blurting out the question.

Knox chuckled at my curiosity, leaning his elbow on the table and his face in his hand. "Plenty of women have tried to flirt their way out of tickets, none of them as cute as you."

Damn, this boy was trouble. Exactly the kind I'd drool over in a bar... until Fletcher came back to town and fucked with my head.

Morganne butted in. "Isn't that illegal? Could you arrest them for that?"

Knox launched into a full-blown explanation of ticket evasion, and Fletcher and I locked eyes across the table. My stomach swirled uncomfortably, and I glanced down at my lap. I shouldn't be thinking about my boss while on a date with his brother.

A server came by and took our drink and food orders, and because I couldn't focus on a single thing on the menu, I asked for a margarita and picked something at random before passing the menu her way.

We'd only been sitting here for five minutes, and I

already couldn't think straight with Fletcher right across from me.

Knox glanced over at me and said, "How do you like nannying?"

"It's the dream job," I answered honestly, earning a smile from Fletcher. "I get to hang out with the coolest eight-year-old in the world every day."

The server came back with our drinks, and after she left, Morganne said. "I bet nannying's a breeze when it's just one kid, older no less, and you don't have a separate job. I love being a work-from-home mom, but I have my hands full with working and watching two under three... I wouldn't trade it for anything, though."

Did I imagine a slight edge to her voice? Like she was trying to say I had it easy compared to her? Before I could think of a reply, Fletcher said, "Liv's the best thing to happen to Maya and me." He glanced down at his whiskey and took a sip.

We all glanced at him, including Knox, but no one looked longer than me.

"Do you mean that?" I asked softly.

He glanced across the table at me, nodding.

An awkward silence spread around the table until Knox stood up and said, "I have to piss."

Gross, but maybe that was a cop thing. Or a guy thing. I'd definitely bring it up if we went on more than one date.

"Fletcher," he said. "Can you come? I have a... um.... mole I've been meaning to have you look at."

Fletcher gave him an incredulous look. "Now?"

"Yep. If it's abnormal, time's of the essence, right?"

Fletcher rolled his eyes at his brother. "We can look tomorrow."

Knox shook his head. "Now feels better."

Fletcher's jaw ticked. "Fine. Excuse me." He slid out of the booth, smiling at Morganne as he went. "I'll be right back."

With both the guys gone, the silence felt even more awkward. I sipped from my margarita and rolled my lips, making the salty flavor spread on my tongue.

Morganne leaned forward, her flirty smile gone. "I'm a single mom, so you'll excuse me for cutting to the chase. Is something happening between you and Fletcher?"

My cheeks instantly heated, and I nearly choked on my spit. "What are you talking about?"

She shook her head, banging her fist lightly on the table. "I freaking knew it."

"What are you talking about?" I asked, starting to get frustrated.

"He can't take his eyes off of you. Even when he's looking at me, his eyes are constantly darting your way."

"Morganne." I leveled my hands on the table to steady myself. "There is nothing happening between Fletcher and me. I'm his nanny. I clock in at seven, clock out at six, and I sleep in the guest house, not even the same building as him and Maya. It is strictly a professional relationship." No matter how much I wished things could be different.

Morgan narrowed her eyes at me, clearly pissed off. "Uh huh. 'Liv's the best thing to ever happen to me.'"

Even repeated in her angry voice, the words made my heart flutter. "He said Maya and him."

"And you're still smiling like a lovestruck teenager!" She gestured her hands at me. "You're all gooey over him." She shook her head. "Look, I don't want to be in the middle of whatever this is. When he comes back, I'm asking him to take me home. I don't need to miss time with my kids for a dinner where my date doesn't even want to be with me."

Guilt wracked my chest. "Morganne, don't do this on my account. Yes, I have a little crush on Fletcher, but it's completely unrequited. I promise, there's nothing between us."

She let out a laugh. "You're either dumb or in denial, sweetheart."

Ugh. I hated when people called me sweetheart like that. It was so condescending. "You can do whatever you want, *sweetheart*. But you're the one doing it, not me."

She shook her head at me, about to say something else when the guys got back. Before they could sit down, she got up. "Hey," she said to Fletcher, standing from the booth. "I'm sorry, but I've got a major migraine. Would you mind taking me home?"

Concern knit his eyebrows together. "Oh no, where are you feeling it? Maybe some water would help?"

She gestured all over her head. "Just this general area. I'll be fine with a bit of sleep and an aspirin, really."

Knox said, "I'll take her home. I actually got a call from the station while I was back there. Someone called in sick."

I frowned. Was my date really leaving right now? "You have to go?"

He nodded, leaning across the table and kissing my cheek. "See you around, Liv."

My stomach sank. That wasn't a we'll-do-this-again-soon kiss on the cheek. It was a goodbye with no promise to call or reschedule. Had I really been that awful of a date already that he wanted to run away?

Knox and Morganne waved goodbye and exited the restaurant, leaving Fletcher and me at our booth... alone.

22

FLETCHER

Liv's wide blue eyes landed on me. "Well this is awkward."

"I'll say." I rubbed my hand over the back of my neck.

"Shall we go back home?" she asked.

My stomach was sinking, and my heart was beating fast. After that conversation in the bathroom with Knox, I felt like the world's biggest jackass. I couldn't date Liv. That much was true. But clearly, I was shit at hiding my attraction to her because Knox refused to date a girl I liked, whether I planned to act on my feelings or not.

He was a good brother that way.

And I was a shitty one. That much had been established.

"We haven't even gotten our food yet," I said.

She nodded, blinking quickly. "I guess we could get our food boxed up and then go home." She let out a sigh. "I was looking forward to dancing tonight. Maybe I can see if Della or Hen wants to go out.... Shit." She lowered her phone. "I forgot they're both busy." She shook her head. "I guess the night's a dud."

I hated seeing her this disappointed, on the verge of tears, all because of me. "You and I can go dancing," I offered.

I knew I was playing with fire.

But I was a doctor. I could handle the burn.

She raised her eyebrows at me. "You seem surprisingly okay for someone who's date just fled the restaurant like it was on fire."

Right. Why wasn't I upset? Or at least acting that way? "Can't control migraines," I said lightly.

"So you'll reschedule with Morganne?"

I drank from my whiskey, the liquid burning my throat. "Probably not."

Her lips parted, sending fire to my stomach to match the whiskey. I needed to stop thinking about those lips as much as I was. "Why not?" she asked.

I leaned forward, my elbows resting on the table. "Have you ever been with someone you knew would be right for you on paper, but you didn't feel it?"

"Feel what?"

What I feel when you're in the room. "A... connection," I said instead.

"But connections are built over time, right?" she asked, watching me carefully. I couldn't pull my gaze from her. Not if I wanted to. Not if I tried.

I shook my head. "They can be destroyed over time." I knew that much firsthand. "You can learn they weren't as strong as you once thought they were. They can be deepened. Strengthened. But you can't light a fire without a spark."

She swallowed, drawing my attention to her throat. It was thick like the rest of her, and I imagined how it would fit in my hand. Suppressing my shudder was almost impossible.

"Will you be going on another date with my brother?" I asked. I couldn't not.

She glanced at the table, shaking her head. "I don't think so."

She didn't seem sad about it.

And some sick, twisted part of me liked that.

A lot.

Our server from earlier brought out four plates of food, and she looked around the table, confused. "Where did the other two go?"

"They weren't feeling well," I answered. "Can we have a couple to-go containers please?"

She nodded. "Do you want me to box it up for you?"

"No." I smiled over the table at Liv. "I think we'll enjoy our own little buffet."

For the next hour or so, Liv and I picked over the food on all the plates while she asked questions about my grossest ER stories when I worked at the hospital in Dallas. I thought the one about a kid putting rabbit poop up their nose might make her sick, but the woman had worked at a feedlot. Her stomach was clearly made of steel.

But then the conversation turned serious again when she said, "I'm pretty sure Wayne's kids have three or four rabbits."

"What happened with Wayne?" I asked. I remembered Rhett telling me that he proposed several years ago but then never got a wedding invitation. After a while, Dad told me they never got married at all.

She frowned at the table. "I guess it was what you're talking about. We were good on paper, but it just didn't feel right."

"And no one's snatched you up since then?" I asked.

She seemed stunned for a moment. Then she laughed.

"Why are you laughing?" I demanded. This wasn't funny. Not to me. "You're a smart, attractive woman in her early thirties. Women like you usually don't stay single long in Cottonwood Falls."

"Did you just call me pretty?" she asked, a flirtatious smirk on her face that reminded me of Rhett. Maybe that was one reason not to be attracted to your best friend's little sister; you could see their similarities. But if I was being honest, a smirk on her was sexy as hell. And her question caught me off guard, getting me slightly flustered.

"You know what you are," I finally said.

Her lips curved slightly. "And what's that?"

"Are you going to make me say it?"

"Say what?" she said, exasperated. "Because unless you haven't noticed, I don't exactly have guys lining up, begging to date me. Knox was the first person to ask me out in six months. I never get more than a dance or two at the bar on the weekends, and it usually stops there. So no, I have no idea what you mean."

I'd like to blame the whiskey, but I'd only had half a glass. More likely it was the anger raging in my chest that made me say the truth. "Olivia Griffen. You are the most beautiful damn woman I've ever laid eyes on. There's no one with a better smile, a kinder heart, or a more contagious laugh. I knew it was true when I was sixteen years old, and it's just as true now."

Her lips parted and closed again. "I... I never knew you saw me that way."

I sat up, squaring my shoulders. "I don't. I can't. Because we have Maya to think about. And she has to come first."

Her eyes searched mine, and she nodded slowly. "Fletcher, if you don't mind." She let out a breath and spoke quietly. "I think I want to go home."

I quickly looked down. Man, I fucked up. When I looked up again, her wide eyes were on me.

"I'm sorry," I said. It was all I could manage.

She shook her head. "Don't be."

But I was. Because not only had I ruined her date with Knox, but I'd clearly upset her with my questions... and with my answers.

We packed up our food into the to-go containers in silence, and when we were done, I paid the bill and we walked to my truck. I wanted to hold the door open for her, but I'd already crossed so many lines, I just got inside and drove back toward the house.

She sat, arms folded across her chest, and stared out the window for the better part of the drive. So I had plenty of time to beat myself up for my idiotic behavior tonight and even more time to worry that I'd messed everything up professionally too.

When we got to the house, she started walking toward the cottage, but I reached out, holding her hand. "Wait."

Her eyes landed on me, heavy.

Warmth spread from her skin to my fingertips and up my arm, and I dropped my hand away.

"Are we okay?" I asked. "I mean... you're not quitting on me, are you?"

Her smile was sad. "I'm not quitting on Maya."

23

LIV

The next day, Henrietta needed to get odds and ends for their apartments from the city, so Della and I piled in her car. For almost an hour of the two-hour drive to Dallas, I told them about the clusterfuck of a date, including how I'd cried in bed the night before, not about the failed date, but about Fletcher.

He'd said he was attracted to me but refused to act on it.

Logically, I knew we couldn't have a relationship. But something about that fact hurt less when I thought it was because he wasn't interested. Not because he was interested and decided I wasn't worth the risk.

Della frowned, looking at me in the back seat. "He's being a total fuck boy."

Henrietta nodded in agreement as she drove. "Either he likes you or he doesn't. He shouldn't be blurring lines like that if he's not going to follow through."

I agreed. But I also... liked the fact that he was

standing his ground. "Am I a masochist for liking him more because he's so dedicated to Maya?"

"Yes," they said at the same time.

I laughed, then tugged at my hair in frustration. "And of course Knox noped out. So I'm back to being single as ever. I know it's melodramatic to say, but I don't want to die alone in this town!"

Della reached back, putting her hand on my knee. "Get on FarmersOnly and find yourself a good southern boy if that's what you want."

I sighed. "I don't. I want to meet someone the old-fashioned way."

Henrietta smirked at me in the rearview and said, "You know, I met Tyler at my job too."

"I know, I know, and it worked out great for you two, and you're living your dream life. But we can't all get that lucky. It's more complicated when you have to worry about a kid too."

Della twirled a red curl around her finger. "I say you just have a good summer with Maya, have fun with us, and leave your feelings for Fletcher in the past. Things will fall into place the way they're meant to."

"You think?" I asked.

She nodded. "What do you say we go out next Saturday and get trashed?"

I laughed.

"I'm in," Henrietta said.

"Me too," I agreed. "Better make up your guest bed for me."

We reached the city, and Della said, "Hen, do you mind if we make a little detour?"

Hen said, "That's fine. Tyler's hanging out with Rhett and Gage all day, so it's not like he'll miss me."

Della pulled up directions on her phone, taking us to some address in a residential neighborhood. Each house looked the same: brick exterior, green lawn, one or two young trees out front. It was clearly a newer neighborhood.

Hen stopped her car across the street from one of the houses. This one had a big yellow wreath on the wooden front door with the letter S on it.

My lips parted when I realized where we were. "Is this Kyle's place?" I asked Della.

She nodded slowly.

"Who's Kyle?" Hen asked.

"Her ex," I breathed.

Della looked out the window, her light blue eyes somewhere else. "I was in love with him, but he always said he didn't want to commit. Didn't want marriage or children.

The front door to the house opened, and Della slid down in her seat slightly.

A willowy woman came outside, carrying a tow-headed baby on her hip, followed by an attractive guy with light brown hair. He was wearing khaki shorts and a nicer shirt, like they were maybe going to church or out to brunch.

"He met her a month after we broke up," Della said sadly.

Hen glanced at Della. "When did you break up?"

"Two years ago."

I reached up, rubbing Della's shoulder.

She turned to me, so much pain in her eyes—the kind

she usually tried to hide. "People *show* you how they feel about you. It's up to us to believe them."

Her words hit me hard.

Fletcher had shown me he felt nothing more than unwanted attraction.

And believing that?

It hurt like hell.

⠀⠀⠀⠀⠀⠀⠀⠀⠀⠀ꕥ

AFTER DELLA'S ADMISSION, we went shopping and got good Chinese food, which put us all in a better mood. We even went to a salon and got our nails done. It made me think of Maya at her first sleepover with girls her age. I hoped she had a good time. I couldn't wait to hear about it when I got back home. Even if it meant facing Fletcher, knowing that he didn't want to feel any kind of way about me.

Fair. Because I didn't want to have feelings for him either.

As I drove toward his house in the country, my phone began ringing, and his name flashed across the screen.

Confused, I answered. "Is everything okay?"

"Livvy!" came Maya's little voice. "I wanted to tell you about the sleepover!"

I grinned so big hearing how happy she sounded. "I'm almost home. Want to come over and tell me everything?"

"Yes!" she said. "See you soon!"

Smiling to myself, I hung up and drove the rest of the way. It meant so much that Maya was starting to see me as a friend. When I got out of my truck, she was swinging in the backyard, the setting sun hitting her pretty caramel curls. This view, this country home? It was perfection. But it wasn't mine. I tried to remember that as she leapt from the swing, her nightgown flying around her.

"Livvy!" She ran up, hugging me, and I spun her around. I set her on the ground, and she was practically jumping up and down.

"Come on," I said. "You can tell me all about it while I bring my groceries inside. Will you help me carry them?"

She nodded, skipping along beside me as we walked to the truck.

"So how many girls were there?" I asked, reaching for a bag out of the back seat and handing it to her.

"Eleven. But there were supposed to be twelve."

Frieda must have been a saint. "That's so many! Did you all have beds or were you in sleeping bags on the floor?"

"On the floor," she said, adjusting her hands on the bag. "We lined all our sleeping bags up in a big circle in the basement. And Jesse's mom had a lantern that looked like a fire inside, so we told ghost stories all night."

I grinned, shutting the doors. "Did you pee your pants?"

"Ew, no." She laughed. "I told the scariest one."

I raised my eyebrows. "Well, I have to hear this."

She told me the classic story about the kid hiding out in the closet saying, "I've got you where I want'cha, now I want to eat'cha." But he was really talking about his booger all along.

I laughed out loud. "I'm pretty sure Uncle Rhett told your dad that one."

"Everyone loved it. And then two girls argued over who got to braid my hair."

I was way too happy about this. Maya, making friends, being the popular girl after being left out for years? It sliced right through the cold feeling in my heart her father left behind last night. "What did you do?"

"I said Jesse could braid one side and Eliana could braid the other. And you were right. I slept in the braids, and now my hair's all curly." She flipped her hair around so I could see it.

"It's pretty," I said, twisting the knob to my cottage and opening the door.

It was just as I left it. Perfectly neat for my date, even though no one ended up coming over afterward.

We set the grocery bags on the counter, and I started putting the cold stuff away. "How late did you stay there today?"

"Dad got me after lunch. We made pigs in a blanket that looked like mummies."

"That sounds super fun. You'll have to show me how you did it."

"Really?" She jumped up and hugged me. "Thanks for taking me to swim lessons, Livvy. If I hadn't gone, I wouldn't have met Jesse and I wouldn't know all those girls in my class."

"Of course," I said with a smile.

"Dad and I are watching a movie tonight. Do you want to come watch with us? Please?"

My heart ached at the mention of her father. I didn't

mind seeing him while I was working, but spending extra time around him? That was last on my list.

"Please?" she begged. "I missed you all weekend."

My heart strings sang like she was playing a steel guitar. "Okay, I'll come, but after I put on my PJs. And we need to check that it's okay with your dad."

I was *so* looking forward to it.

24

FLETCHER

I looked up from the stove where I was making popcorn in the kettle to see Maya and Liv crossing the yard together. Liv had on a white nightgown, such a contrast to the neon yellow one Maya wore, and they were laughing, talking to each other.

Maya adored Liv; you could see it in the way she looked at her, like she personally invented Uncrustables. And when Maya got home from the sleepover, she immediately was disappointed when Liv's truck wasn't in the drive.

The door opened, and Maya said, "Dad, Liv's watching the movie with us. If it's okay. Which it totally is, right?"

She'd said *totally* at least seventeen times tonight, which was both adorable and exasperating. I swear just yesterday she was calling lemonade "lemalade" and crocodiles "cockadoddles." Where had those days gone?

But Maya was watching me expectantly, so I said, "Totally," not making eye contact with Liv.

Maya tugged Liv's hand, and they sat on the couch. From here I could see Liv's bare shoulders, her dark hair trailing down her back. I had to bite my lip against the thoughts running through my mind.

I wanted to sink my teeth into her shoulders, pull her hair until her head fell back, baring her neck to me.

So many fucking thoughts I should not be thinking about my nanny, my patient, especially with my daughter in the room.

Maya went to the blanket chest and pulled out her throw that looked like a tortilla. Hayes had gotten it for her birthday last year, and it made me chuckle every time. But now I was having a hard time on focusing on anything other than Liv.

So I trained my eyes on the popcorn I was cooking. The oil was hot now, so I poured in the kernels and covered them with the lid to begin cooking.

"Livvy, roll me into a burrito!" Maya said.

I made the mistake of looking up at exactly the wrong moment, seeing Liv on her hands and knees as she positioned Maya in the blanket.

Fuck.

If that nightgown rode up any higher, I'd see her underwear.

If she's wearing any, a salacious voice added in the back of my head. I could already see most of her full thighs, the way her tits hung down in the loose fabric. My cock strained painfully against my pants, and I had to adjust it behind the counter.

From the living room, Maya called, "Is something burning?"

"Shit," I mumbled, gripping the handle of the kettle

and taking it off the heat so the popcorn wouldn't burn anymore. It was already ruined anyway.

Irritated, I put the pan in the empty sink.

I should have loved the sound of Maya and Liv giggling, but it just distracted me. Frustrated me.

I wanted to be the one making Liv laugh. Wanted her to be over me, her full chest hanging in my face, close enough to taste. My cock got harder, and I gripped the counter with my hands.

Get it together, Fletch.

I let out a silent, frustrated sigh and put a bag of popcorn in the microwave. I focused on the popping kernels, slowly cooling down. I could handle this. It was just a movie night with the nanny. We'd been together a million times before without my cock standing at attention.

The microwave went off, and I made a bowl for each of us with apple slices and a pickle. It was mine and Maya's favorite movie snack.

When I gave them each a bowl, Liv said, "It's been forever since I've had a pickle with popcorn. I think since our families did movie nights in the backyard."

"It was one of my mom's favorites," I replied honestly. "I think of her every time I have it."

Maya looked to Liv. "Did you know Grammy?"

My chest ached as Liv swept Maya's hair over her shoulder. "I did. She was the *best*. Always had a big smile like your uncle Ford and an ornery streak like your uncle Hayes. And she was so nice to everyone, just like Bryce. But she had a good heart like your uncle Knox and always took care of everyone like your daddy does. I miss her a lot."

"I do too," Maya said. Then she got a confused look on her face. "Can you miss someone you've never seen?"

Liv nodded, smiling gently. "Of course you can."

The pain in my chest reached new heights as I blinked quickly. "What do you want to watch?"

Maya picked *The Parent Trap*, making Liv laugh.

"What?" I asked.

"Nothing," they both said in unison.

An inside joke between the two of them.

Maya lay on the floor in front of the TV, her chin resting in her hands as she watched the beginning of the movie, the girls going to camp and seeing each other for the first time.

But then Liv shifted on the couch, tucking her feet beneath her, and I glanced over to see her nightgown riding up her thighs, sliding down her chest to show her cleavage.

I grabbed a pillow, hugging it to cover my cock. I felt like a fucking teenager, the way she was turning me on without doing a damn thing.

After a few minutes in, Maya asked Liv to braid her hair.

"Sure," Liv said. "I'll go get the stuff." She rose from the couch, her hips swaying under the nightgown as she walked away.

That fucking nightgown was a blessing and a curse.

I reached under the pillow, into my pants to adjust myself and get some relief. And when Liv came back, I looked straight at the TV screen, hugging my side of the couch, trying to gain some self-control.

Liv sat down on the couch, a little closer this time, and I could smell her vanilla perfume. My cock got ramrod straight at the thought of licking that scent off her skin.

"Can you do a fishtail braid?" Maya asked. "Daddy can only do regular braids."

"Sure," Liv said with a smile and began carefully braiding her hair. It took all I had to keep my eyes glued to the screen.

Regina had never done Maya's hair unless we were going out to an event in public. Maya was just an accessory to her that she could discard at the end of the night.

But Liv, she took time with Maya, even when she didn't have to.

It fucked with my head, made it harder to ignore the attraction I had for her.

And that fucking nightgown didn't help. It should be a crime for her not to wear a bra with it, her full nipples strained at the fabric like that.

And why couldn't I keep my mind out of the gutter? It wasn't like Liv was seducing me or anything. She was braiding my daughter's hair, for fuck sake. And women were just fine wearing a bra or not. As a doctor, I knew there was a decent amount of research that pointed to the harm of wearing those undergarments, after all.

This was what I got for the world's longest dry spell. My dick was thinking more than my head.

"I'm going to use the bathroom," I said. Neither of the girls seemed to care or even notice. So I got up and went to the en suite in my bedroom, locking both doors, just in case.

My dick was already straining against my sweatpants, and I pulled them down, freeing my cock. It was hard as a fucking rock, full of blood at the thought of

Liv's body, her touch. I took it in my hand, pumping twice.

Why Liv had made that comment about no one lining up to date her, I had no fucking clue. Just the sight of her luscious thighs in those shorts had been enough to capture my attention. And her ass jiggling in that swimsuit?

It made me think what she would look like bent in front of me, her ass rippling as I slammed into her over and over and over again. I pumped myself angrily. Angry at myself for not being in control of my desires. Angry at her for not seeing how fucking perfect she was. Angry I couldn't have her right here, right now.

I imagined her looking over her shoulder at me as I railed her and came undone, spilling thick ropes of cum into the bathroom sink. My breath came in quick pants, and I pressed my hand into the counter to hold myself up.

When I looked in the mirror, I didn't see myself. I saw a tortured man who couldn't have what he wanted. Because I'd only mess it up. And that little girl out there, looking at Liv like she hung the moon?

She deserved better than for me to ruin her relationship with the first good woman in her life.

꧁ꕥ꧂

I WENT out and watched the rest of the movie with the girls, only comprehending about half of it. I knew I had to talk to someone about what I was feeling, but I didn't know who. I couldn't tell Rhett. Last time I even hinted at a crush on his sister he threatened to castrate me. And he knew how to do it too. Not Knox. He was probably still pissed at me for telling him he could go out with Liv without mentioning that I liked her.

Ford was busy training for the upcoming pro football season, and Bryce was so occupied with college we rarely saw him. Which left Hayes. He had been single for as long as I could remember. He'd probably be single for the rest of his life.

So Hayes. As the movie neared its happy end, I texted him, asking if he'd eat lunch with me tomorrow so we could talk.

And then the end credits began rolling and I said to Maya, "Time for bed, kiddo."

She looked at Liv behind her, braids swinging about her shoulders. "Can Livvy put me to bed?"

Liv looked at me in question. "I don't mind."

"Sure," I said, trying not to feel rejected by my eight-year-old. "I'll clean up the bowls out here."

"Thanks, Daddy!" Maya said, wrapping her arms around me. "Goodnight."

I kissed the top of her head and told her goodnight before letting them go together. This was just more proof that I couldn't cross that line when it came to Liv. Now Maya didn't just want Liv during the week, but the evenings and weekends too.

I took my time, washing the bowls and the pan of burnt popcorn, but when the sink was empty and clean, Liv still hadn't come out yet.

I crept toward Maya's bedroom and heard Liv singing the song my mom always sang to me. "Red River Valley."

Moisture pricked at my eyes, and I covered my jaw with my hand as the words to the song came to a close. In the silence, I could hear Maya's soft snores, and Liv said, "Goodnight, sweetheart. I love you."

There was the soft sound of a kiss, and I squeezed my eyes shut against the sting of tears.

Liv tiptoed out of the room and stopped when she saw me. "Are you okay?"

I slowly opened my eyes, shaking my head.

"What's wrong?" she breathed.

I stared at her. "Can't you see what you're doing to me? Treating Maya like a mother would?"

Her eyes searched mine. "What?"

I shook my head.

"Say it."

"I..." My voice broke, and I shook my head. "I can't."

After a charged weekend with Fletcher, I knew I had to get out in the country with Maya and distract myself from the constant ache in my heart. Tubing sounded like a fun idea, so we loaded up my truck with a cooler full of drinks and food, aired up some inner tubes, and drove to the slow-moving creek near my parents' house.

Since the river only went one way, we'd park the truck at a starting point and then Dad offered to leave a vehicle for us further down. We'd ride on our tubes until we got to the end and drive back to our truck.

The early August heat was already making me sweat, and I couldn't wait to get the tubes in the water, but I slathered both of us with sunscreen first.

Maya pointed at my face, giggling. "You look like a snowman."

I chuckled, pointing my finger out from my nose so it would look like a carrot nose.

She took my finger and pretended to chomp it, making us both giggle.

"This snowman is about to melt," I said, rubbing in the rest of my sunscreen. "It is so dang hot."

She nodded. "Uncle Hayes always says it's sweating balls outside."

I cackled. If Hayes were a few years older, he and Rhett would have been hell on wheels together, but he was five years younger than me and seven younger than Rhett. "Do not repeat anything at school that Uncle Hayes says."

Her cheeky grin made me smile more.

I got the tubes out of the truck bed, handing her one, then grabbed my mesh bag, putting a couple bottles of water inside, along with some packaged snacks. I put a life jacket on her just in case, and we stepped into the water.

The cool stream swirled around my feet and legs, such a contrast to the hot and humid summer day. Maya splashed in less cautiously, romping around like a little puppy. She was completely happy, carefree, so different than the first day I met her.

She could be herself around me.

And I realized I could be myself too. I loved this girl with my whole heart. She was more than just the kid I nannied for. She was practically my best friend outside of Della and Henrietta.

After swimming around the water in her life jacket while I held her tube, she climbed in, resting back so her wet, tangled hair fell over the black tube and skimmed the water. She let out a happy sigh. "I like this."

"Me too," I agreed. It was exactly what I needed to set my aching heart at ease.

"You know my dad went on a date Saturday?" she asked.

My heart hitched, her words such a contrast to the carefree moment we just had. "He did, huh?" I said nonchalantly.

"He told me."

That was sweet, Fletcher keeping Maya in the loop about that. Me on the other hand? I was definitely going to hell, because I couldn't hold back my next question. "What did he say about the date?"

Maya shrugged her little shoulders, making the pink ruffles of her swimsuit strap move. "He said they were just friends."

I couldn't decide whether to be happy he was talking about Morganne or sad because the same applied to me. "It's good to have friends." I tried to convince myself.

"Yeah, but I want Dad to have a girlfriend."

"What about your mom?" I asked. Just a couple months ago, she was wishing her mom would come back.

With a frown, she said. "Mom called me last weekend. She said she has a new boyfriend."

My heart broke for her, for the way she wouldn't quite meet my eyes. "Are you okay?"

She nodded sadly, wiping at her nose. "I want Dad to be happy too."

"What makes you think he isn't?"

"Because he smiles more when you're around."

My heart wrenched. This sweet girl noticed more than we gave her credit for. "Are you sure he's not smiling because I have a booger hanging from my nose?" I lifted up the tip of my nose for good measure and made pig sounds.

"Liv-*vy*." She gave me an exasperated giggle.

I smiled back at her, dipping my toes in the water.

"Your dad will date when the time's right. But until then, he's already got a great girl in his life."

She smiled sheepishly back at me, and we changed the subject, talking about the upcoming school year, what kind of school supplies she liked, and what kind of books she wanted to read.

We'd done so much outside in our time together, but I made a mental note to take her to the public library later this week. We could do some reading in the air conditioning to get her back in the habit of focusing on schoolwork, especially when she didn't have swim lessons.

Up ahead, I spotted our ending point. "There's Candycane," I said, pointing at the old pickup my parents had left for us. It had a red cab with a white truck bed and was at least twenty years old. It wouldn't drive over forty miles an hour, but it was great for bopping around the pasture.

"It has a name too?" she asked.

"We name everything," I said. "Well, I do at least."

"What's your truck's name?" Maya asked.

"Bernice," I replied.

We got out, carrying our tubes toward the sandy creed bed. Mom had left a couple towels in the pickup, so we dried off and ate our snacks before heading back to my pickup with the windows rolled down and warm wind pouring in the cab.

"We should have a tubing party for my birthday," she said. "And invite all my uncles!"

I smiled over at her. "I bet you could sweet talk them into it."

"Will you come?" she asked.

"Of course," I replied, not sure it was a good idea for

me to spend more time around her dad. I was having a hard enough time keeping my feelings in check. "When is your birthday?"

"September third." Her little eyebrows came together, and she pointed toward the side of the road. "What's that?"

My eyes widened as I saw a small brown and white animal heading out of the grassy ditch toward the road. I slammed on the brakes, making dust fly through the air and pour into the open windows.

Coughing, I put the truck in park, praying I hadn't hit it. "Wait there," I said to Maya, opening the door to get out.

Of course, she followed me.

I hurried forward, hoping to find an unharmed animal as the dust cleared. And right there on the edge of the road, I saw it.

A sweet, furry puppy sprinting my way. It bounded toward me, putting its paws on my leg, and I immediately picked it up. "What are you doing here, little guy?" I asked it.

"A PUPPY?" Maya yelled.

"I know!" I said, examining what looked like an Aussie mix for any harm. But he looked perfect. A little dirty, some matted fur, but overall healthy and oh, so sweet.

It licked my cheek with its rough tongue, and I giggled. "What a sweetheart."

"Can I hold it?" Maya asked.

I nodded, passing her the puppy. She carried it so carefully in her arms, petting it and sweet-talking it.

I peeled my eyes away from her to scan the countryside. Had it run off from someone's truck bed? Maybe a neighbor was out building fence or something?

But there was no one to be seen for miles, and the closest house was five miles away—my parents' or her Grampy's home. No way had this little guy run from there.

"Where did it come from?" she asked, hugging it close to her chest. He nuzzled under her chin, its white head with a brown patch looking so sweet with her hair dangling around it.

"I have no idea." A nervous feeling settled in my stomach. I hoped someone hadn't just dumped this puppy by the road to die. "Let's drive around a little and see if we can find someone."

She nodded, carrying the puppy to the pickup. I had a smile on my lips the entire time we drove back to my truck, seeing her interact with him. She petted his fur, gave him little pieces of her graham cracker snacks.

"You're such a good boy, Graham," she said sweetly.

"Graham?" I asked.

"He likes graham crackers, so I thought it would be a good name."

"You named him?" I asked, already worried for the fallout that would come when she had to part with him.

She pinned me with a look. "We name everything, right?"

I let out a small laugh, shaking my head. I was in trouble.

FLETCHER

I walked to the diner from work, feeling more stressed than usual. A little boy had fallen out of a tree, breaking both of his legs. He was in so much pain, and it gave me flashbacks from my years working in the emergency room at the children's hospital in Dallas.

I shuddered, trying to suppress the memories I thought I had worked through. Even though it was still so hot out, I had goosebumps under my button-down shirt. I rolled up my sleeves, taking deep gulps of fresh air and grounding myself in the moment until the memories weren't so strong and it didn't feel like they were happening right now instead of years ago.

Then I walked into the diner, seeing Hayes sitting toward the back. Saying hi to a few people on the way, I took a seat across from Hayes, saying, "Do they serve beer here yet?"

"I wish," he muttered. "We should talk to someone at the bar about serving more than peanuts and chips too."

"Agreed." I loosened my tie, pulling it over my head

and setting it in the seat next to me. Then I raked my hands through my hair, trying to ease the tension tingling my scalp.

Hayes eyed me, seeing way too much. "You okay?"

"Fine," I mumbled. "How's the shop?"

He shrugged. "Got a new guy working on tires. He's eighteen, but he's strong."

"That's what you need for that job," I said. I remembered working at the shop one summer in high school. It got hotter than hell in that metal building—I think I lost fifteen pounds that summer, and I didn't have anything to lose. "Please tell me you put a better fan in there. I was too distracted to notice the last time I was there."

"Got one of the big gym fans from the school."

"How?" I asked.

He smirked. "I would tell you, but..."

"Then you'd have to kill me?" I teased.

"Then you'd have to hear about my tryst with the athletic director," he retorted with a smirk.

My jaw dropped. "*Sheridan?*"

His cheeks and neck flamed red under the tattoos that crawled up from his collar. "Those fans cost like five hundred dollars."

"Now I know how you price your dignity," I teased.

He arched an eyebrow, his smirk making his lip ring glint. "She's flexible."

"I'm going to puke before I get my food," I replied, laughing.

Agatha came over, smiling at both of us. "It's good to see you boys together again. What can I get for you?"

We both ordered, and as soon as she walked away, Hayes said, "So when are we talking about Liv?"

Now it was my turn to flush. "How..." I frowned. "Knox."

"Tells me everything," Hayes said. "Including about Saturday. What the hell happened?"

Agatha brought our drinks, and I took the sweating cup of ice water in my hands. "I fucked up. I should have just let it go, but clearly he can read me like a book."

"He's a cop. It's his job to read people."

"I'm his brother. It's my job to put his happiness over my own."

Hayes frowned at me. "He's your brother too. And it didn't take a genius to see how you felt about Liv back in high school."

"That was over ten years ago," I replied. "A lot's changed since then."

"A lot hasn't."

I frowned, thinking about Liv. She was older now, but there were a lot of similarities from the past too. She was kind, fun to be around, made everyone feel included.

"Why didn't you date her back then?" he asked.

I shook my head. "Couldn't lose my best friend when I didn't know if it would work out with his sister."

"And now?"

I smirked sadly at my water, wishing it was something stronger. "Now I'd lose my best friend and my nanny. Maya can't take losing another woman in her life."

"So what's the plan?" he asked. "You keep Liv on as a nanny until Maya's eleven or twelve? Hope she doesn't fall for someone else?"

It was a terrible idea, and we both knew it. "It doesn't really matter because we both know I don't deserve her."

Hayes shook his head. "You're still beating yourself up over—"

I cut him off, not wanting to relive my past. "Liv's gold. And even if I did want to risk Maya's nanny for a relationship, it would end the way everything else has ended. I need you to tell me how to keep my head on straight when it comes to her."

"You keep expecting shit to fail. That's my thing," Hayes said with a sad smile. "But what if it works out? I mean, you still like Liv after what? Twelve years?"

"Fourteen," I corrected.

"That's the same amount of time that Dad and Mom were married."

I shook my head, not able to handle it. "That didn't work out either, if you don't remember."

He frowned, about to say something, but Agatha brought us our food.

Hayes looked at me across the table now filled with our meal. "I know you say this is to protect Maya, but I'm not so sure that's the only thing you're worried about protecting."

I glared across the table at him. "Bad decisions have already cost her enough," I said.

"Bad decisions have cost both of you."

✌

I DROVE home with the windows down, breathing in the fresh country air and trying to steel my nerves.

I didn't like what Hayes had implied. That I was only staying away from Liv to protect myself. You couldn't keep safe what was already broken. Liv deserved better than damaged goods, and Maya needed a stable mother figure in her life.

I had to beg Regina to call Maya the other day, and even that call had only lasted five minutes. Maya spoke more on the phone to Liv, even though we lived on the same damn property.

The house appeared over the hill and I pulled into the driveway, rolling the windows back up and then getting out of the truck.

I heard Liv and Maya in the backyard, playing, and then I heard another strange sound. Something like a bark? But we didn't have a dog.

Maybe they were watching videos outside or something.

I walked around the house toward the backyard and squinted. I couldn't be seeing right.

Maya was romping around in the grass with a little furball. A puppy.

Just as I realized what it was, Liv turned toward me, guilt written all over her face.

Oh, hell no.

She got up, rushing toward me, but Maya saw what she was doing and picked up the dog, running toward me with it in her arms. Its little tongue hung out happily in the wind created by Maya's speed.

"What is that?" I asked.

Maya held him up so I could see his big brown eyes. "Dad, this is Graham."

Fletcher's eyes were going to pop out of his head to match that vein throbbing on his neck. "Maya," he said, "will you take *Graham* to the front yard so I can talk with Liv?"

Her eyes darted between her dad and me. "You can't take him away, Daddy."

"Front yard. *Now.*"

She scurried off, whispering to Graham. "Don't worry, baby, I won't let him take you. You're my doggy, and you'll be my doggy forever. He'll learn to love you."

I fought back a smile at her words, but Fletcher snapped, "Something funny, *Olivia?*"

"Don't call me that." I scowled. "I'm not in trouble."

"Are you sure about that?" He folded his arms across his chest, and my eyes followed his exposed forearms. I swear, rolled sleeves were like arm porn.

Eyes up here, Liv. I huffed out a breath. I hadn't expected him to take a surprise puppy great, but I knew if we asked him on the phone, he'd say no without a second thought. And he hadn't seen how happy that puppy made Maya all day as we drove around looking for its owners. I'd also put a post in the community Facebook group with no luck, even after several hours.

"Look, we were driving out by my parents' house, and we saw him in a ditch. We went to every neighbor in a ten-mile radius and asked all of them about the dog. None of them were missing a puppy. I posted online and still nothing. If you were missing a puppy, don't you think you'd be looking all over the place to see if someone found it?"

He pressed his lips together and rubbed his hands over his chin. "Someone dumped it."

I nodded. "And you should see how sweet Maya has been to that dog all day. She even set out three bowls of water for him."

"Three?" he asked.

"One from the sink, one from the fridge, and then one from the bottled water you keep in the garage. So he would have options."

He raised his eyebrows.

I nodded. "She loves that dog already. Even though I told her if he belongs to someone else, she needs to give it back."

"But if no one claims him?"

"That's up to you."

He scoffed, shaking his head. "I'm supposed to say no?"

"I don't think you should," I admitted. "I think it would be good for Maya to have something to worry about and take care of other than herself."

"But a dog's a lot of work."

"And you have a nanny here full-time to take care of it. Graham can even stay in my house at night so you don't have to worry about cleaning up accidents."

His lips twitched. "Now I feel like I'd be saying no to Maya and you."

I fought a smile, because at this point, he was definitely right. "You saw how cute he is, right?"

He shook his head. "Puppies are always great the first few days. What happens when Maya gets bored of him?"

"Then I'll keep him," I said. "I like dogs. I just wasn't allowed to have one in company housing."

He eyed me suspiciously, then shook his head. "There better not be any more surprise pets."

"There won't be," I promised, already grinning.

"I'm serious. You keep so much as a cricket in a jar, and it's going to the pound."

"Heartless," I teased.

He pinned me with a glare. "You're on thin ice, Olivia Griffen."

I glared at him. "Use my full name again and you will be too, *boss*."

He stuck out his tongue.

The playful gesture surprised me so much I let out a laugh and hit his arm.

"You have no spine," he grumbled, walking toward the front yard.

"Okay, pot," I teased, following him.

Up front, Maya lay in the grass, Graham jumping over her chest and licking her cheek. Fletcher glanced my way and muttered, "Okay, maybe I understand."

I smirked at him. Of course he did.

"Maya," he said.

She jumped up, taking the puppy in her lap, holding him in a way that said, *you can take him over my dead body*. I kind of agreed with her.

"You can keep Graham," he said, cracking a smile warmer than the hues of orange coloring the sky.

Maya screamed happily, running up to him.

He hugged her, closing his eyes, and then said, "I have a few ground rules. The puppy does not come in the main house until he's potty trained. He will have plenty of chew toys so he doesn't ruin our furniture or shoes."

She nodded eagerly at every demand.

"He will sleep in the cottage with Liv, and you are in charge of making sure he has food and water every morning and every night before bed. You'll bathe him once a week and save money for his veterinary visits and obedience training. Okay?"

"Yes, yes, I promise!" she said.

"Now let me see the little guy," he replied.

She carefully passed the puppy to her dad, and I swear my ovaries exploded.

This strong, beautiful man with a jawline like stone and arms of chiseled muscle smiling at a puppy with his eyes crinkled and his beautiful teeth on full display?

He was already in love.

And me? I needed to remember that I couldn't be.

GRAHAM CURLED up in his kennel next to my bed, breathing softly and whimpering every so often as he slept. With a sigh, I rolled to my back, staring at the whitewashed plank ceiling, the rustic fan spinning in slow circles. I tracked one blade as it spun, trying to settle the aching in my heart.

Fletcher was the perfect guy... in theory. He loved his daughter. He had an amazing job. He was tough with just the right amount of sentimentality. And he was attracted to me too...

But we couldn't pursue a relationship. I knew that, and he'd said as much on our failed double date. Still. I wondered what it would feel like if he had enough faith in us to risk it. What kind of life we could live...together.

I tossed and turned, eventually finding a restless sleep... until I heard a scream outside.

My heart jolted, and I bolted upright shooting out of my bed to find the sun just barely rising.

That was Maya's scream.

And it curdled my blood, turned it to ice in my veins.

I pushed out the door to see her standing in the yard, a coyote just feet away from her.

Instinct took over, and I ran to her, taking her in my arms and shouting at the coyote to run away. They usually never got close to houses in the country like this. Coyotes were afraid of humans.

They had to be.

I yelled again, standing my ground with Maya scrambling and shaking in my arms so it wouldn't go on the hunt and chase after us.

The door to the house banged open, and the animal turned, sprinting under the fence and away from the house.

Fletcher ran to both of us, wearing only sweatpants low on his hips. He reached us, cradling Maya's face with one hand and mine with the other. "Are you okay?" he asked forcefully, looking from her to me.

I nodded, but Maya was breathing fast. He tried to take her into his arms, but she clung to my neck, sobbing quietly.

His lips pressed into a line. "Let's go inside."

I nodded, moving to carry her into the main house, but Maya shrieked. "Graham! I need Graham!"

"He's in the kennel," I told Fletcher.

He nodded sharply, going to get the puppy while I carried Maya into the house, stroking her hair and soothing her softly.

"It's okay, baby girl; you did the right thing," I said.

Through gasping breaths, she said, "I just wanted to check on Graham."

"I know you did, honey. And you went outside to find him, then you yelled for Daddy and me. We came right out to get you."

She hugged me harder. "I'm so glad you came."

"I'll always be there for you," I promised. I didn't know how, but I knew I'd always fight to keep this girl safe.

28

FLETCHER

"I'll always be there for you," Liv said fiercely to my daughter, just as I walked in the door.

Maya held on to her for dear life, and my heart ached. Liv had done for my daughter what I couldn't. This morning, when I went to help her, she reached for Liv.

What happened when Liv wasn't here anymore? Would Maya survive it?

Would I?

Graham barked, announcing our presence.

Both girls spun their heads my way, and Maya scrambled out of Liv's lap to get the puppy from me. He jumped out of my arms, eagerly going to her. She shushed him, saying, "It's okay. I'll get you food, sweetie."

I looked up from my daughter and connected gazes with Liv. I waved my hand toward her, indicating she should follow me. "Maya, stay inside. Liv and I need to talk. Privately."

"It wasn't Liv's fault," Maya said quickly.

My heart jerked. A few months ago, Maya never would have defended someone else like that, human or animal. I could see the changes in her more now than ever.

I walked back to my bedroom, feeling Liv's gaze on my bare back. The second she shut the door, I couldn't hold back anymore. I took Liv in my arms, holding her close. She was warm under my touch, safe. And I held on longer than I needed to, saying, "I'm so glad you're okay. Thank you for protecting my daughter."

Her hands gripped my back like we were both rattled from the experience.

"What the hell happened?" I asked, stepping back. "One minute I'm sleeping, and the next I hear screaming and see a goddamned coyote running away."

Liv's blue eyes were wide and worried. "I heard Maya scream, and I ran out to see what was going on. She was face to face with a coyote. I picked her up and started yelling to scare it off. Thank god she was okay."

My eyes stung with unshed emotion. "Why the hell was she outside?"

The realization dawned just as Liv said, "She said she wanted to check on Graham."

"That's it," I replied. "Today we're packing your things and moving you into our spare bedroom."

Liv's plush lips parted. "What? Why?"

"I can't have Maya running out there, and I can't have you walking outside early in the morning when I know there are coyotes getting that close to the house."

Liv tilted her head. "I've lived in the country all my

life, and that's the first time something like that has ever happened."

I shook my head, closing my eyes at the memory. "I did a pediatric plastic surgery rotation in med school. A child got attacked by a coyote on the outskirts of Dallas." Images of that poor child flashed through my mind like it was yesterday. "Like hell I'm letting that happen to Maya or you."

"Fletcher—"

"I have to keep you safe," I snapped. "And this is the only way I know how."

Her expression softened as she nodded. "I'll move my stuff over when it's daylight." She glanced over my chest, and I became very aware that I wasn't wearing a shirt. That my chest was heaving with adrenaline. When her eyes stayed on my bare body a second longer, heat spread through my veins.

I took the back of her neck in my hand, twining my fingers through her hair. "I'm so glad you're okay."

Her breath hitched as she looked up at me, her full lips parting. "Fletcher, I..."

"I know," I breathed, leaning closer.

"Dad!" Maya yelled.

I cringed, but Liv took a pronounced step backward. She wasn't disappointed by the interruption. Not like me.

"I'll make breakfast," she said.

I nodded roughly. "Thank you."

♡

I DROVE INTO THE OFFICE, and when I arrived, I had a text on my phone from my brother Ford.

Ford: Coming home this weekend. Dad said we could have a barbecue.

Fletcher: What time?

Ford: Six on Saturday.

Fletcher: I'll be there.

Ford: You should bring the nanny. Heard you have the hots for Liv still.

I rolled my eyes toward the ceiling of my truck.

Fletcher: Like you said, she's my nanny.

Ford: Hottt

Fletcher: I see Hayes is rubbing off on you. Catch you Saturday. Which is Liv's day off.

I put my phone in my pocket and walked into the clinic, seeing Brenda had already opened it up.

"Morning," she chirped. "Coffee is in the pot, I have your schedule for the day here"—she handed me a sheet of paper with all my appointments—"and your insurance coverage for Liv went through. Her first bill will come through at the end of the month."

"Perfect," I said. "Can you submit a referral for her to Dr. Shelly Robinson in Dallas?"

"What office?"

"Gynecology, at the Memorial hospital."

"Will do," Brenda said.

I walked back to the kitchen at the back of the house-turned-office and poured myself a cup of coffee while looking over my schedule for the day.

Doctor Deb had the first appointment for a checkup on her shingles. My chest tightened because I still didn't have an answer for her. I knew Maya was settling in and doing well here. Plus having Liv made me feel like I could handle something this big. But after I almost crossed a line this morning, I worried I'd mess it up and be on my own with Maya again... I only had a couple weeks left to make a huge decision.

I let out a sigh, scanning the rest of my schedule. There were few back-to-school physicals, and... I rubbed my jaw. Rhett Griffen was coming in for his yearly checkup.

We hadn't talked much lately because this was rodeo season for him, but I knew he'd see right through me if he asked about Liv. I couldn't keep my feelings a secret in high school, and they were so much stronger now.

When I saw her protecting my daughter, saw her in danger, all I wanted to do was keep her safe and never let her walk away from my side. Thoughts a boss shouldn't be having about his nanny, the only person who'd been able to stick it out with Maya and see the amazing little girl she really was.

I let out a silent groan and went to my office, filing paperwork until Doctor Deb came in.

"You look a helluva lot better than the last time I saw you," I said.

She smirked at me, her papery skin wrinkling deeply. "You look a lot more comfortable at my desk."

I chuckled, leading her back to the exam room. "How's your nerve pain?" I asked her.

"Comes and goes," she said.

"I'll prescribe you a painkiller to use as needed, but I think you're out of the woods on this one."

She nodded happily, standing from the exam table after I looked her over. "Have you given any thought to purchasing the practice?"

I stood from my rolling chair. "I've given it a lot of thought but haven't found any answers."

She studied me for a moment, her sharp brown eyes seeing too much. "How do you like being back in Cottonwood Falls?"

"Maya is doing great here," I said.

She studied me for a moment. "And you?"

"Why do I feel like I'm not the one doing the examining anymore?"

"You can sit on the table if you'd rather," she said with a wink.

I chuckled, folding my arms across my chest.

"Can you humor an old woman by letting her give you some advice?"

I nodded. "But I'd hardly call you an old woman."

She pinched my cheek. "You charmer." She looked at me closely before saying, "This job is different than being a city doctor. You're this town's lifeline, and that means you see it all, the good and the horribly, terribly bad... Make sure you're doing things that make you happy and fill your soul outside of work as well."

I nodded, feeling understood. There weren't a lot of people who got what this job was like or even really wanted to talk about it. But she did.

"Thanks, Doctor Deb, for everything."

She gave me a wink. "It's just Deb now."

I walked her out of the office, but I thought about her words long after she left. By the time Rhett came in for his appointment, I was ready to talk to him about Liv. Because of all the things that filled my soul since I'd been home? It had been moments spent with her and Maya.

Watching movies together, seeing her braid Maya's hair, teasing each other, walking down memory lane.

And with Liv's promise to Maya this morning, I knew she wouldn't break it.

29

FLETCHER

Rhett sauntered into the office, still wearing his jeans and boots from work. He looked so out of place sitting on the exam table, boot-clad feet dangling over the edge.

"Never thought this day was coming, did you?" Rhett teased, his smile deepening the dimples on his cheeks.

I chuckled. "I'm glad you actually show up to your yearly checkups. I thought I'd be seeing you here for a bull-riding injury or some other fall."

Rhett laughed. "I never fall."

"Uh huh." I rolled my eyes, glancing down at his chart. All his previous checks had come back healthy as a horse, great blood pressure, cholesterol and blood sugar levels. "Anything that's been bothering you lately?"

"Yeah, there's this girl at the bar who won't go home with me... yet."

I smirked at him. "I don't suppose I could help you with that."

"Don't say that. You could come along and make me look better by standing next to me."

"Ha ha," I said.

Rhett shook his head. "I feel great. But this chick I was with this weekend said I have an ugly mole on my back. Can you cut it off?"

"Are you sure it's not a third nipple?"

He pinned me with a glare before breaking out in a smile.

"Let me have a look," I said, walking along the exam table.

He reached over his head, lifting his shirt, and my stomach sank.

"Is it a nipple?" he teased, not seeing my expression.

I swallowed, fighting the tightness in my throat. I was a doctor first right now. I needed to remember that. I stepped forward, saying, "Rhett, I'd like to biopsy this and send it in for testing."

His permanent smile fell, barely lingering on his lips. "Is it cancer?"

"It's hard to tell without a test, but it doesn't look right."

He swallowed, his Adam's apple moving. Suddenly, the room felt tight, stuffy.

Because I wasn't just a doctor and he wasn't just my patient. He was one of my longest friends. Basically a brother.

"Hopefully we caught it early and it'll just be a simple surgery to remove it," I said to myself as much as him. "Don't borrow trouble until we have any definitive answers."

Rhett nodded, forcing a smile back on his face that didn't look natural. "Whatever you say, doc."

We were silent as I got the tools to biopsy the spot and

then as I did blood tests to send in. I said a silent prayer that it would all come back normal, that the mole was nothing or that we'd caught it early enough for it to be taken care of without radiation or chemo.

But when we finished, my stomach was churning.

He pressed a cotton ball to the spot on his arm where I'd drawn blood and asked, "How are things going with the girls?"

"What girls? All I do is work and come home," I said.

He smirked. "I meant your daughter and my sister."

My cheeks felt hot. "We had a scare this morning. Coyote ran up to the house."

His brows drew together. "They usually don't approach people. Was it rabid?"

"I don't know. Liv scared it off when she saw it close to Maya."

His smile was back. "Atta girl. I bet that was scary for Maya though."

I nodded, wondering how I could broach this subject after the appointment we just had... "I told Liv she needs to stay in the main house, so she doesn't get hurt on the way over or Maya doesn't run out in the morning again alone. But thank god she was there for Maya this morning. Liv sure is something else." My heart warmed just thinking of her.

"She is..." He studied me. "You're not getting any ideas, are you?"

I didn't know how to answer. I couldn't lie to him, but his reaction wasn't exactly positive.

Without waiting for my response, he stood up, toe-to-toe with me, and said, "Look, Fletch, I love you like a brother, but we both know my sister deserves better than what happened with Regina."

My head jerked with the force of his words. "What happened with Regina is different." I was trying to convince myself too.

"Really?" he asked, studying me. "Because I see it in your eyes. You're still hurting."

"It's better," I told him. "I'm better."

"I hope so. For you and for Maya. But I don't want you using my sister to make you feel better. She deserves someone whole. Who could give her a family and put her first. I love you like a brother, Fletch, but we both know that isn't you. Not right now. Maybe not ever."

Before I could respond, he walked out of the office, leaving me feeling more alone than ever.

MY STOMACH WAS STILL CHURNING as I drove up to the house. And I was having that conversation with myself again.

The one where I reasoned with myself.

I was better than I was eight years ago, a new resident with no idea how it would affect me to see so many children hurting.

I'd done the therapy, I'd taken the medication, my PTSD was under control. But it wasn't the kind of thing that was ever truly gone. I still had flashbacks from time to time, nightmares that felt real as anything else in my life. But I could recover faster now. I was more me than I'd been back then.

And it pissed me off that Rhett couldn't see that.

I didn't like Liv in the same way I'd been attracted to Regina.

And the way Liv loved my daughter... she understood. She knew that Maya had to come first.

These feelings I had couldn't be one sided. Not with the way Liv looked at me this morning.

I let out a heavy breath as the house came into view.

Because none of it mattered if Rhett wouldn't give me his blessing. That woman I cared for? Her family meant everything to her. It would kill her if she had to choose between Rhett and me. If we didn't have her family's full approval and support.

I was right before to keep this strictly professional. I shouldn't have let my thoughts get away from me. I wouldn't let them get away from me again.

And I couldn't blame Rhett for being on edge this morning. I couldn't have picked a worse time to talk to him about my feelings for his sister.

As I transferred my clothes from a laundry basket to my new dresser in the guest room, Maya lay on my bed, her chin propped in her palm. Graham slept next to her on his dog bed. (What Fletcher didn't know wouldn't hurt him.) "So we're going to have a sleepover, like every night," she said, giddy.

"Pretty much," I replied with a smile. "Except for the nights I go to my parents' for dinner or hang out with my friends."

She pouted. "Me and Dad are your friends."

I reached over, tweaking her nose gently. "The best friends."

When she smiled, I went back to folding clothes.

"Why do you think that coyote came after us?" she asked.

I shook my head. It still threw me for a loop, too. "I don't know."

"You know my mom called last night?"

I drew my eyebrows together, facing her. "She did?"

Maya nodded happily. "She said she moved into a new house with her boyfriend."

I tried to keep a smile as I replied, "That sounds nice."

"She said it has a bedroom for me."

My stomach squirmed because I knew Maya hadn't stayed the night with her mom since Regina left. I didn't like Regina getting Maya's hopes up like that. But I tried to remind myself that I wasn't Maya's mom. She had a mom, who had every right to see her daughter.

"What are your favorite things to do in the city?" I asked her, trying to distract myself.

She began counting off everything under the sun, from her favorite trampoline park to bowling with her dad, getting ice cream with her mom, visiting playgrounds, or seeing the botanical gardens.

She looked around the room. "Is it okay if I draw a picture for your walls?"

"I'd love that," I replied. "Remember where all the colored pencils and markers are?"

She nodded, carefully getting off the bed so as not to disturb Graham. As the mattress shifted, he let out a sleepy huff, rolling to his back and stretching his front paws in the air. It was so stinking adorable.

While Maya worked on her art, I continued moving my stuff over from the guesthouse. I didn't have all that much, but I was surprised how empty the cottage felt without my things in it.

In the short time I'd been here, I'd already come to think of this place as home, and that was a hard thing to accept. Because Maya was already eight. In a couple years, she'd hardly need a nanny, and I doubted Fletcher would want to continue paying me as much as he did.

And then what would we be?

I'd be there for Maya, always.

But Fletcher? In the next two years I worked for him, he could date, fall in love, marry, even have another child with someone else.

That thought ate at me all day until he came home from work.

I had supper ready early and carried some to my room so I could hide out and lick my emotional wounds.

While I ate my food, I could hear him and Maya talking. The low rumbling of his voice and her chirped replies were soothing in a way I didn't want to admit. This place really was home, and I didn't know if I could find another without them.

$$\mathcal{Y}$$

THREE SOFT KNOCKS sounded on my door after Fletcher finished putting Maya to bed.

I knew because I'd heard him quietly sing the song his mom always sang to them and us Griffen kids on the nights we'd stay over. His voice singing those words in memory of her all these years later did strange things to my heart. I was falling for him. And I didn't know how to stop.

But I couldn't ignore him either, so I climbed out from under my covers and walked to the door, cracking it open.

In the dim hallway night-light, his sharp features fell into relief, dark eyes studying me.

"Everything okay?" I asked.

His nod was jerky. "Can we talk?"

I opened the door, stepping back and sitting on the edge of my bed. He glanced around my room for a moment before joining me.

"I see Maya put her touch on your room." He nodded toward the drawing thumbtacked over my bed.

I smiled at the drawing. "She sure did." She'd taped nine pieces of paper together to make a poster of her, me, Fletcher and Graham playing with one of his many new toys. There were hearts instead of clouds, and the image made my chest swell with love.

Fletcher clasped his hands in his lap. "I know you think I'm probably being overdramatic, but I feel better with you in here."

I wished I could say the same. My heart had been racing knowing I'd be sleeping just feet away from him. "It's nice that you look out for me," I said instead.

"I think Maya's happy to have Graham in the house too. She made me give him three kisses goodnight."

I chuckled. "Big, bad Fletcher kissing the puppy?"

He smiled softly, rising from the bed. "Goodnight, Liv," he said, my name like honey on his tongue.

"Goodnight, Fletcher."

The room felt so empty without him in it, but I lay in bed, trying to rest. I wasn't sure how long I slept, but the house was pitch black when I heard Fletcher's voice coming from his room.

He was saying something, breathing hard. I could hear it even through my closed door. Worry gripped my heart.

I got out of bed, walking toward his room. On the

way, I glanced in Maya's room, seeing her sound asleep despite the noise.

I tiptoed to his door and found him thrashing in his bed, sweat on his forehead, illuminated by the night-light by the door.

He was saying something.

"Please. Stop. Help her."

A nightmare. One that looked really bad.

I rushed to him, gently shaking his shoulder as my heart sped faster. "Fletcher, *Fletcher.*"

His eyes snapped open, wild and crazed like he couldn't tell the difference between his dream and reality.

"It's okay," I soothed, running my hand over his arm. "You were having a nightmare."

His breathing slowed inch by inch, and he ran his hands through his sweat dampened hair. "I'm sorry for waking you."

I shook my head, studying him. His skin looked clammy, his eyes haggard. "Are you okay?"

He nodded, his jaw tight.

"Does this happen often?"

He didn't quite nod or shake his head. "I'll be fine. You can get some rest."

I hesitated, not wanting to leave him after what I'd just seen. He'd seemed so distressed, both before and after he woke. "Okay... Goodnight." I started walking away, but then I heard his voice.

"Can you sit with me... just until I fall asleep?" he asked.

My heart ached for him. "Of course." I went to the bed, but instead of sitting, I lay beside him. Next to me, I could feel his thoughts going a million miles an hour, but I stayed quiet beside him. And then it came to me.

I started singing "Red River Valley."

And by the end of the song, he was asleep.

31

FLETCHER

When I woke up in the morning, Liv wasn't in my bed anymore. I already missed her lying next to me, her voice soft as she sang me to sleep. In the daylight, something like that might have been embarrassing to ask for. But in the darkness, when my heart was still racing, I knew I needed her. I didn't want to tough it out alone, knowing I'd sleep terribly and then feel like shit the next day.

I got out of bed and went to the kitchen to find her and thank her. Apologize if I stepped over a line, but when I got to the kitchen, I only saw Maya playing on the floor with Graham.

"Where's Liv?" I asked her.

Maya shrugged. "Can you let Graham outside before he pees in the house?"

"Sure," I said. I took Graham outside, thinking maybe Liv missed her alarm because she'd been up late with me. But when I got back in, Liv still wasn't up.

"Why don't you start combing your hair," I said to Maya. "I'm going to wake up Liv."

"Sure," Maya said with a shrug, then gestured for Graham to follow her to the bathroom.

As she got ready, I went to Liv's door, knocking softly. "Liv?"

"I'm up," she said, but her voice sounded off. "Can you come in?"

I went into the room to find her lying on the floor, dressed in sweatpants and a T-shirt, a heating pad under her back. It might have been comical if her face wasn't pale and tight with pain.

"Oh my gosh." I dropped to the floor next to her. "Are you okay?" I felt her forehead, damp with sweat but a normal temp.

She rolled her head to the side. "I'm sorry, but my monthly started this morning and I feel like I'm dying."

My eyebrows drew together. She'd mentioned having bad periods, but this was worse than last month. "How's your flow?"

Her cheeks finally got a hint of color.

"I'm not asking as your boss; I'm asking as your doctor."

"It's heavy," she answered.

"How heavy?"

"I've filled a super tampon in the last two and a half hours," she said. "I'll be fine, but it will have to be an easy day with Maya. We can watch TV, and I'll see if Mom can bring us some food."

I shook my head, pushing up from the ground. "Nonsense."

"What?" she said.

"You rest. Maya and I will take care of you."

"But your work..." she began.

"Allows for sick days," I finished. "You rest up. Don't worry about us."

I could see from the tightening around her eyes how much it bothered her. But she didn't need to be ashamed. It hurt knowing she was in this much pain. "Can I get you anything now?"

"Some ice water?" she said. "I already took some ibuprofen."

"That was the right thing to do. I'll be right back with some water." I went and got her the water, and when I came out of her room, Maya was waiting for me in the living room, looking concerned.

"Is Livvy okay?" she asked.

I patted her back, giving her a half hug at my side. "She's not feeling so well today, so we both get to be doctor and treat her like our very best patient."

She got a scheming grin on her face. "Only if Graham can be our nurse."

I chuckled, looking down at the dog who tilted his head at us. "He might as well come along."

Ten minutes later, we had Graham stuffed into a reusable grocery bag with his furry little head sticking out because Maya refused to leave him at home while we went shopping.

Unfortunately, we only made it through the front door of the grocery store because the cranky woman at the front register wouldn't let him in. No matter how much I begged or even offered to slip her a twenty. (Not my finest moment.)

In fact, I think it insulted her more, because she threatened to put my picture up on the window as a banned customer and refuse service to me ever again.

Maya stuck her tongue out at the woman.

I only gave her a high five once we were outside in the truck. I couldn't exactly leave Maya in the car, and she wasn't old enough yet to go into the store by herself. So I got out my phone to call Rhett.

It was instinct, leaning on my best friend. But I felt awkward too because of our last interaction.

This was for Liv, though, a way to show him that I was putting her first. So I went ahead and dialed his number.

"Hey, can you come into town?" I asked when he answered.

"I'm actually at the bank right now... Do you need something?" The offer to help made me feel better. Maybe things weren't as off between us as I feared.

"Yeah, I'm at the store and they won't let me bring Graham inside."

"He's a dog," Rhett said, nonplussed. "Of course, they wouldn't let him in."

"And you really think we could leave him in the car when it's a hundred degrees outside? Our parents might have left us outside with the car running when they went shopping, but that shit gets the cops called on you nowadays."

Rhett made a sound. "I'll be there in five. I need to get a few things anyway."

While we waited on Rhett, I wrote down a list of items I'd need for Liv, and he arrived in a few minutes, as promised. When he got to the truck, I rolled the window down, and Maya said, "Uncle Rhett!"

He grinned at her. "Heard you're stirring up trouble. Good girl." He reached past me and fist-bumped her.

I rolled my eyes at him. "Still a terrible influence, I see."

"You know it. Now what do you need?"

I passed him the list of items, and he scanned it. "Tampons? You're a little young for that, aren't you, Maya?"

"Rhett," I said, exasperated.

Maya only giggled. "It's for Livvy."

"Right," he said. "That's why she needs the... seven-inch, mega-thick tampons?" His cheeks were turning red. "You're fucking with me."

I fought to keep a straight face. "I'm a doctor, Rhett. You think I'd joke about feminine hygiene?"

He let out a grunt and said, "Be right back."

Maya was playing a game with Graham in the back seat, trying to put barrettes in his hair, and I couldn't help but laugh at how cute he looked. What would she do without that dog when she was in school all day?

After a bit, a knock sounded at my window, and I looked up to see Rhett carrying a couple of bags. Rolling down the window, I said, "That was fast."

"You owe me fifty bucks," he replied.

"Sure. Let me make sure you got everything first." I looked through the bag and found a box of super tampons, frowning. "Rhett, these aren't the right ones."

The tips of his ears were already turning red. "I didn't see any with what you said on it, so I figure 'super' was good... right?"

I shook my head. "Imagine a waterfall, gushing blood. Are you gonna walk out with a Dixie cup to catch it?"

His face turned green. "God, just stop talking." He

turned around and walked back into the store, and I had to fight laughter in case he looked back.

I waited a few minutes, just imagining the conversation he'd have with an associate, and when he came back out, he put both his hands on my open window, his face blushing red. "You asshole!"

"Hey, there are children around."

He looked at Maya. "Cover your ears, little girl."

She just laughed.

"What did she say when you asked her?" I asked him, holding back laughter.

His cheeks went bright red. "I'm gonna get you back for this," he said, pointing a finger at me.

I was laughing too hard to care. Rhett and I were back.

He walked away, flipping me the bird.

32

LIV

I tried to sleep, but it was hard with the cramps battling a massive headache. *Yellowstone* played on my phone on the bed, but I couldn't really focus on it much. The only thing comforting me was Fletcher's confidence as he said he'd take care of me today. *He cared for me.* It might not have been the romantic way I wished for, but he did care.

A knock sounded on my door, and I blinked out of groggy half-sleep, saying, "Come in."

The door opened, and Maya walked into my room carrying a tray full of food. There was a pretty green smoothie, eggs with sauce drizzled on top, and a little fruit salad with a sprig of mint. Not to mention there was a tiny glass with a single cut flower. Lilac.

She looked so proud as she carefully carried it to me.

"This is so sweet of you. Thank you so much, Maya." I sat up, taking the tray and folding it over my legs.

"That's Doctor Maya to you," she said sternly. "Have you been getting plenty of fluids?"

I smiled incredulously at her and then noticed her dad

standing beside her. He looked so freaking good in a tight navy shirt and faded jeans. The wink he sent me was just the cherry on top.

"Thank you, Doctor Maya," I corrected with a smile, despite the cramps that felt like barbed wire in my gut.

Fletcher came forward with a little ramekin and handed it to me. I looked at all the pills inside and asked, "What's this?"

"They're a few supplements that should help with your symptoms and replace some of the nutrients you're losing with your flow. If you need a list, I can write them out for you."

My eyes started to water, and I blinked quickly, trying to wipe away the tears.

"Oh no," Fletcher said. "Are you okay?"

"It's not that. It's just so sweet that you and Maya would..." My tears choked off my voice, and I had to take another breath. "This just means a lot is all."

Maya came to my side, hugging me, while Fletcher tried to keep Graham off the bed. He stood with the dog in his arm, looking caringly down at me. "Of course we're here for you, Liv. You're not just a nanny. You're family."

My heart was melting so damn hard, I said, "Get in here, Fletch. Group hug."

He held me close, and something about the three of us, plus Graham, just felt right.

After a couple minutes, Fletcher stepped back, saying, "Eat your breakfast, and then we'll all hang out on the couch and watch a movie if you're up for it."

"I'd love that," I said.

Maya glanced at me. "*Parent Trap?*"

"You know it," I replied. "Then I'll introduce you to an old friend of mine. *Uncle Buck*."

She looked confused. "Like Uncle Rhett?"

Fletcher and I both laughed. "More than you know," I finally said.

I ate my food, which was so delicious I half wondered if I should start making Fletcher cook breakfast every day. When I finished and went out to the living room, they had the space looking so cozy with blankets and *The Parent Trap* ready to play on the television. Maya curled up on the floor in her little burrito blanket with Graham sitting next to her, and Fletcher gestured at the couch, long enough for me to lie down on while he sat on the other side.

"You get situated, and I'll grab an extension cord for your heating pad."

Tears pricked at my eyes, but I blinked them back, not wanting them to think of me as an emotional mess. So I just lay down, and he was so sweet, getting the cord from the garage and laying the heating pad under me.

Then he pressed play on the movie and went to the end of the couch where my feet were resting. "Lift your feet up?"

I did, moving my feet back so he could have room to sit, but then he reached for them, setting them on his lap.

"What are you doing?" I asked.

"Giving you a foot rub," he said, like I was the crazy one.

"Did they teach you that in med school?" I teased.

He shook his head, taking a foot in his hands. "This one comes naturally."

I leaned my head back, the massage feeling so

freaking good. "I think you wasted money on student loans," I told him over the opening credits.

"Is that so?"

I nodded, with my eyes closed. "You missed your calling as a masseuse."

"*Shhh*," Maya said. "Graham hasn't seen this yet."

Fletcher and I shared a smile. And as the movie played, I was finally able to sleep.

33

FLETCHER

The last few days with Liv had been... different. After her symptoms improved, we were friendlier with each other. More comfortable. There was an ease that hadn't been there before, and I'd be lying if I said it didn't make me feel invincible. Like I could do anything with this woman at my side.

When I got out of work Wednesday evening, Liv and Maya were already parked in the small lot out front, waiting to take me to the Griffens' Wednesday night dinner. Liv had insisted I come along, despite the awkwardness between Rhett and me that I couldn't explain to her. It was one thing, seeing him at the grocery store and another still for him to see Liv and me together. But we'd have to deal with it one way or another.

As I walked down the front steps, I could hear the music spilling from the open truck windows. Through the windshield, I watched the girls holding their fists to each other's mouths, shouting at the top of their lungs to Shania Twain.

Deb's words echoed in my mind. *Find what fills your soul.*

This was it.

Liv caught sight of me first and turned her microphone to me like she wanted me to sing.

And it was Shania Twain, after all. How could I not?

I belted out the lines as I walked to the car, and Maya covered her face.

"What?" I asked as I got in the front seat while Maya crawled to the back with Graham and Liv turned down the music. "It's cool when Liv does it and embarrassing when I do?"

"Livvy's cool," Maya said with a roll of her eyes. Eight going on eighteen.

"And me?" I retorted, buckling in. "I *invented* the word cool."

"You're a doctor, not an inventor," Liv teased.

"Hey, who's side are you on?"

"The one who calls me cool. *Obviously.*" She grinned at me before glancing over her shoulder to back out.

Just a mile out of town, my phone vibrated with a text message.

Miles: Emailed you the results.

My stomach dropped. A friend of mine had placed priority on Rhett's biopsy results, but part of me wished he wouldn't have because now I had the truth. Once I opened that report, there would be no more hoping for the best if my worst fears were confirmed.

"You okay?" Liv asked, glancing my way.

I nodded, forcing a smile I didn't feel. "I'm fine. Hungry."

"We're going to the right place then," she replied.

I shifted slightly in my seat, tapping through my email to the results. And discovered they had also been sent to Rhett.

Shit.

I read over the report, and time seemed to slow as we drove past the sign to my family farm and underneath the metal arch that read GRIFFEN FARMS. How could I pull Rhett aside to talk about this without making a scene in front of his entire family?

"Do you think Deidre made cookies?" Maya asked from the back seat.

Her question brought memories flooding back. Deidre had brought us chocolate chip cookies when they put my mom on hospice, dying of cancer. They were the only food she would eat at the end...

"You know I can make those cookies, right?" Liv asked her, slowing as we got closer to the white farmhouse.

Both Maya and I stared at her. My mind wasn't moving fast enough to comprehend this conversation.

"WHY DIDN'T YOU TELL US SOONER?" Maya asked, bringing me back to the present. Out of the past.

Liv parked in their gravel drive alongside a white minivan. "I like to keep a few tricks up my sleeve." She winked and turned the vehicle off before getting out.

The gust of fresh air that blew through her door cleared my head, if only a little. But it did absolutely nothing for the boulder in my stomach.

Being in this driveway felt like coming home in a way. Except all the kids I used to play with? We were the adults now. Back then, the parents seemed to have it all together.

I wondered if they were like me—playing it by ear half the time, doing their best.

We walked together into the house and were greeted with a bustle of activity. All of Liv's family was there. Her oldest brother, Gage, with his new wife and three stepchildren. Then her brother Tyler and his wife Henrietta. And of course, Rhett and their parents, Jack and Diedre.

Everyone said hello, but Rhett merely lifted his chin at us and said, "Want a beer?"

"Sure," I replied, not quite meeting his eyes.

"Make that two beers," Liv said. "And get my girl a lemonade."

Rhett just turned around, saying, "Will do."

"I'll come help," I offered.

Rhett simply said, "Don't."

Liv gave me a questioning look, but when I had no explanation, she began introducing Maya to a little girl named Cora and a boy named Andrew who were around Maya's age. The three kids took off to the backyard, where Deidre said there were three buckets of water balloons to play with.

"I'm going to see if Jack needs help on the grill," I told Liv.

"I don't think so," she replied. "Come with me." Before we reached the door, she called over her shoulder, "Fletch and I have a bet about the swing in the hayloft. He thinks the rope won't hold him, but I said it's sturdy as steel."

No one seemed too curious about that, but Liv didn't mind either way as she marched me down to the red barn about a hundred yards from the house.

"We're not really going to the hayloft, are we?" I asked.

"Yes, but only because we need privacy," she replied.

She knew something. "Did Rhett talk to you already?"

"He didn't need to." She opened the barn door and marched to the ladder leading to the upper floor, where we used to hang out as kids.

When we crested the top, it looked the same: hay stacked along the walls, a rope swing dangling from the rafter, plenty of dust and cobwebs. But this time was different, because Liv was staring at me with upset blue eyes.

"What is going on with you two tonight?" she asked. "You were so off in the car, and then Rhett barely acknowledged you when you got here. No one made a dumb joke or even smiled."

My eyebrows rose. It depended on what he'd told her about our last appointment. If anything.

"You aren't hiding anything," she snapped. "So I'm going to ask you again. What happened between you two? And don't you dare lie to me."

My stomach churned. I couldn't tell her about the skin test because of HIPPA. But there admittedly was some awkwardness between Rhett and me because of my growing feelings for Liv. I could be honest about that.

"Rhett had a talk with me," I admitted. "About you."

Her lips parted. "Me?"

I nodded, rubbing the back of my neck. We were adults. And in light of what I read on the report, Rhett's protectiveness over his sister seemed so trivial in comparison. "He guessed that I had feelings for you."

Her breath hitched, catching in her chest. "You have feelings for me?"

I nodded, slightly.

"He's upset?"

"He doesn't think I'm good enough for you."

Confusion colored all of her features. "But you're his best friend."

"Which means he knows me better than anyone else."

Her voice was gentle. "I've known you since we were kids, Fletch. There's no one better than you."

Each word was an axe to my heart. Because she thought I was a hero, and I needed to tell her the truth. "I'm not the guy you think I am."

"Fletcher." Her voice was breaking. "What is going on?"

I paced the weathered wooden floor beneath me. "You know Regina and I divorced, but do you know the reason we got together?"

She shook her head. "Because you liked her? Why does anyone get together?"

I scoffed, the sound rough on my throat. "I wish that was why."

"What do you mean?"

"When I worked at the children's hospital in the emergency room, I saw things I couldn't unsee... Some people, they're able to go home and leave work at work, but I couldn't. I started having panic attacks, nightmares. I'd get mad for no reason and lash out. Stopped visiting my little brother Bryce when he was just twelve because I knew if I went home, I'd see all my patients in him. The only thing that helped was drinking and..." I shook my head, ashamed of how I used to be. "I used girls, sex, for a release, a distraction."

If she was breathing, I couldn't tell. She was just watching me. Waiting for me to tell her what a piece of shit I was. She would be right.

"I was a doctor. I should have been ready for it, should have fucking known to go to a psychologist and get some help, but everyone around me was fine. I thought I should be too. But one night at the bar turned into every night, and one hookup turned into more. Regina was one of the girls I slept with the most. After work, I'd get drunk, I'd take her home, and pretend I forgot about it all the next day."

"Fletch, you were going through a hard time..." she said gently, giving me far more understanding than I deserved. I needed to crush that belief in me now, before it hurt us both even more.

"Regina kept hoping for me to turn our hookups into something more. But I couldn't handle more because..."

"It kept you sane," she whispered.

"But then she got pregnant." I shook my head, ashamed of my first response to the pregnancy. "When I found out, I kicked her out of my house. I yelled, screamed, demanded a paternity test. I treated her like shit... And when I found out that Maya was mine, you know what I told her to do?"

Liv covered her mouth, her eyes shining. But I had to say it anyway. Because if Liv thought I was a dick, she'd stay away. I might lose a chance with her, but maybe I could keep my best friend.

"I told her to get rid of it. Gave her the pills to do it," I said.

Liv pressed her hand to her heart like the words physically pained her.

"If Maya ever knew that my first thought about her existence was wanting her gone..." I shook my head, my throat closing with emotion. "But Regina refused to get an abortion. She still hoped I would come around, when I saw Maya's sonogram."

Liv nodded, hope in her eyes.

I took a heavy breath, knowing I would crush it. "I ripped up the sonogram. And Regina did the only thing she could think to do. She found my family online, called my dad. And when he found out about my drinking problem, he signed me up for outpatient therapy and told me to put my head on straight. He told me..." I shuddered on the words. "He told me that my mom would be ashamed of the man I'd become."

A tear slid down Liv's cheek. "Fletch..."

"She would have," I said, sure of it. "A daughter on the way and I wanted nothing to do with her." I shook my head. "So I turned it around, because for all the mistakes I've made, I never wanted my mom to be disappointed in me. I proposed to Regina, we had a small elopement with family around. I did the therapy. I stopped drinking. Started taking antidepressants. And Maya was born."

As I thought back to that day, my eyes stung with tears, and I covered my mouth with my hand. "She was the most beautiful thing I'd ever seen. I loved her with my whole heart the second I saw her. I really did."

Tears spilled down Liv's cheeks, but she wiped them away.

But I knew more would come, because this was the worst part.

"A girl needs her mom. But I couldn't love Regina." I shook my head. "She helped me through my pain, got me cleaned up, gave me the most amazing baby girl, but I couldn't love her. Not the way she deserved."

Liv said, "She wasn't the one..."

"No, she wasn't *you*."

The words were heavy between us, Liv's perfect lips parting and closing again.

But it wasn't the end. "Regina knew I didn't love her, and after a while, she started going to the bars again, seeing different guys. One night, she got drunk and told me that Maya looks so much like me, she was just a reminder to Regina of all that I'd done. It hurt to see Maya, and it hurt to be married to a guy like me... And Maya heard her say it. That's why I'll never blame Maya for her behavior this last year. She's been through hell and back, and it's all my fault."

My chest heaved with emotion, of all that I'd told Liv. She'd seen all the ugliest parts of me, and I waited for her to pull away. To run.

Instead, she stepped closer.

She took my face in both of her hands, so close I could smell her vanilla perfume. Her gaze held mine, and she said with so much conviction, "Fletcher, I want you to hear me."

I stared into her blue eyes, light in the dim barn. A life raft for a drowning man.

"You are a good man."

My throat got tight, and I swallowed down the pain.

"You are a good man who let his hurt lead him to bad choices. But it doesn't matter how low you got, only that you found the strength, the courage, the *love* to get back up. That's *exactly* the kind of parent Maya deserves and the kind of man I'm lucky to have in my life."

I was speechless, hanging on to her every word. She'd seen me, for all that I am, and she found the gold inside me. And somehow, it let me see just a little bit of light in myself. Helped me somehow believe that maybe I could earn the love of a woman like her.

It wasn't hard to spot the gold in Liv. This woman was pure, incredible, and I couldn't hold back anymore.

I took her face in my hands and kissed her like I'd been wanting to do ever since I left Cottonwood Falls. Ever since she walked into my office that day and into my daughter's heart.

She met my kiss with passion, teasing her tongue along the seam of my lips and deepening our embrace.

I held her close, feeling like we would never get close enough.

Until I heard Rhett's shout. "GET YOUR FILTHY FUCKING HANDS OFF MY SISTER."

Fletcher and I jumped apart, reeling as Rhett hauled himself up in the hayloft.

"What are you doing here?" I demanded of him. There was no reason for him to follow us up here. No reason to talk to Fletcher like that.

Rhett glared between us, his hazel eyes narrowed. "I just knew he was going to take you out here and try something."

"He didn't 'try' anything," I said angrily. "I'm an adult. I can't believe you said Fletcher wasn't good enough for me, like it's your decision to make."

Rhett swung his gaze to Fletcher, a look of betrayal plain as day. "You told her?"

Fletcher's jaw flexed.

"Did he tell you why he got married to Regina?" Rhett demanded.

"He did!" I said.

"And you still want to be with him?" He said it like it

was some kind of judgement on my character, wanting to be with Fletcher.

"You still wanted to be his friend," I argued. "If he's *so awful*, how could you stand to be around him?"

Rhett's hand cut through the air. "It's different, and you know it."

"All I know is that you've been interfering in my life, and it is not okay!" I yelled. "Why do you think people never change? That Fletcher hasn't learned from his mistakes?"

Rhett looked between Fletcher and me. "This was your plan? Huh?" he demanded of Fletcher. "Sneak around my back, turn her against me? You couldn't just wait until I drop dead?"

"Of course that wasn't the plan," Fletcher said, trying to calm him. "And you're going to be okay, Rhett."

My eyebrows drew together. "What are you two talking about?" They were acting like Rhett had some kind of incurable disease.

Now both of them fell silent, their chests heaving as dust motes swirled around them.

My stomach sank. There was something else I didn't know. "What?" I demanded. "What aren't you telling me?"

Fletcher looked at Rhett. "I can't tell her without breaking confidentiality."

"Now you can't tell her something," Rhett muttered. He stared at the ground, saying, "I got a spot tested on my back, and the results came back right before y'all got here. It's cancer."

My legs felt weak underneath me, threatening to send me crumbling to the dusty floor. "Rhett..."

Fletcher said, "We need more information before we know how serious it is."

"How much more serious can it get than *cancer?*" Rhett demanded.

I wanted to know the same thing.

Fletcher's voice was rough. "It's the difference between it spreading to other parts of your body or having a simple surgery to remove it. And Rhett's white cell count wasn't too elevated, so I want to hope for the best."

Rhett shook his head. "You want to talk to me about hoping for the best when I know my best friend is going behind my back to be with my sister when I flat out said I thought it was a bad idea? I never thought you would betray my trust like that."

"Rhett..." Fletcher said.

But Rhett was already climbing back down the ladder.

Fletcher moved to follow him, but I put my hand on his chest. "Let him go. He needs to cool down, and he won't do it with you around." At Fletcher's hurt expression, I added, "He'll take it out on you, and I don't want your friendship to have to survive that too."

Fletcher covered my hand with his. "I never should have..."

I shook my head at him. "I just found out my brother has skin cancer. Please don't tell me you thought that kiss was a mistake. I couldn't take that too."

A look full of emotion crossed Fletcher's features, and he cupped my cheek with his hand, slowly kissing my forehead. "We can't pursue this, Liv. Not now."

Angry tears threatened to fall, but I didn't want to let

him see. I turned and left the hayloft before he could say anything else that would break my heart.

I'd barely reached the barn door when Fletcher said, "Liv, wait!"

I spun on him, light illuminating him through the open barn door. "What, Fletcher? Are you going to tell me that I repulse you? That you'd do anything to push me away? Because I see right through it! You want to be with me, and you're too fucking scared to admit it."

He stepped back like my words hurt him, but then he recovered, coming closer and kissing me again. It was everything...pain, hope, and all the feelings in between.

His voice was rough as he spoke against my lips. "I don't regret it. Not for a second."

My eyelids fluttered open to catch his heavy gaze.

But he backed up and started walking toward the house, three steps ahead of me. Dust billowed down the dirt road in the distance as Rhett's truck raced away.

When I made it back to the house, all eyes were on us, like they could see the heat of Fletcher's kiss on my skin, the guilt of being caught, and the sadness of Rhett's diagnosis.

I was scared as hell and wanted to know that my brother would be okay. But I also didn't want to ruin everyone's night when Rhett clearly wanted to keep things to himself.

So I fought to keep a happy face. Sat through dinner with my parents, listening to them talk with Fletcher about his new house and Maya about her swimming lessons.

But after dinner, when I went to put away the plates, Henrietta said, "Come upstairs with me."

There wasn't a question in her voice, so I followed her up, finding our other sister-in-law, Farrah, already sitting in my old room. She stood up when she saw us, worry in her eyes.

"What's going on, Liv? Is Rhett okay?"

I looked between the two women, sisters who'd joined my family by love, and knew they understood as much as anyone could.

"Did Rhett say why he left?" I asked finally.

Henrietta shook her head. "He got in his truck and drove out of here like a bat out of hell after giving some lame excuse about cattle getting out. He was pale as a ghost."

I glanced between her and Farrah.

Farrah asked, "What happened in the barn? We saw him follow you and Fletcher, and then he took off."

I realized I couldn't tell them Rhett's news before he could do it himself. So I bit my lip, blaming it on the second reason Rhett flew off the handle. "I kissed Fletcher."

They both acted surprised. But more than that... they seemed worried.

"What?" I asked. I thought for sure Henrietta would be happy for me after how much I talked about him. "You think it was a bad idea?"

The glances they exchanged confirmed just that, putting me on the defensive. "Great, Rhett has an issue and now you do too," I said, backing toward the door.

Henrietta held her hands out gently. "It's a lot to take in, Liv. That's all."

Farrah nodded. "You live with him, you care for his child, and adding a relationship can get messy... And trust me when I say co-parenting with another woman is a huge challenge, even if she has good intentions."

"Co-parenting?" I asked, shocked. "We just had one kiss, and I'm already his nanny."

Henrietta said, "Did you discuss how a relationship would affect your job?"

My cheeks burned with embarrassment. Because I'd kissed Fletcher without ever asking how things might change. And instead of being happy like I thought I would when Fletcher showed me his feelings, I was on the verge of tears. I hadn't anticipated such terrible news about my brother or having Fletcher back away when I finally got what I wanted. "I think I need to go home," I said, reaching for the door.

"Wait," Farrah said, "we were just worried about you. But if you're happy, of course we're happy too."

My eyes stung because of I knew the truth, but it wasn't my news to share. "Then throw a party. Because I've never been better." I pushed my way out the door and wiped my eyes on the way down the stairs.

Forcing a smile, I went outside to find Fletcher talking with my dad. All it took was a lame excuse about not feeling well and the three of us were in the truck.

Maya talked the entire way home about her new friends, missing the fact that the adults up front hardly spoke at all.

35

FLETCHER

I had nightmares that night. Terrible ones, where the kids I tried to help in the hospital turned into my best friend dying.

When Liv shook me awake, my skin was slick with sweat and my breaths came fast, like I was running.

"Fletcher," she soothed. "It's okay, you're here now. It's Wednesday night, we just had dinner with my parents, then we came home. You're in your bed, it's two in the morning. Maya is safe in her bed and Graham is in his kennel..." she continued, reminding me where I was, and I realized... she was grounding me without my ever having asked.

"Where did you learn to do that?"

My eyes were slowly adjusting to the dim lighting, seeing her kind eyes as she said, "That first night you had the nightmare, I looked up how to help someone with PTSD."

My breath stopped at her words. Liv was more than a godsend... She was an angel. "You did that for me?"

"I want to be there for you, Fletcher. If you'll let me."

I reached out for her, pulling her closer, and she came to me, letting me cradle her against my chest.

And I started to cry, because I realized Liv was there for me in a way no one had been before. She didn't want me to get my shit together like my dad had or support her like Regina had. She wanted to help me for... me.

"Oh, Fletch," she said gently, taking my head to her chest, running her hand over my hair until I wiped my eyes and steadied my breath.

"I love you," I admitted, the words rough on my tongue. "I've been trying not to, but I can't help myself."

She adjusted herself, so we were in the bed, lying face to face. "Why do you try?" she asked. "Why can't you follow your heart?"

"Because you know it's not just you and me," I said. "Ever since we were kids, it's never just been you and me. You have a family, a brother, who has been there for you always. And I have a daughter and a best friend who need me more than ever."

She pulled back, the distance palpable. Painful. "Why do you keep trying to find reasons not to be with me?" Her voice quavered. "Why can't you have faith that you and I will figure it out, together?"

I looked up at her, wishing I could have the faith she did. But I couldn't. "I lost my faith a long time ago, Liv Griffen."

She stood from the bed, wiping angry tears from her eyes. "Then maybe you were right. I should keep my distance until you can find a way to believe in me like I believe in you."

♡

LIV HARDLY SPOKE to me the next few days, aside from things I needed to know about Maya. But that was only part of the problem... The other was the way Liv looked at me.

I could see it in her eyes. She thought I had betrayed her. And that was worse than anything I could imagine. I hated not seeing her smile in the morning. Not hanging out with her before Maya went to bed.

She thought I didn't have faith in her, but she couldn't have been further from the truth. I believed in her, I saw all the good in her, and I didn't want to be the one to make her cry ever again like I did the other night.

I didn't trust myself.

I never wanted to be the one coming between her and her brother while he fought for his life. Because as much as I loved her, I loved him too. He would need both of us to make it through.

He had an appointment coming up on Friday with the best dermatologist in Dallas as a special favor to me. They would remove the spot completely and have him do a CT scan to see if the melanoma had spread then go from there. So I had Brenda cancel all my appointments for that day and drove to Dallas to meet Rhett at his appointment.

When I walked into the waiting room, he looked up from the magazine he was reading and said, "What the hell are you doing here?"

A woman a couple chairs over glanced our way and quickly looked down when I caught her staring.

"I came to support you," I said, steeling myself for a fight. He wouldn't be Rhett if he made things easy.

He huffed, straightening his magazine. "You want to support me? Leave my sister alone like I told you to. She doesn't know you like I do."

I sat a couple chairs away from him. "I'm not here to argue."

"Then why are you here? Because I didn't ask you to come, and I don't need your 'support.'"

"Rhett... you're my best friend. You were there for me when my mom..." My voice broke. "You were there for me through it all, and you're fucking crazy if you think I'm not going to be there for you when you go through this. Especially since you aren't telling anyone in your family, and you know Liv's too damn loyal to say a word."

His jaw ticked, and he was quiet for a long moment. Finally, he folded the magazine, staring hard at the floor. "I don't want to die, Fletch."

Emotion clogged my throat, but I swallowed. "We don't know anything yet, Rhett. It could be easily treatable with a simple surgery."

"And it could have spread to my lymph nodes. We don't know."

"We don't know," I conceded.

He lowered his voice. "Fletcher, this whole thing has sent me into a tailspin. You know, I'm thirty-two years old. And what do I have to show for it? When Gage was my age, he'd made his first billion. Tyler's married, has a business he loves. You're a fucking doctor. And what am I? a second-rate bull rider with a job on someone else's ranch. I pushed away the only woman I ever loved and hold every other woman I meet at arm's length. This can't be it."

His words echoed in my mind. *This can't be it.* "It won't be," I promised him and myself. "Why do you think I became a doctor? I couldn't let what happened to my mom happen to anyone else I love. And no matter how pissed at me you are, I love you just as much as any one of my brothers."

Rhett looked at me. "I'm sorry for what I said about—"

I shook my head. I wanted him to give Liv and me the clear to date, but I could wait. "You love Liv," I said. "You were doing what any good brother would do."

He shook his head. "I've made all the mistakes a person could. I'd hate to see her have anything less than..."

"Everything," I finished. Because that's what I wanted to give her.

He nodded.

"Rhett Griffen?" a nurse called from beside the door.

"That's me," Rhett said as we both stood to follow her.

"And him?" the nurse asked.

Rhett studied me for a moment, then put his arm around my back. "That's my brother."

36

FLETCHER

I offered to take Rhett out for dinner after his test, but he said he needed some quiet time to think. Which left me to reminisce on my drive back to Cottonwood Falls. So much had already changed since I'd moved back home. A lot of it for the better. But in some ways, I felt more confused than ever.

I didn't know what to do about this practice. I definitely didn't know what to do about Liv.

Since I still had time before I needed to be back home, I drove by the Cottonwood Falls Cemetery. It was a small plot of land outside of town, surrounded by a tree row of evergreens. I drove around the gravel path skirting all the headstones.

The way was familiar. I came here every Mother's Day, every year on my mom's birthday, and every time I felt at a crossroads in my life, because even if my mom wasn't here anymore, this was where I went to see her.

I got out of the car, the afternoon sun hot on my skin and the grass crunching slightly underfoot until I reached her headstone. There were new silk flowers in each of the vases along her grave. I noticed a figurine of the football team, a ceramic truck with flowers hanging out the back. A Cottonwood Falls Police Department badge and a set of dog tags.

All of my brothers had been here. But it had been a while for me. I traced my fingers over the rock Maya painted for her grandmother for Grandparents' Day, the paint already fading.

Then I looked at the words, etched into marble and seared into my mind.

Maya Madigan
   Beloved wife and mother
   "Lead with love."

I RAN my thumb along the last line. "If you did anything, it was love, Mom," I said softly. I hitched my jeans and sat in the grass beside her stone. I still remembered when the dirt was fresh and hilled over her casket.

But time had changed things, settling the slope, reclaiming the dirt with buffalo grass. She was as much a part of the earth as anything else.

"Maya's starting third grade next week," I whispered. "You would be so proud of her. She can swim across the pool and back now. She has the sass of a teenager, but she speaks her mind. And you should see the way she loves her puppy. Graham. I know she had to ask permission to have him, but no way could I ever turn her down." I raked my hands through the grass, watching the green blades part around my fingers. "But that's not really why I came here."

I sighed, tilting my head back toward the cloudy blue sky. "I've got a lot of decisions in front of me. Ones I'm having a hard time making."

Mom always used to tell me I had a lot of thoughts in my mind. She would get out Tupperware, which were really just used butter and sour cream containers, and tell me to put a worry in each one. So I tried to do that now and started with one worry at a time.

"Doctor Deb offered for me to buy her practice, and I'm worried I won't be able to handle owning the practice and being the dad Maya deserves."

I wished she could answer me, but I let my words hang in the silence instead.

But a big gust of wind came through, and a flower fell from the vase beside her headstone and landed on all of the items my family had left.

A soft smile befell my lips as I picked up the flower, uncovering the reminder. It wasn't just me. We had a whole family that was here for each other always.

I could do this.

Tears streamed down my eyes as I realized Mom gave me the sign. That I wasn't alone in this, no matter how much it felt that way sometimes.

"Thanks, Mom," I said, my voice cracking.

I rubbed my face, pushing away the moisture.

"That last year before you... when you were still here... you told me you were proud of how good of a friend I was to Rhett's little sister by letting her tag along. But I don't know if I'm being a good friend anymore. I love her mom. But I can't pursue anything without risking

Maya's nanny and Rhett's friendship. And he needs me right now."

I wished she could reply. Waited for a sign like the flower. Mom always had a way of giving the best advice. But there was no gust of wind. No flower to point me in the right direction.

"Mom, I need you," I said.

Nothing. But I could close my eyes and imagine what she would say.

Life is too precious to wait.

Because even before she was diagnosed with terminal cancer, she knew time was better spent baking together in the kitchen than watching TV. She knew riding along with Dad to check cattle made him happy even if she got bored hearing him talk about cattle prices every day.

And she knew, when push came to shove, a true friend would understand. Forgive.

I lay on my back, allowing myself a moment to breathe.

To let myself be a son instead of a father.

But then I got up to drive home, because I knew... it could be gone all too soon.

Maya flicked through my closet as I finished putting in my earrings.

"You have to wear this one," she said, pulling out a sparkly dress I hadn't worn in years. It was fancier than my usual choices, but that was fine for tonight. Della and Henrietta were taking me out to the bar to get my mind off Fletcher.

These last few days had been hell, living in his house, smelling his cologne, seeing him love his daughter, and knowing that he wouldn't risk loving me too.

"Thanks for picking the dress," I said, taking it to the bathroom to change. When I came out, Maya clapped her hands together happily.

"You look like a disco ball," she said.

I laughed. "Exactly what I was going for." I went to the closet, digging through my boxes for a pair of sandals, then slipped them on my feet. Good thing I remembered to shave my toes last night. "What do you think?" I asked her, doing a spin.

She gave me two thumbs-up.

"Awesome, let me get you settled with some dinner before your dad gets home." We went to the kitchen, and I started making her a sandwich. "Are you getting excited for school to start next week?"

She nodded. "Penny said she would give me one of her lip balms when school starts. It's flavored like Dr. Pepper."

"They still make those?" I asked.

She nodded. "Will you help me pick out an outfit?"

"I'll do you one better," I said with a smile. "I'll take you back-to-school shopping for a special new outfit. Maybe we can even find Graham a matching bowtie."

She grinned, looking down at Graham, where he sat at her feet. "You'd be a fancy dog."

I chuckled, loving how sweet she was with him. I finished making her sandwich, then put it on a plate with some baby carrots and ranch. "Bon appetit."

She picked up the sandwich and was taking her first big bite when the door opened, and Fletcher came inside.

He looked a little ruffled, his button-down shirt slightly wrinkled. "Hey, Maya. Liv, I need to talk to you."

I shook my head. "It'll have to wait. I'm off the clock and already running late."

"To where?" he asked, eyeing my disco ball dress.

"I'm off the clock," I repeated. I went and gave Maya a hug, then scratched Graham behind the ears, and walked past Fletcher to the front door, getting my purse from the hook and putting it over my shoulder.

Behind me, Fletcher said something to Maya and then followed me outside. "Liv, wait!"

I kept walking toward my truck, frustrated with him

after the last several days. We'd barely spoken this week, and *now* he wanted to talk? Couldn't he see I needed to forget him? At least for the weekend?

I put my hand on the truck door handle, wanting to drive away and leave him in the dust.

Instead, he stopped me, covering my hand with his own.

It was like an electric shock, having his rough hand on mine. Feeling the heat emanating from his body. Smelling his cologne that wouldn't scrub itself from my mind.

"What?" I demanded, not looking at him. I hated how my body reacted to him without my permission.

"What are you doing? Can't you stay here and talk this out with me?"

I glared up at him. "No, I can't, because I need to get over you, Fletcher. I need to go to the bar and drink too many shots. I need to dance with a guy who puts his hands too low on my ass. I need to sleep with someone and not have him tell me he loves me but can't be with me. I need to *move on* so I can open my heart to someone who actually wants to be with me."

His jaw tensed. "But what if I don't want you to move on?"

I shook my head at him, angry tears forming in my lashes. "I'd say it's too damn late."

"Liv, let's talk. I—"

I yanked my door open, getting in and driving away as he stood in the driveway, watching me.

Just a minute down the road, my phone chimed with a text. I pressed the button for it to play over the speakers.

Fletcher: Come back.

I shook my head at the robotic voice. "No! I've been

too stupid already, chasing after a man who clearly doesn't want me!" When a truck drove by on the dirt road, I realized how crazy I must look, just talking to myself in the middle of the country.

So I cranked up the radio, letting the music drown out my thoughts until I got to Della's house. I let myself in the front door, sitting on her couch with the TV on. She looked gorge in ripped jeans, ankle boots and a flowy, lacy tank. Her curls were loose and voluminous, dancing around her bare, freckled shoulders.

"I'm loving the dress," she said when she saw me.

I did a spin as I walked to where she sat on the couch. "Maya picked it out."

She waggled her eyebrows. "I bet Fletcher's going crazy with that image of you in his mind."

"Apparently... He tried to stop me from coming out tonight."

Her jaw dropped. "No freaking way."

I nodded. "I told him I needed to move on, and he was all 'What if I don't want you to?'"

"What did you say?"

"I said it's too late and left!" I leaned back on her couch and covering my face with my hands. "We both know I would have just held on to what he was saying and never moved on. He showed me what he wants, right?"

Della patted my leg. "Fletcher seems like a nice guy, and I adore Maya, but it's not okay for him to string you along. He needs to be in or out." She got a salacious grin on her face. "Maybe both, multiple times, in the span of half an hour."

I laughed out loud. "I need to be more drunk for jokes like that."

A knock sounded on the door, and Della called, "Come in!"

Henrietta walked into the house wearing a cute cotton dress and sneakers. "My girls!"

We gushed over her for a minute, and then I filled her in on Fletcher drama while Della got us shots to pregame.

"Make Liv's a double," Henrietta said.

Della grinned. "Already on it."

I shook my head at them, taking the plastic cup with the Woody's Diner logo on it while they both had shot glasses.

Henrietta held up her shot. "To Liv moving on tonight."

"To moving on," Della echoed.

I drank to it, even if it tasted bitter.

38

FLETCHER

Maya and Graham were asleep in her room, but I sat up in my bed, back against the headboard, trying to read a book. Trying to watch TV. Trying to do anything that would get my mind off Liv.

And failing miserably.

I picked up my phone, looking at the last text I sent her, and seeing no reply.

She was right. I'd been a jackass, scared of my own feelings and taking it out on her. But how could I fix it if we didn't talk it out or make a plan?

A picture slid over the screen, and I squinted to make it out. There was a part of Liv's shiny dress. Was the photo taken by accident?

Then another message slid over the screen.

Liv: Do you see that? It's my ass. You can kiss it.

My eyes bugged out.

Fletcher: How much have you had to drink?

Liv: Not enough because I'm still thinking about you.

Liv: Butthead.

That made me way happier than it should have. I was smiling as I typed back my response.

Fletcher: Did you just call me a butthead? I haven't been called that since seventh grade.

Liv: Then you clearly don't have anyone in your life being honest with you.

Liv: Butthead.

Fletcher: How much have you had to drink? Tell me.

Liv: Eleventy seven.

My eyebrows lifted.

Fletcher: 1107? Sips? Is that an exact count?

Liv: I've lost count. There's a nice man here who likes that I like whiskey. It's freeeeeeeee for meeeeee.

Oh, dear lord.

Fletcher: Are you with someone right now?

Liv: The handsome bearded mannnnn?

Fletcher: Where are you friends?

Liv: They're here.

Liv: somewhere.

Liv: Not here here. Like I'm in the bathroom. I had to poop. But somewhere. I think.

Liv: Not like you. You're HOME. BECAUSE YOU DON'T LIKE ME.

Liv: It's FINE.

Liv: Really fine.

Liv: Perfect actually.

Liv: Because the mountain man is getting me shots.

Fletcher: There aren't any mountains in Texas.

Liv: But he's wearing plaid and has a beard and drinks whiskey so he could be a lumberjack.

Liv: Maybe that's why he asked me to come home with him. Because my dress reminds him of a chainsaw.

My eyes bugged out of my fucking head.

Fletcher: DO NOT GO HOME WITH HIM. DO YOU HEAR ME?

Liv: You're not my boss.

Liv: I'm off the clock.

Liv: boss.

Liv: haha.

I blinked, hard, and dialed my brother Hayes's number. When he answered, I swore I heard a woman in the background.

"Did you seriously answer the phone while you're having sex?"

A giggle sounded on the line.

Gross.

"Hayes, I need you to come watch Maya. Now."

"Give me a minute. I'll be there."

I rolled my eyes toward the ceiling, ignoring the pings of additional texts coming through my phone. "Get here soon."

I hung up and looked at my screen to check the million texts Liv had sent.

Liv: The cool thing about dresses is that you can pull them up when you go to the bathroom. That's kind of fun.

Liv: Fletcher, why aren't you texting me BACK?

Liv: Ugh. I'm out of toilet paper.

Liv: Don't worry. The girl next to me got some.

Liv: That was a close one.

Fletcher: Wash your hands.

Liv: Gah, you're such a doctor.

Fletcher: I am a doctor.

Liv: Going to dance.

Fletcher: NO. STAY IN THE BATHROOM.

She sent me an emoji of a plant.

Liv: Shit. Wrong one.

Then she sent me an emoji with its tongue sticking out.

"God damnit, Liv," I muttered to myself. I pressed call, holding the phone to my ear as it rang. She didn't answer.

Liv: Don't call me.

I called her again.

This time, she answered.

"Fletcher," she said over sound of a toilet flushing. "What do I owe is the pleasure?"

"You're drunk," I said.

"AND?"

I smiled to myself. She was so sassy. "And, I think you need to leave the mountain man alone."

Suddenly, music played loudly over the phone. She must have left the bathroom and walked back into the bar.

"Oh, there he is. BENTLEYYYYY!"

"Put Bentley on the phone," I ordered.

I heard her yell, "My BOSS wants to talk to you."

After a second, *Bentley* came on the phone. "Yeah?"

"Bentley, you don't know me, but I'm a doctor. I know seventy-one ways to kill a man, forty-eight that could never be traced back to me, and I will use every fucking one of them on you if you lay a finger on that woman. Got it?"

He stumbled over his words before finally saying, "Sorry, I didn't know she was taken."

"She is. Now get the fuck out of there before I show

up and handle you myself." I heard the front door to my house open, and I said, "I'll give you a head start." Then I hung up and got out of bed, throwing on a pair of shoes and meeting Hayes in the living room.

"Watch Maya. I've got some business to handle."

Hayes gave me a knowing look. "Liv?"

"Just stay here."

39

LIV

I rolled over in bed, feeling like absolute dogshit.

What the fuck happened last night? I thought I was staying at Della's?

But I was in my room at Fletcher's house.

I looked up at the nightstand, seeing a bottle of Gatorade, a couple ibuprofens, and my phone. I took the drink and pills first, thanking god I didn't feel nauseous. When the night went fuzzy, I'd had four shots... Maybe five...

I got my phone to check in with the girls, but when I got to my messages, I stared at the screen. Fletcher had been my last text.

I scrolled through the thread in abject horror.

What the fuck was wrong with me? Why hadn't Della hidden my phone in my purse? I was the *worst* drunk texter.

I looked at my phone calls, seeing two on my screen, and wracked my brain for what happened last night. I got fuzzy flashes that made me even more embarrassed.

Fletcher driving me home.

Hayes in the living room, watching as he walked me inside.

Asking Hayes to dance with me.

Hayes agreeing. Until Fletcher picked me up and put me over his shoulder to carry me to my room.

Dear lord.

I texted my friends group chat.

Liv: WHAT THE HELL HAPPENED LAST NIGHT?

Della sent three cringe emojis.

Henrietta: It wasn't *that* bad.

Liv: I have a million texts to Fletcher that say otherwise!

Della: It was really hot though, the way he showed up at the bar and took you home. I mean, except the part where you sang a Disney song on the way out.

Liv: *facepalm emoji*

Liv: This is very important.

Liv: Which song was it?

Crickets.

Liv: Tell me.

Henrietta: I'll make a man out of you. From Mulan.

I squeezed my eyes shut.

A knock sounded on the door, and I wished with all I had that the bed would swallow me up. "Yes?" I finally squeaked.

"Liv, I need to talk to you," Fletcher said. "Meet me in the office when you're done getting dressed and ready."

I squeezed my eyes shut. This was it. I was getting fired all because I couldn't turn my phone off like a rational freaking person.

Well, if I was getting fired, it was not going to be looking like a tired, hungover wreck. I had to spare some of my dignity—if any was left.

I chose a pair of clothes I knew I looked good in and went to take a shower, brushing out every tangle, washing off the mascara and eyeliner smudged around my eyes that made me look like a hungover panda.

I may have been stalling, but I even shaved everywhere and put on a facial mask for my skin. When I ran out of hot water, I got out and took my time doing my makeup, drying my hair, occasionally cringing at those texts I sent.

When I couldn't stall any longer, I took a deep breath, looking at myself in the mirror. "You, Liv Griffen, are a grown woman. You're an amazing nanny. *You are turning off your phone next time you go out.* Everything will be fine."

I only half believed myself.

Squaring my shoulders, I walked out of the bathroom and into the office. I hardly came in here, except to get extra paper for Maya's crafts, but Fletcher sat at the rustic desk like he belonged there. He had on glasses and his hair was messy, his shirt unbuttoned, with five o'clock shadow darkening his jaw. And now he was that much hotter, knowing he could sling me around like I weighed nothing.

When he looked up at me, his eyes were just as dark, tortured like they were that night we kissed. "Can I talk to you?" he asked.

I nodded, stepping through the doorway. "Where's Maya?"

"I had Hayes take her for the day." He took off his glasses, rubbing the bridge of his nose, then stood up.

The invisible weight of the world clearly rested on his shoulders.

My stomach sank. "Please don't fire me. I promise I will never text you about toilet paper or lumberjacks again. And I certainly won't be singing Disney songs to you..."

His lips lifted in a sad smile, and he shook his head. "I could never let you go."

The words did strange things to my heart as I looked up at him and saw how much he meant it.

"I wanted to tell you the truth about our kiss." He rubbed his hand against his chest like he had a physical pain.

I braced myself for him to tell me it was a mistake after all, that it would never happen again. That I needed to move out of the house and find a place to live in town so we couldn't tempt each other anymore. Instead, he whispered, "I didn't want it to end."

My lips parted in shock. "What?"

He stepped around the desk, reached out, running his thumb over my chin. "I've been wrapped up in you since we were kids. But we're not kids anymore."

He removed his hand, making my entire body go cold. "What do you mean?" I asked, my voice barely rising above a whisper.

"I mean..." He tilted his head, taking me in. "I would like nothing more than to date you, see where this could go. But it's not just us in this relationship. I have a child who needs you, and you have a brother who needs me."

"And you think dating me would tear that apart?"

"It could," he said. "But I'm willing to believe in us, if you are."

I lifted my chin, because even if he'd been steered by worry, I was guided by what I knew in my heart. "They aren't worth risking."

He nodded, looking more dejected than I'd ever seen him.

"But," I continued, making him look up, "it's not a risk when it comes to you and me."

He pinned me with a questioning stare. "What do you think happens if we break up? Rhett forgives me for breaking his little sister's heart? You live in my house and stick around for Maya when seeing each other tears us apart?"

I stepped closer to him, taking his face in my hands. He needed to see me. To *hear* me. "It's not a risk because I know our hearts. You would never turn your back on Rhett, and he might be hotheaded, but he would never write you off completely, because whatever breaks us apart, if anything does, will not be unforgivable."

"How do you know that?" he asked. "Because I've crossed so many lines in my life."

"I know because I *know you.* Remember? I've seen you every morning when you hug Maya like it's the most important part of your day. I see you come home from work and jump out of your truck instead of sitting out there and stalling to come inside. I've seen you call your ex, no matter how much it hurts, to make sure Maya stays connected to her mom. You've told me every dark bit of yourself, and I still care for you, Fletch. No matter what happens, I still love you."

He leaned into my touch, closing his eyes. "But Maya..."

"I love that girl," I said. "And if you think so little of

me that I'd let a breakup take me away from her, then you never really knew me at all."

"You really want to do this?" he rasped, tortured eyes on mine. "Because if we start, I don't think I can hold myself back again. These last few days have been hell."

I reached up, running my thumb along his bottom lip, and then I kissed him instead of saying what I really thought. *If we start this, I hope we'll never have to stop.*

He wrapped his arms around my waist, pulling me close and kissing me with that same hunger from before at the barn. Except this time, we both knew what we were getting into. We knew the terms, the people we'd affect with our relationship, and we trusted ourselves to handle it, together.

Still kissing me, he backed me up to his desk, and when I butted up against it, he lifted my leg, pulling it around his hip.

Heat pooled in my center as I felt his growing erection pressed against me.

He tugged my hair, making my head fall back as he trailed kisses along my jaw, his short stubble scratching deliciously along my skin. His voice hummed against my throat as he said, "You are so fucking beautiful."

My heart warmed at his words, at finally hearing what I'd always wanted him to think. I held on to him as he continued his assault of kisses to my collarbone, shoving aside the straps of my tank. His hand slid down my waist to my slit, giving me pressure in just the right spot.

"Fletcher," I breathed, reaching for his shirt and undoing the buttons one by one until his chest was fully exposed and I could run my hands over the ridges of his muscled torso.

My fingers played along the edges of his waistband, and he ordered in my ear, "Don't make me wait."

Emboldened by his words, I unbuttoned his jeans and slid my hand into his underwear, taking his thick cock in my hand. He let out a guttural moan as I pumped. "Fletch..." I never expected him to be this big, this ready.

He met my eyes, holding my gaze and took off his shirt, leaving his chest bare to me.

This was really happening.

I stepped back. "Do you want to get the light?" I whispered, suddenly shy. He had the perfect physique, and I was far from a Victoria's Secret angel.

"Not a chance in hell. I've waited twelve years to be with you; I'm not missing a second of your beautiful body."

My cheeks warmed with his words, but I couldn't help feeling shy. "I'm..." Nervous, I couldn't say out loud. Hooking up with a guy was one thing. Making love to Fletcher...

He was my high school crush, the guy I idolized as a teen, the person I thought of over the years, far more often than I cared to admit. And now, he was the man I loved, the one I could see a future with. What if I didn't live up to his expectations?

Understanding crossed his features, and he closed the distance between us to take my face in his hands. "You, Olivia Griffen, are going to see exactly what you do to me."

He kissed me, hard, and ground his erection against me. His fingers teased the bottom of my tank top as he said, "These are the rules. Every time I remove a piece of your clothing, I'm going to tell you what I see."

I nodded, anxious butterflies filling my stomach.

"And you're going to repeat after me." His tone left no room for negotiations. "Got it?"

"Okay." My voice was breathy.

He gripped the hem of my shirt, lifting it up, and took me in, a slight smile on his lips. "I can't wait to have a handful of those breasts in my hands, your nipples on my tongue."

I whispered an echo of his words, but he stepped back, making me cold.

"Say it," he demanded.

I felt more naked than ever as I said, "You can't wait to have my breasts in your hands. My nipples on your tongue." I shuddered at the words. At the heat they brought to me.

"Good girl," he breathed. Then he pulled me back toward him, removing my jeans.

"These thighs are going to feel so fucking good wrapped around my waist."

My breath hitched. "My thighs are going to feel so fucking good wrapped around your waist." I clenched at the words.

"That's my girl," he said, coming closer and pressing two fingers to my clit, sliding them in a slow, tantalizing circle over my panties. He hooked his fingers over the lace, dragging them down. "I'm going to eat your pussy like it's my last fucking meal."

My breath hitched.

"Say it."

"You're going to eat my pussy like it's your last fucking meal."

He raised his chin in approval. "Lift your arms," he ordered.

I did as he asked, and he pulled the lacy bralette over my head. My dark brown curls came cascading back down, tickling my bare shoulders as he stared at me, brown eyes full of heat.

"You're the most beautiful woman I've ever seen," he breathed, nothing but truth in his voice.

"Fletcher..." I whispered. I knew what Regina looked like... imagined the other women he must have been with before me.

"Repeat it," he ordered.

Something caught the words in my throat.

"Now," he said, a gentle force to his voice.

Completely bare to him, this man looking like a muscled god with his jeans unbuttoned and his shirt rumpled on the floor. Me, with all my curves and stretch marks and cellulite. I lifted my chin and said, "I'm the most beautiful woman you've ever seen."

"You are," he breathed, coming closer, sliding his jeans over his hips.

And my lips parted because I realized, just like I'd dreamed, it was him and me, bare to each other. All his secrets on display, all my curves not just seen, but desired. And we wanted each other anyway. Not in spite of our flaws. Not because of them. But in honor of them.

He reached into his wallet and retrieved a condom, rolling it on, and then he stepped closer.

Anticipation had my heart hitching, my breath catching, but he closed the gap between us, our bodies pressed together, skin to skin. He lifted my hips, putting me on the desk where he wanted me, and I wrapped my legs around him like promised.

He filled and stretched me so hard I was gasping into his kiss.

But he held me tight, easing in and savoring this moment, knowing it could never be undone.

"You feel so good," he said, rolling his hips again.

I moaned against his kiss, using my legs to pull him closer. All I could say was his name.

He pumped a steady rhythm into me, the friction delicious, but his words were even better. He cradled my face as I held on to his shoulders, and he said, "Olivia Griffen, you are everything good about this world. Your body, a soft place to land." He tucked my hair behind my ear. "Your eyes, that see the good in everyone. Your heart, that loves harder than I thought was humanly possible." He picked up speed, all my insides turning to mush around him, his words. "You're perfect." He grabbed my hips, pushing into me. "You're mine."

Tears flowed down my cheeks as I came around him, my heart soaring, my body shuddering, all of me... falling.

40

FLETCHER

I lay in Liv's bed with her, cradling her against my body and brushing my thumb over her cheek as I stared in her eyes. She was beautiful in the dim lighting, her eyes deep blue pools catching the little light in the room.

She lifted her arm to brush her hair behind her ear, and I noticed something I hadn't seen before. I tapped on the black ink contrasting her pale bicep. "What is that?"

She glanced at it, a soft smile forming on her lips. "My brothers and I got matching tattoos about fifteen years ago now... I was seventeen, and they used all their extra cash to bribe the artist into doing mine too."

I chuckled. "Rhett got Tyler on board for that?" Liv's second oldest brother usually played by the rules, taking fewer risks than her oldest brother Gage and definitely less than Rhett.

"He can be convincing when he wants to be." She bit her lip. "That was a tough time for Gage. He and Dad had just fallen out, and I think he felt like he was losing everything. I convinced them to get this tattoo as a reminder."

"Of what?" I asked.

She leaned forward, kissing right above my heart. "Of home."

"So the windmill?"

"It's a symbol... of life, the water it gives. Of keeping your eyes where it matters. Because you can always spot it, like a country lighthouse. And mostly, of how it's constantly moving, but no matter how much it moves, it's always there. Rain or shine, sun or snow. Just like us Griffen kids are always there for each other."

Her words made my chest fill with warmth, emotion. She spoke so beautifully about her family. That was one thing I knew for sure—we had so many similar values we could build a life around. "Your brothers are so lucky to have you."

"We're lucky to have each other," she replied earnestly.

I bit my lip, looking at her. Because I knew I was seeing the rest of my life. "I think we need to tell Maya and Rhett."

"Is it too soon?" she asked.

I shook my head. "Liv, I'm in. I'm *all* in. If you want to wait, I'll respect that, but I don't want to hide how happy I am from anyone."

She smiled, her eyes somehow even brighter. "Me neither. We can tell Maya. But I don't think she should know we're sleeping in the same bed right away."

I raised my eyebrows. "It's not like she's lying between us or anything."

"No, but she still loves her mom so much. I don't want her to feel like I'm trying to take Regina's place."

My stomach dropped, because Liv was right. She was always right. Maybe I'd have a turn sometime. "Okay, we'll tell her that we're dating. But once she's asleep... we're fucking."

Liv squirmed beside me. "Damn, do you have to be so hot?"

I grinned at her. "You think I'm hot?"

"Don't be coy. Whatever magic you worked earlier gave me the best orgasm of my life, so shhh."

"The best of your life, huh?" I couldn't help my grin. "I guess those anatomy classes paid off."

She put her hand over my face. "Shhh."

I chuckled, pulling her closer. "And what about Rhett?" I asked. "Do you think he can handle this?" He was my best friend. And I didn't want to push him away when he needed me most.

"We'll tell him together," Liv said. "Sometimes he forgets I'm not just his little sister. I'm a grown woman, and I can make my own decisions. He'll come around."

I leaned my cheek against her head and hoped like hell she was right.

"What do you think your mom would say if she knew we were together?" Liv asked.

I couldn't help but smile. "I think she'd say it's about damn time."

♡

WHEN HAYES BROUGHT MAYA HOME, Liv was making dinner and my chest felt tight with nerves. This was the second woman I'd dated since the divorce, and Maya hadn't handled news of the last one very well.

I tried to keep things positive leading up to the news, asking about her time with Hayes while Liv plated the dinner she made.

Maya said, "Uncle Hayes showed me how fast the four-wheelers go at Grampy's farm."

I groaned at the same time Liv chuckled.

"Typical Uncle Hayes," she said with a smile.

Maya added, "He told me people race four-wheelers. Can I do that?"

"When I'm dead," I grunted.

Liv thought that was funny too, but Maya pouted.

"But, Daddy—"

"Too many kids get hurt that way. I hope your uncle was safe with you today," I said, but I already knew he was. Hayes might be a risk-taker, but he loved my daughter like his own. He'd never get her in a position to be seriously injured. And I remembered being a little kid. Picking up just a bit of speed felt like flying.

Maya dug her fork into the spaghetti. "Grampy said he could make me a four-wheeler carrier for Graham."

Liv leaned forward on the counter. "You have the coolest grandpa and uncles."

She nodded happily, focusing on her food.

Liv and I exchanged a glance, and she nodded.

"Maya, I need to talk to you about something," I said, sliding into the chair next to hers at the counter.

"What is it?" she asked, looking up at me. She had a Parmesan crumb on her cheek, and I reached out to wipe it away.

"I asked Livvy to go on a date with me, and she said yes," I told her.

Maya's mouth fell open, and her eyes pinballed between Liv and me. "Really?" she asked.

I nodded with a smile.

She looked at Liv. "Really?"

Liv smiled and nodded. "I hope that's okay with you."

Maya jumped up, running and wrapping her arms around Liv. "Yay! Will you wear that dress again?"

"Which dress?" Liv asked, drawing her eyebrows together. "The disco ball one?"

"No, the purple one?"

Liv thought it over for a moment than laughed, squeezing Maya just a little tighter. "I don't have my prom dress anymore, but maybe you can help me pick one out for our first date... on Friday?" She looked to me for confirmation.

I nodded with a smile. "Friday at seven."

I couldn't wait for our date... and all the things I wanted to do to her after. But there was still a pit of worry deep in my gut.

We still had to tell Rhett.

On Sunday morning, Maya and I got ready for a trip to the city. I'd promised to get her a back-to-school outfit, and there weren't a lot of options for cute little girl clothes around here. I wanted her to feel extra special on her first day at a new school.

We were just about out the door when Rhett called. My stomach instantly filled with that guilty feeling because Fletcher and I hadn't told him about our relationship yet. Even though there was no way for him to know, it still felt like getting caught with my hand in the cookie jar or being pulled over when I knew I'd done nothing wrong.

"What's up?" I asked, opening the back door for Maya so she could climb in.

"Hey, I was hoping you could do me a favor?"

Only because you'll be doing me *a big favor by not blowing up about Fletcher and me...* "What is it?"

"We have a sick cow, and the vet ordered medicine for it, but the clinic in Rutlage is closed, and I don't have time to drive to Dallas today. I'm not sure what you have planned, but—"

"—you were wondering if I could go pick it up?"

"Only because Mom said she can't because she's getting ready for school to start, and Dad's working with the cattle, and Tyler and Henrietta are busy, and Gage is watching Levi's baseball game, and I'm *begging*. Pretty please with extra cherries on top"

Maya buckled up, and I grinned at her. "How do you feel about running an extra errand for Uncle Rhett today?"

"Can we get ice cream?" she asked loud enough for him to hear. The little negotiator.

In my ear, Rhett said, "I'll buy her a whole truck load if you go!"

Chuckling, I said, "I'll hold you to that. Just text me the address and we'll get it."

We hung up, and I went around to the driver's side.

"Can we go to Sugar Rush?" Maya asked from the back seat. "My mom always used to take me there."

I glanced over my shoulder at her, my heart melting. "Are you sure you don't want that to be you and your mom's special place? We can try another spot if you want." I just realized I might already be overstepping with the clothes shopping. Even though Regina hadn't offered, it did feel like something a mom and daughter would do.

Maya looked down at her hands in her lap, orange fingernail polish shining against her tanned skin. "If you and my dad get married, you'll be my mom."

Oh my heart. I took a deep breath and looked at her. "Honey, your daddy and I are just beginning to date. It will be a long time before we get married, if that's what we decide. But even if we do, I'll never take your mama's place. Okay? She'll always be your mom."

"I wish you were my mom," she muttered.

And that statement hit me in the gut, because even though I was here with Maya every day, even though I knew she liked her pancakes with two squares of butter and a dash of powdered sugar or that she put one sock and one shoe on before moving to the other foot like a complete weirdo, I would always be the nanny. The stepmom. "I love you, Maya."

Maya nodded sadly. "I love you too."

I tilted my head. "I know this is hard."

Another nod. A quiet sniff. "Can we have a jam sesh on the way?"

I smiled. "That, I can do. Queen Shania, our hero, we're ready for you!"

I cranked the radio to my Shania Twain playlist, and we sang along as we drove. When Maya was tired of singing, she got out the art supplies she brought along to make her birthday invitations for the tubing party coming in a few weeks. And soon enough, we were at my favorite boutique, Dress Your Heart.

They had cute clothes with a little western flare, and I could just imagine how cute Maya would look in a pair of flair-cut jeans with a Holstein print and some turquoise jewelry.

A sweet woman with big blond hair greeted us as we walked in. "Hey, you two! Looking for anything special today?"

Maya nodded, and I said, "We need an extra cute first-day-of-school outfit for her!"

"How fun. Our little girls' section is over there. Let me know if you need anything!"

Maya smiled and I thanked her before we walked over to the racks of clothing. There were all sorts of styles, and before I knew it, Maya had picked so many outfits to try on I could barely hold up all the hangers.

"Let's take these to the fitting room before we look for more?" I suggested.

She nodded, and we walked toward the dressing room, but she froze in her tracks, almost making me bump into her.

"Those boots are totally cute!" she said, looking at a pair displayed on the wall. They *were* cute, light tan with pointed toes and pink cutouts up the sides. I picked one up, glancing at the tag.

"They're a little pricey. Maybe we can save up for them?" I suggested.

She looked disappointed but nodded anyway and continued to the dressing room. I got her set up, pants on one hook and shirts on another and then stepped out while she started changing. As soon as the door was shut, I hurried to the saleswoman at the front desk of the small shop and said, "Can I order those and have them shipped?"

She grinned. "Girlfriend has great style."

"I totally agree."

The woman got out a card and said, "Fill this out with your address, and I'll ring it all up when you check out."

"Perfect," I said. I set the card on the glass counter and began filling it out, but then a hint of silver caught my eye.

There was a stunning heart locket and, next to it, a bigger, matching bracelet. Instead of hearts or a cutesy design, it had metal ridges running across it in a simple pattern. "What is this?" I asked her.

"Oh, that." She smiled at the pieces. "It's a daddy-daughter set. I thought it was adorable, just got it last week at an auction."

My heart completely melted. "I'll order those too."

"Perfect." She grinned.

"Livvy?" Maya called. I turned to see her stepping out of the dressing room in a denim skirt and a graphic black T-shirt.

"Oh my gosh, is that Taylor Swift I see?" I gushed, going up to her. "Give me a spin!"

Grinning, she did a turn with her socked heel kicked up, the flared denim swinging around her. "I like it!"

"Me too... Is this the one or do you want to have a whole fashion show?"

She got a cheeky smile and said, "Fashion show!"

A COUPLE HOURS LATER—AND my wallet signifi-cantly lighter—we went to the veterinary pharmacy in Fort Worth, getting medicine in a Styrofoam cooler.

"We need to get this back to Rhett, but first..."

Maya smiled. "Ice cream! Can we please go to Sugar Rush? *Please?*"

A worried feeling hit my gut, but I couldn't say no to her when she just wanted to feel close to her mom again.

"Okay, we'll go."

I followed the map directions until we were in a

fancier part of town with high-end stores in the same shopping center. I felt a little out of place in my cutoff jeans and dollar-store flip-flops with my hair thrown up in a messy bun, but Maya was so excited, so I smiled like I was the most confident woman in the world. After all, clothes didn't make the woman—her heart did.

As we walked on the sidewalk, Maya hung on my arm, practically bouncing up and down and telling me about her favorite mint chocolate chip ice cream with gummy bears mixed in. It sounded disgusting, to be honest, but her enthusiasm made me smile.

"If you're bouncing now, you'll take off with some sugar," I teased.

She hopped forward to the front door and yanked it open, making the bell chime inside.

But once we got through the door, I almost ran into her, because she stood frozen.

"Mommy?"

My stomach dropped as I scanned the store and found the woman I recognized only from her pictures. Regina sat toward the corner of the shop with a little girl not much younger than Maya.

"MOMMY!" Maya yelled, running to Regina.

"Maya, wait," I whispered, but she didn't hear me, already running to her mom.

Regina seemed confused at first, but then registered it was her daughter and stood up, wrapping her arms around Maya. "Honey, what are you doing here?"

Maya gestured at me. "Livvy and I came to get ice cream like you and me always did."

That's when Regina's eyes landed on me, and I hated it, but in that moment, I felt small. Regina wore designer clothes, jeans that were ripped in a factory instead of from wear, high-heeled shoes that probably cost more than my first car. Her honey-colored hair fell in perfectly done waves, and expensive sunglasses rested atop her head. Not to mention, she was wearing makeup while my face was bare.

"You're Maya's nanny, right?" she asked.

I nodded, extending my hand and forcing a smile. "Hi, I'm Liv. Maya's said such sweet things about you. She adores you."

Regina smiled, and the little girl with her tugged at her hand. "Oh, this is my boyfriend's daughter, Phoebe. Phoebe, this is my little girl, Maya."

My heart ached as Maya looked between Phoebe and Regina.

"Hi," Maya said shyly, looking like she wanted to disappear in the speckled marble floor.

My little girl was not one to fade away. Where was the wild child belting Shania Twain just a few hours ago?

"Do you want to sit with us?" Regina asked.

Maya nodded, and I said, "That would be great. Maya, let's go order some of that delicious ice cream you were talking about earlier."

She stayed quiet beside me as I walked to the register, but she wasn't bouncing anymore. It was like she'd been deflated. I tried to cheer her up by offering a double scoop of ice cream, but her lips barely moved. I ordered myself a scoop of cappuccino ice cream, but with the leaden feeling in my stomach, I doubted I'd be able to eat it.

We walked back to the table, Maya and me sitting across from Regina and Phoebe. And I thought what I couldn't say earlier. *I wish I was your mom too.* Because this was breaking my heart.

Regina asked Maya, "How's your ice cream?"

"Good."

Regina and I exchanged a glance.

"Fletcher says you're doing a great job with our girl," she said.

I wanted to puke, because I knew Regina called once, maybe twice, a month. But I tried to remember the story Fletcher told me about her and feel compassion. If not for Regina, then for the girl beside me. "I've had the best time hanging out with Maya. She's doing so great in her swim lessons! She even dove off the diving board Friday!"

Maya smiled slightly.

"Wow," Regina said, "is that true?"

Maya nodded shyly.

"Good job, Maya."

Silence fell on the table. I had to wonder what little Phoebe thought of it all, caught in the middle of a weird situation.

Maya perked up. "I have your invitation to my birthday party in the truck. Can I go get it, Livvy?"

"Sure," I said. I got my keys from my purse and turned to aim the fob at the window. "It's unlocked."

As Maya ran out, Regina said, "Phoebe, why don't you go use the bathroom?"

Phoebe set down her spoon and slid out of the chair, doing as she was asked, then it was just Regina and me.

Regina rushed out, "I'm sure Fletcher's told you a lot about me, but—"

I shook my head, not wanting to dive into the drama between her and Fletcher. "Maya loves you. She misses you like crazy. And seeing you with this little girl was a slap in her face. If you care about your daughter at all, you'll start showing up for her, no matter how much it hurts, because she deserves that from her mom, do you understand? That means calling her to tell her goodnight. It means sending her notes in the mail. And it means when she comes here with that invitation, you tell her it's the most beautiful thing you've ever seen and that you wouldn't miss her party for the world, or I *promise*, I'll make you regret it."

Regina's eyes were wide, but she didn't have time to answer before Maya came running back to the booth with her carefully decorated card made of construction paper and covered in her favorite bubble stickers. She'd worked so much harder on that invitation than the others.

Maya slid it across the table to her mom, watching with eager but nervous eyes.

Regina's jaw shook as she looked at it, ran her manicured fingers over a sticker. She swallowed. "It's the most beautiful thing I've ever seen." She looked up at Maya, their eyes a perfect match. "I wouldn't miss your party for the world."

Maya jumped up happily and wrapped her arms around her mom's shoulders.

Regina closed her eyes as she held on to her daughter.

And I hoped, with all my heart, she would start being Maya's mom. The one Maya deserved.

RHETT

Liv's white truck bounced over the dirt road toward the shop where I was welding a fence panel while I waited for her to bring the medicine. I set down my electrode holder and tossed my helmet and gloves into the bucket where we kept them. As I walked to the garage door opening of the shop, I wiped the sweat from my forehead, thankful for the breeze, even if it was just hot August air.

They pulled up, and Maya got out first, running to me with a Styrofoam cooler while Liv walked behind, her flip-flops slapping the cement.

"Here you go, Uncle Rhett!" Maya said, handing it to me.

"Thanks, sweet pea," I said, taking it from her. "You're a lifesaver!"

"Livvy says you better pay up for the ice cream," Maya told me, a cheeky smile on her face.

I laughed. "Did she say that?"

Liv stopped beside us and folded her arms across her

chest. "Gas isn't cheap either. Even if we were already in Dallas anyway."

I dropped my jaw. "You really let me go on begging so long when you were already going to the city?"

Liv smirked. "It was a little fun."

I shook my head at her and got out my wallet, pulling out a couple bills and handing them to Liv. "Thank you. I really appreciate it. Both the other guys have the weekend off, and with it just being me here, I really couldn't leave."

"No worries," she said, but she seemed distracted.

"Everything okay?" I asked.

"Totally!" Maya answered. "It's been the best day ever! First, I found out Daddy and Livvy are going on a date! Then I got new clothes for school tomorrow. And then I saw Mommy at the ice cream shop and she said she'd be at my birthday party!"

My mind got stuck on the first sentence. "Daddy and Livvy are what?"

"They're going to fall in *love!*" Maya spun in a circle, casting a spinning shadow on the sun-soaked cement. "Liv and I are going to pick out a dress for her to wear this week! AND!" She reached into her back pocket, taking out a folded-up piece of blue construction paper. "This is your invitation to my birthday party. I like makeup, cowgirl boots, and Squishmallows for gifts."

With my mind still spinning, I said, "Is that so?"

Liv was staring at me like a fish flopped ashore, no idea how to get air, much less speak.

"Maya, you know there's a new horse in that pen over there. Why don't you go say hi? I haven't even named it yet. Maybe you can come up with something good."

"I'd love to!" She sprinted away, leaving my sister and

me alone, but all I could do was grind my jaw. "Are you fucking kidding me?"

"Don't talk to me like that," Liv snapped. "I'm a grown woman. I can make my own choices without big brother weighing in."

"A grown woman who can't think straight," I gritted out.

She put her hands on her hips. "What the hell's that supposed to mean?"

"I mean, you're already living with the guy and now you're going to make it complicated by sleeping with him?" I waved my hands around as I spoke because, really, couldn't she see it wasn't smart to live with your new boyfriend, let alone Fletcher? "It's going to blow up in your face."

Liv aimed a glare at me that could have sent weaker men to ashes. "*You're* really going to judge *me* for sleeping with someone?"

"It's not that."

"Then what is it?"

I put the side of my hand in my palm. "You deserve *better.*"

She narrowed her eyebrows and stuck her chin forward. "Better than your *best* friend?"

"Fletch is a great friend, but he has a daughter, baggage. He's done some pretty fucked up shit in the past."

"I know all of this," Liv said angrily. "And I happen to love his daughter. I don't see how she is baggage."

Frustration rose in my chest. My sister had a heart of fucking gold. She'd do anything for anyone, give them the shirt off her back. She was smart, strong, and determined as hell. She deserved a relationship out of a fairy tale. And if I was being honest, I didn't see that happening with Fletcher.

"Of course you love Maya," I said. "She's an amazing kid, but that's the thing about dating Fletcher. Even if he's changed and grown a lot since he did all that shit in the past, he has a daughter he needs to put before you. Maya comes first for him, always. You need a man who'll put *you* first, Liv, damn it. Don't you see that? You can't have waited this long just to settle!"

Liv's eyes were already shining, something she did when angry. "How could you say that about Maya? Being her stepmom wouldn't be 'settling,' Rhett. If I'm so great, isn't that what she deserves too? Someone who will love her and stick around? And Fletcher puts everyone first before himself! Including you. You know he didn't want to date me because he's afraid of upsetting you while you're going through this diagnosis?"

I opened my mouth to argue, but she cut me off. "Fletcher is an *amazing* man, and I'd be lucky to have him. I've liked him since I was sixteen years old. You pushed Fletcher away from me then, and I let it slide because you were an eighteen-year-old dumbass. But you're doing the same thing now. It's got to stop. You're my big brother, and I love you, but if you can't handle this choice I've made for *my* life, maybe you'll just need to stay away so you don't have to see it."

Tears fell down her cheeks as she turned, walking back to her truck. "Maya!" she yelled. "Come over here. We're leaving."

"Liv, wait," I said, following her.

"No!" she yelled. "You want me to have this 'perfect'

life because you drove the woman you loved away all those years ago, and now you have cancer and you think it's over for you. But it's not over. Not for Fletcher, not for you, and definitely not for me. My life is far from perfect, but I know what I want. I probably won't be able to have kids, Rhett. And being Maya's stepmom isn't a step down. It's an amazing opportunity to be part of her life. This might not look like a fucking fairy tale to you, but it's life, and it's a pretty damn good one...flaws, mistakes, children, divorces, and all."

Maya's footsteps got louder, and we watched as she closed the last dozen yards between us. When she got close, she told me, "I think you should name it Flivvy, like Fletcher and Livvy since you love Daddy and Livvy so much."

My throat got tight, and my voice was rough as I said, "Thanks, kiddo."

"Come on, sweetie," Liv sniffed. "Time to go."

All I wanted to do after that fight with Rhett was curl up on the couch with Graham and watch movies, but Maya wanted to drop off her birthday invitations. With only a few weeks left to her birthday and school starting tomorrow, we didn't exactly have time.

Fletcher said he had work to catch up on at the clinic anyway, so this would be a good way to use the afternoon.

First, we drove out to the Madigan farm to find Grampy. I knew him as Gray Madigan, short for Grayson. A good-looking older man with an impressive work ethic, a great friend to my dad, and the kind of guy who let his kids get up to trouble with a wink and a gravelly "be safe."

Their house was a similar style to my parents, two stories with a big front porch, but theirs was white with a red tin roof to match the barn. Fletcher's mom had been so proud of her home, and Grayson still kept flowers growing in the boxes under the windowsills.

As we drove down the gravel path, Maya rolled the

back window down and stuck her hand out, catching the wind. It felt like the last glimpse of summer.

I scanned the lot in front of the house, not seeing his truck, but then I spotted it by a big line of round haybales near the barn. "There he is."

Maya followed my pointing finger and said, "Let's go!"

We bounced over the trail formed by years of trucks driving over the pasture, green grass passing below us and blue skies bright above us. As we got closer, his truck started driving our way. The driver's side window rolled down, his tanned arm resting on the door. "If it ain't my two favorite girls!"

Maya was already on my side of the truck, her window rolled down too. "Grampy! We have something for you!"

"What's that?" he asked.

She held the folded invitation across the gap between our vehicles. "For my birthday party."

He read the invitation and scratched his chin. "Sounds like a good time, sweetie. I'll be there."

Maya smiled so big, it made my heart melt.

"Can I bring anything?" he asked.

"Do you have a few extra innertubes we could have in case someone doesn't have one?" I replied.

"Sure thing... and wait a second..." He reached into his glove compartment and pulled out a sucker from the stash he'd kept there ever since we were kids. We could always count on him to have a sweet for us. "Here you go." He passed it to Maya.

"Thank you!" she said, taking it.

Grayson's smile deepened the creases around his eyes.

"You're welcome." Then he handed me one. "We sure appreciate you and all you've done, Olivia. You're a fine young woman."

My heart melted at his sweet words. "Gray."

"I mean it." He pointed at me. "Now I gotta check the windmill on the east section. Stick around too long, and I'll put you both to work."

"GO, GO!" Maya said with a giggle.

I laughed, peeling my truck away and waving out the window to Gray.

For the rest of the day, we made all the stops around town, from her uncle Hayes at the body shop to Della at the insurance agency, and all her friends' houses too. It was so fun to see how excited Maya was to invite them, but I was completely wiped out as we started home.

I just hoped Fletcher would be okay with all the news I had to share about my run-ins with Regina and Rhett.

FLETCHER

I went to the clinic Sunday morning while the girls were in Dallas, and I spent the day barely getting up from my desk as I went over the information regarding ownership of the practice. I'd need to meet with my accountant, but from what I could tell, it was a good investment.

And now that I knew Liv and I were solid, I felt like I could really take this on. I couldn't wait to tell her about this new step in my life. Our life. And I realized, that's what love felt like—wanting to share life with someone. I'd finally found that person in Liv.

My cell phone rang, and I checked it to see Regina's name. An uncomfortable feeling swirled in my gut as I walked to my office door and closed it out of habit. She never called.

"Hello?" I said, holding it to my ear.

"I met the nanny today," she replied.

My eyebrows drew together. "What?"

"She was in Dallas with Maya."

"How did they run into you?" I asked. I hoped Liv

hadn't planned a meetup with Regina without even consulting me... That would be a big overstep. "Did they go to your house?"

"Nothing like that. They were at Sugar Rush."

My chest ached. That was Regina and Maya's place. One of the few things they had that was special to both of them. "Regina..."

"I like her," Regina said. "Just tell her she doesn't need to threaten me again."

My eyebrows rose. That didn't sound like Liv at all. "Threaten you? What the hell?"

There was a resigned smile in Regina's voice. "She said I needed to start showing up for Maya more. Or she'd make me regret it."

My heart turned liquid. Liv had stood up for my daughter to the most important woman in Maya's life. Not to separate them further, but to repair what had become so broken.

"The thing is, I already regret the way I've behaved," Regina said. "Seeing Maya today... for the first time, I didn't see you. I saw our daughter." Her voice broke, and she took in a shaky breath. "I miss her."

"She's misses you too," I said.

Banging sounded on the front door, along with muffled shouts. Adrenaline started pumping through my veins. "Regina, I'm sorry, but I have to go."

It was never a good sign for someone to be banging here. My mind covered every possibility from drug addict to a medical emergency. But when I made it to the front door, I saw Rhett yelling at me through the glass.

"I need to talk to you," he bellowed.

I opened the door, stepping aside so he could come in,

then shut and locked it behind him. "What the hell is going on?" I asked Rhett as he paced a hole in the waiting room floor.

"When were you going to tell me about you and Liv?" he demanded, still marching back and forth.

My breath caught. "Will you stand still for a second? You're making me nervous," I said.

He beat his chest. "*I'm* making *you* nervous? I'm the one waiting on a cancer diagnosis while you're fooling around with my little sister!"

His words nearly took the air from my chest. "Liv and I wanted to talk to you together, but regarding your diagnosis, we'll have information soon. We can't make any big decisions until then."

Now he seemed taken aback. "As far as I'm concerned, this is the only time to make big decisions. Don't you want the clarity you get when you know you might have limited time?"

I shook my head. "I got that when my mom died. I'd do anything not to have known what was coming to me. To enjoy a day where she was just my mom and not a dying woman."

He gave me a smile that had no joy. "Are you using cancer to keep me from kicking your ass?"

"Is it working?"

"No, I'm pissed."

"Why?" I asked. "I know you have your reasons for thinking Liv can do better, but you know as well as I do that love doesn't always follow logic."

He let out a sigh then stopped on his path and looked at me. "You have to see it my way."

"What's your way, Rhett? Because honestly, I'm

starting to feel hurt. I know we don't talk about our feelings much, but you're my best friend. After everything we've been through, all the ways you've seen me change in the last eight years, do you really think I wouldn't do everything I could to keep your sister happy?"

"It's not that." He sat in the chair, not meeting my eyes.

"What is it?" I asked, sitting across from him and resting my elbows on my knees.

"It's Maya."

"Liv's great for Maya," I said, flattered that he worried so much about my daughter to care for her happiness. "And Liv and I already agreed; if something happens between us, Maya will still take priority."

"That's the problem," Rhett said.

My eyebrows drew together. "You're calling Maya a problem."

"Maya's amazing. But Liv deserves to have someone who'd put her first." I could tell he meant it, could see the earnestness in his eyes. But he couldn't have been more wrong.

"Your parents had four kids."

"What does that have to do with anything?"

"You think they put Gage first? Tyler? Liv? You?"

Rhett frowned.

"They did a good fucking job with you, because that's what parents do. They love their kids; they give them what they need. Sometimes they fucked up, like they did with Gage, but then they made it better. You don't have just one kid because you're worried you'll love one more than the other. Your love grows and you show up because *that's what you do.* It's not Maya *or* Liv. It's Maya *and* Liv. For the rest of my life it will be *and* not *or*."

Rhett took a deep breath and stood up from the chair. "Here's the deal. You promise to treat Liv like a goddamn queen, and I'll back off. But if you ever mess up, I swear to god I'll castrate you, and you know I don't have to be a doctor to know how."

We both knew he meant it. "I promise," I said, making each word carry meaning. "Whether Liv and I are apart or together, I'll only treat her with the respect she deserves."

"Good." He was quiet for a moment, rolling his ballcap in his hands before putting it back on his head. "And I'm sorry for what I said about Maya. I really think she's a great kid."

I smiled. "I know."

He nodded, walking toward the door.

"Rhett?" I said.

"Yeah?"

"I think there's a favor you can do to make it up to Maya and me..."

"I'm all ears."

Last night, Rhett called to apologize for his initial reaction, giving me his blessing to date Fletcher. Regina called to wish Maya good luck for her first day at school.

And this morning, Fletcher, Maya, and I stood at the end of the driveway, watching the big yellow school bus blaze a path down the dirt road. Maya wore a pair of flared denim jeans, a cow print shirt, and white sneakers. I'd done her hair in a couple fishtail braids, and she even asked to wear a little lip gloss, a request I happily obliged.

But by the tense set of her shoulders and the tight way she held on to Graham's leash, I could tell she was nervous watching the bus approach. I was too. It was like a piece of my heart was going out on its own, unprotected.

I knelt beside her and looked in her eyes. "Maya, you are going to do amazing at school today. You have a big heart, a bright mind, and a creative soul. If people can't see and appreciate that, it's a them problem, not a you problem, okay?"

She nodded, giving me a hug.

Then her dad picked her up, backpack and all, hugging her tight. "You've got this, Maya. Find one of your friends from swim lessons and have the time of your life."

The bus slowed to a stop in front of us, its flashing stop sign swinging out to the side. The doors opened, and the driver, an older woman named Jeanie, smiled at us. "Good morning, dears."

"Morning," I said with a wave.

Fletcher gave his daughter a pat on the back and said, "Take care of my little girl."

Maya grunted. "I'm not little."

"My big girl," Fletcher corrected.

"I will," Jeanie promised with a wink.

Maya passed me Graham's leash and knelt in front of him. "I'll be home so soon you won't even know I'm gone."

He licked her cheek like he knew.

"I love you sweet boy," she said to him, scratching him behind the ears.

She stood back up and walked up the steps, looking so small with her backpack behind her, and the door swung shut. Fletcher put his arm around me as we watched her taking a seat toward the front and sitting at the window. As the bus drove down the dirt road, she waved goodbye.

Graham whined and pranced beside me, and I picked him up. My eyes watered, watching the bus disappear in the distance, and I tried not to let Fletcher see.

"Oh my gosh, are you crying?" he asked.

"No," I said too quickly. "Shut up."

He laughed.

I hit his chest. "I'm sad! She's been my bestie for the last three months, and now I'm all alone! I feel like a puppy dog waiting for her to come home."

He took Graham, setting him down, and then gave me a hug. "Can I tell you a secret?"

I nodded, wiping at my eyes. I swore the tears just kept coming thinking of Maya being all on her own. Of being away from her all day and not knowing who she was sitting next to at lunch or when she'd get picked for teams in gym class or how her teacher would treat her.

He walked beside me toward the front door of the house. "I had to cancel all my appointments Maya's first day of preschool. I couldn't stop crying."

"Really?" I asked, stepping through the open door. The second I took off Graham's leash, he ran to Maya's room, disappearing through her doorway.

Fletcher nodded. "I was a mess every morning for a month."

I let out a groan. "You mean it's going to take a *month* for this feeling to go away?"

"It never goes away," he said, wiping my eyes with the pads of his thumbs. "But it does get more bearable."

I nodded, taking a breath.

"You know, there is one benefit to having Maya in school."

"What's that?" I asked.

He bit his lip, eyes tracking my body. "We can have sex anywhere in this house, as loud as we want."

The thought, the heat behind his words, had my thighs clenching. "But you have to go to work," I whispered.

He was already on me, dropping kisses on my jaw, my neck, his short facial hair scraping as he went. "I had Brenda schedule my first appointment late. We have time."

I let my head fall back, giving him better access. "Are we going to your bedroom? Because I don't want to waste a second."

"Fuck no. I'm taking you right here in the picture window."

My jaw dropped. "What if someone drives by?"

"Then they're getting one hell of a view," he said, reaching for my shirt and pulling it over my head.

"Naked?" I breathed.

"Like I'd have you any other way." He reached for my shorts, pulling them over my hips and leaving me bare in his living room, the sun shining through the massive front window.

Normally I'd be nervous at the risk of getting caught, but Fletcher was so into me and wanting to show me off that it was turning me on even more.

If sixteen-year-old Liv could see me now...

He walked me back to the window, practically prowling with fire in his eyes as he stripped out of his shirt in one swift movement and then took off his pants. Fletcher Madigan, broad shoulders, short hair trailing down his abs, his long, thick cock growing harder by the second... he was sheer perfection.

He backed me against the window, the sun-filled glass warm against my skin, and took one nipple in his mouth, sucking and nipping at one and then the other until moisture pooled between my legs. I reached down and took his cock in my hand.

"That's it, baby," he said roughly in his assault. "You know how to make me feel good."

Emboldened, I began pumping, using my other hand to claw at his back. Not enough to break skin, but enough to match the delicious pain he was giving me.

"Fuck, Liv," he roughed out.

I lowered myself between his legs, and he braced his hands on the window over me as I took the tip of his cock in my mouth. His full sack hung heavy, and I gripped it with my other hand, tugging in a way that made him beg for more.

"Open your mouth. Wider," he ordered.

I did as he asked, resting my head back against the window and holding my jaw open as he fucked my mouth. Made me gag. Made precum drip from his thick head and spill over my tongue. Knowing what we must look like from outside made it that much hotter. I used my free hand to touch myself, getting more turned on by the second.

He stopped his assault and reached down, pulling me up and making my skin slide against the window until we were face to face. He lowered his face, nipping my breasts, and then hooked my right knee over his elbow.

Standing sex had never worked for me with past partners, but Fletcher's long cock easily met my entrance and filled me in the hottest way.

I gasped at his size, gripping his shoulders.

"That's it, baby, hold on tight," he said, his voice hot on my ear as he rammed into me.

"Fletcher," I moaned loudly, uninhibited, completely overcome with the sensation.

"I'm jealous of the person who drives by, getting to see your ass pressed against that window."

"Fletch," I gasped out the only word crossing my mind.

"Your tits are so fucking hot bouncing against my chest."

My eyes rolled back in my head, completely overcome with the sensation.

"And the way your thighs ripple with each, fucking, trust."

I had to hold on. Tight. Because I was tipping over the edge.

"Your mouth, open it for me. Open that fucking mouth."

My lips parted, and he slid two fingers over my tongue. I sucked, rolling my tongue along the seam, and I came undone, clenching around his cock as he railed into me.

He waited until every last wave was done before coming, shuddering inside me.

When he pulled out, he kissed my shoulders, then my lips.

Resting his forehead against mine, his breath beginning to slow, he said, "It's good to spend time with Maya, but we need time for us too."

I smiled to myself. So much of the last few months had been about Maya and getting her to a good place emotionally. Fletcher was right—we deserved this time that was purely for ourselves and our pleasure.

"Come shower with me?" he said.

"I'd love too."

He linked his fingers through mine, leading me back

to his bathroom while I enjoyed the view of his naked body in motion.

"Is it weird that I want to watch you work out naked?" I asked.

He looked over his shoulder at me, grinning. "Isn't that what we just did?"

I laughed. "No! I want to see all your muscles moving without your clothes in the way."

We reached his bedroom and he gave gestured at the exercise bike near his bed. "You know, I'd do anything for you."

"Even get on the bike?" I batted my eyelashes.

He chuckled. "I'm pretty sure there's not supposed to be any loose material on the bike..." He gestured at his thick sack.

"Pretty please?"

Chuckling, he said, "Okay, but no way I'm doing burpees without underwear on."

I laughed at the thought, going to lean on his bed. I bend over, resting on my forearms.

"God that's hot," he said, walking toward the bike.

I shimmied my shoulders, making my breasts sway.

He bit his bottom lip. "Fuck me."

"Stop stalling!" I said.

He shook his head, put his hand on the handle, then his foot in one petal. He swung his feet over, and then sat his bare ass on the seat. "Are you happy now?"

I nodded, giddily, as he started pedaling. Just like I expected, all his muscles rippled and flexed. So freaking hot. But then I got up and went to get a view from the front of his chest muscles.

. . .

AND I BURST OUT LAUGHING.

"What?" he asked, looking down at himself.

"It's like a little bean bag chair." I gasped for breath through my laughter.

"I fucking hate you," he said, getting off the bike.

I covered my mouth, talking through laughs as I said, "I promise I'm trying to stop laughing."

He came to me, taking my arms and walking me back to the bed, laying me down forcefully. He had a wicked smirk as he said, "I'll fucking make you stop. And then you'll be screaming my name."

My already tender sex clenched. "Try me," I breathed.

He covered my mouth with his and followed through on every. Last. Promise.

*

I WAVED goodbye as he left to work, and soon after, the mail carrier drove by. I smirked to myself and waved as they deposited mail in the box. If only they'd come by half an hour earlier.

FLETCHER

I looked over the chart for my first patient of the day, still doing my best to stop thinking about the way Liv screamed when I made her come for the second time this morning.

Dennis Phillips
Age: 34
Complaint: Shortness of breath since this AM, no history of asthma, no history of anxiety or depression, no viral symptoms, no chest pain, no temperature, no known allergies.

I DREW MY EYEBROWS TOGETHER. That was strange.

I knocked and walked into the office to see Dennis on a chair, his elbows resting on his knees. At the sight of me, he looked up and stood, shaking my hand.

"Heard you were back in town, Fletcher. Good to see you."

I smiled back at him. He'd been a couple years ahead of me in school, played on the same football team. But now his widow's peak was more prominent, and he had slight crow's feet around his blue eyes. Sometimes seeing other people my age reminded me of my own. We were all getting older.

"I'd say it's good to see you, but it looks like you're having some trouble breathing? What's going on?"

He sat back in his chair, trying to take deep breaths, and I pulled up the rolling stool to listen.

"Well, it started this morning after..." His cheeks were slightly red, and he looked down, trying harder to catch his breath.

"After a workout?" I guessed.

He snorted. "You could say that?"

Confused, I asked, "What?"

"The kids started back at school, and the wife and I were, uh, enjoying our morning, if you know what I mean."

Now I fought to keep a straight face. "I think I follow."

"And, uh, about halfway through it was pretty... vigorous..."

Dear god, please don't laugh. "Go on."

"Well, that's the thing. I couldn't. I got to breathing too hard and couldn't catch my breath, but it didn't feel like normal exertion, you know? I figured maybe I was too tired or something, but I'm still having trouble catching my breath, and my wife wanted me to get checked out."

I nodded, still holding back laughter because we'd had the same damn idea this morning. "It was good that she did. Shortness of breath can be a sign for lots of things. Did you eat anything different today?"

He shook his head. "Eggs and toast like usual."

"Been around anyone with the flu or Covid?"

He shook his head. "Not that I know of."

"Let me have a peek in your ears and nose, just in case."

He waited patiently as I shined a light in all the places and checked the back of his throat.

"It all looks good."

"What do you think it could be?" he asked.

I shook my head, not wanting to worry him but needing to be honest. "Maybe a blood clot or even a collapsed lung. But I'll have Brenda do an EKG on you first and then a chest X-ray, and we'll know more."

"Shit... Thanks, Doc," he said.

I nodded, stepping out and letting Brenda know the next steps.

While she took care of his testing, I saw another patient, a little kid with an ear infection that would be easy enough to treat, then went back to my office to see what Brenda had for me. I looked at the reports on my desk and carefully scanned the X-ray over the light box. Then I shook my head slightly before walking back to the exam room where Dennis waited.

He stood up as I walked in and then sat back down as I did. "What's it look like?"

"Your EKG was normal, and your chest X-ray is clear. I think you have something called respiratory alkalosis. It's when you take in too much CO_2 and your blood gets alkaline. Usually happens to people with panic attacks, but I'm guessing your rapid breathing this morning brought it on."

He nodded slowly. "So it's not serious?"

I shook my head. "Get some rest today; no working out because that could make it worse. And if you're feeling better tomorrow, you can resume your regular... activities."

He smiled up at me. "And if I'm not?"

"Then come see me."

He nodded, standing up, and shook my hand.

"Oh, and Dennis?" I said.

"Yeah?"

"Must have been some pretty good sex." I smirked. "Good for you."

His cheeks flamed as he walked out the door.

I walked back to my office to do some charting, and then I saw the message come through my email. Rhett's results.

I took a deep breath and opened the email. Tears came to my eyes as I read the results. My breath shaking, I picked up the phone and dialed Rhett's number. After a few rings, he answered, wind and cows in the background.

"Rhett, I got your results back."

I heard his breath catch over the line. "What is it?"

My voice cracked. "You're all clear."

He let out a breath that almost sounded like a laugh.

"You need to get checked every six months for new spots, but they were able to remove all of it, and it didn't spread." I wiped at my face, all the happiness, relief, and worry spilling from my eyes.

"Thank God," he said.

"Come over tonight," I replied. "We're going to celebrate."

I drove to Rutlage so I could pick up plenty of food and decorations to celebrate Maya's first day of school. Fletcher texted me and said Rhett would be coming over too, so I wanted it to be extra special. This would be the first night Fletcher and I had Rhett over as a couple since he gave us his blessing.

My heart warmed at the thought as I meandered down the aisle, and then a candle caught my eye.

Safe Haven was its name, in a decorative ceramic container. I picked it up, breathing in the scent of vanilla and lavender. It smelled like home, and that gave me an idea.

I hustled through the store, getting everything I needed, and then checked out.

I had work to do.

AT THREE O'CLOCK, I had a cheese dip warming in a slow cooker, little smokies cooking in another one, and chili in the biggest crock. The house smelled amazing. But the best part was a little snack sitting on the island: cheese and crackers, a cutie orange, and a glass of water.

Graham danced around my feet like he knew it was time for Maya to come home soon. So I leashed him up and walked outside with him. We walked around the house a few times, Graham getting distracted by each grasshopper that flew in front of him or blade of grass that waved off to the side.

He'd get used to walking on a leash eventually, but today was not that day.

When we could hear the bus coming down the road, he tugged on the leash, pulling me toward the stop. We got there, and I held on tight to the squirmy dog as Maya got off the bus.

She grinned at us as she walked down the steps and ran to hug me and her dog. As the bus drove away, she took Graham's leash, and we walked inside as she told me all about her day.

She had Mr. Knotts as her main teacher, absolutely loved banging drums in music class, and wanted me to pack her a lunch tomorrow. We took her snack to the living room and sat on the couch while we talked more about her day.

"Can I call and tell Mommy?" she asked.

I nodded. "Let me call and get her number from your dad first."

"I know it by heart," she said, putting her plate on the table.

I hesitated, not wanting to cross any boundaries like

I'd done in Dallas. I wanted to respect Fletcher both as her parent and as my partner. "Let me check with him."

"Why?" she asked, a grumpy tone in her voice.

I raised my eyebrows. It had been a long time since Maya had taken that tone with me. "Excuse me?"

"Let me call my mom," she ordered. "Now."

"Why don't you take some time to cool down in the backyard. I'll call your dad while you do."

"FINE!" she yelled, stomping outside with Graham on her heels. The slamming door rattled the house.

I closed my eyes and took deep breaths, trying to remember that she was tired. That even though it had been a good day for her, she had used up a lot of her energy learning the ropes.

Once I'd calmed down a bit, I called Fletcher and filled him in. "Sorry, I didn't know what the rules were with Regina and me and calls. I know I overstepped at the ice cream shop and didn't want to do it again."

"It's fine if you call her," Fletcher said with a sigh. "But maybe keep the phone on speaker just to make sure everything's okay. I'll text you her number."

"Thanks."

"Thanks for watching Maya," he said.

"Of course," I replied. "Like you said, I'm not just the nanny... I'm here for you."

"I love you, Liv."

My heart warmed at the words. "I love you too. See you in a couple hours."

"If I make it that long," he teased.

We hung up, and I went outside, dialing Regina's number. Still a little grumpy with me, Maya sat at the picnic table, talking with her mom, and soon Rhett and

Fletcher were there with us. We all had plates full of Frito chili pie, drinks in hand, as we talked about Maya's first day at Cottonwood Falls Elementary School.

When she went to change for bed, I wanted to address the pit of worry in my stomach for Rhett. I didn't know if it was okay to talk about or not, but I needed to ask him if there was any news. "Rhett, have you heard anything more about the spot?"

He and Fletcher exchanged a glance, and Rhett's expression was unreadable.

He cleared his throat, looking down, and when he looked back up at me, his smile was brighter than I'd ever seen it. "They were able to remove all the cancer. I'm going to be okay."

I literally screamed, jumping out of my seat and hugging him tight.

When Fletcher met my gaze, I swore I saw moisture in his eyes.

Rhett cleared his throat, pulling back. "So I'll be around when you two finally tie the knot."

Fletcher laughed. "I'm not getting married again."

Rhett drew his eyebrows together and looked from Fletcher to me. "You're kidding right."

Fletcher opened his mouth, but I quickly said, "Of course he's joking, Rhett. We've barely started dating. You know you'd run to the hills if someone mentioned you marrying one of the girls you've dated for a week."

Rhett eyed us suspiciously, about to ask something, but Maya came out and said, "Livvy, can you help me pick out my clothes for tomorrow?"

"Sure, sweetie," I said. I gave Rhett one last hug and said, "See you at Wednesday night dinner?"

"Of course," he said. "I'll need someone to run inter-ference between Mom and me when I tell them I had, and then subsequently didn't have, cancer."

"True," I said. I sent Fletcher a half smile and walked inside to help Maya.

But my stomach churned because I knew the conver-sation was far from over.

48

FLETCHER

Rhett raised his eyebrows at me, but when I didn't offer an explanation, he said, "Let me help you clean up, then I'll get home."

While Liv helped Maya, we made quick work of the mess, tossing out the paper plates and putting the chili, cheese, and little smokies into Tupperware. I sent some home with Rhett and put the rest in the fridge for Liv and me to have as leftovers.

When Rhett was out of the house, I poured myself a glass of water, then walked to Maya's room to check on the girls. But when I peeked through the cracked door, I found Liv and Maya curled on the bed, Liv reading to Maya while her eyes slowly closed.

Need help? I mouthed.

Liv shook her head.

I pointed toward the bedroom, and she nodded.

I turned toward my room, running my hands through my hair, but when I flipped the switch, my legs wouldn't carry me any farther.

My room had been completely transformed. Instead of the blinds that came with the house, there were now thick, taupe drapes hanging over the windows. The simple white quilt on my bed now had a mustard-color throw draped over it and gray gingham throw pillows at the headboard.

The simple booklight beside my bed had been replaced with matching gold and glass lamps on each nightstand. A hanging plant added greenery in the corner of the room. And now a blue, gray, and yellow-flecked rug contrasted the wood floor. There was a pretty painting of a meadow hanging over my bed and framed photos of Maya on my dresser.

Liv had transformed this room in the span of a few hours.

How?

But I knew why. Because she loved me.

And suddenly, I felt guilty for how the marriage conversation had gone down earlier. I'd meant to talk about this with her instead of reacting quickly to something her brother said offhandedly.

"What do you think?" Liv said behind me.

I turned to see her coming into the room.

Overcome with gratitude, I pulled her into my arms and kissed her. "This is more than I deserve."

She shook her head. "It's the bare minimum, Fletcher. You spend so much time taking care of everyone else. Maya, me, Rhett, your patients at the clinic. You need to add yourself to the list."

I hugged her tight, letting her soft curves ease the sting in my chest. "I think I thought I didn't deserve it after everything that happened..."

She rubbed her hand in a slow circle at the small of my back. "Maybe it will become a habit to be spoiled by me."

I smiled, kissing the top of her head. "We need to talk about what Rhett brought up earlier."

She shook her head, stepping back. "It's too soon to talk about marriage, Fletcher. I understand."

My hands felt empty, cold without being able to hold her. And I'd need to get used to that if she couldn't accept where I was coming from. "The thing is, it's never going to be enough time, because I don't want to marry again."

Her lips parted, closed, parted again.

"You can say it," I said.

She gave me a sheepish smile, then sobered again. "I guess what I want to know is... why?"

I guided her to the bed, where we both sat at the foot. I drew my knee up beside me so I could face her more easily and took a deep breath. "This isn't about my feelings for you, Liv. I *know* I want to be with you. If I were interested in marriage, I'd propose right now. Yesterday."

Her eyes were full of curiosity mixed with something else I couldn't quite parse out. "Then what is it?"

My chest felt heavy. I made this decision so long ago, I didn't realize how hard it would be to discuss it out loud. "When I married Regina, I made those vows. For richer, for poorer, forever." I shook my head, looking at my lap. "Forever lasted eight years."

She tilted her head, waiting for me to continue.

"I can't make the vows I made to Regina to you. It wouldn't feel right. Especially not when you mean so much more to me than a piece of paper could ever cover."

Liv swallowed, and I waited for anger. Frustration. Confusion. Arguments. Instead, she said, "I never thought of it that way."

I reached for her hand, needing to feel her. To be close to her in some way. "I understand if it's a deal-breaker to you. But I really do love you, Liv, and I'm not going anywhere."

Her smile faltered. "I meant it when I said it was too soon to consider marriage." She put a hand on my cheek. "And I mean it when I say I love you, Fletcher."

Our lips met, and we kissed, teased, made love in this room she had transformed from four walls with a bed into a home.

49

LIV

I drove into town, wearing my leggings and a T-shirt. I had so much time during the day, and I had half a clue of what to do with myself.

I even worked out this morning. Like, put my earbuds in and walked/ran/stumbled down the dirt road.

I could do the walking part again, but running was pure torture, just like I remembered from high school gym class. I had no idea why Fletcher would run of his own volition. Surely there were less torturous ways to break a sweat.

Then I cleaned. Like, a lot. All the baseboards in the house were spotless.

At this rate, I could have a full-blown side hustle while Maya was in school with no one knowing.

But I called up Della and Henrietta and invited them to lunch. I was so excited to hang out with them in the middle of the day when we weren't all exhausted from work or had Maya's little ears to worry about.

Because I had some serious tea to spill.

I walked into Woody's Diner, full of the lunch crowd.

Miss Rhonda, the hairdresser in town, waved me over. "Liv Griffen! It has been more than four months since your last trim. When are you going to come see me?"

My cheeks got a little pink. "As soon as we get off lunch?"

"Good girl," she replied with a wink.

Her response just made me think of Fletcher, and I should not be having sexual thoughts in front of a sixty-plus-year-old woman. "See you soon, Rhonda!"

I beelined back to an open booth and sat down, trying not to make eye contact.

"Why are you looking like you're hiding?" Della said, standing in front of my booth.

I breathed out a sigh of relief. "Rhonda called me 'good girl', and my mind went to dark places."

Della cackled so loudly several heads turned our way. Ignoring them, she sat across from me, reaching for a menu from the stand. "So you're either sexually frustrated or your mind's in the gutter because something happened."

Walking up to our booth, Henrietta said, "Something happened? With Fletcher?"

As Hen took her purse off and slid in next to me, they both waited for an explanation.

But my expression must have been enough because Della clapped happily. "Oh my gosh! Something happened!"

I nodded, smiling far too wide. "We hooked up Saturday after he took me home from the bar..."

"I knew it!" Hen said. "I swear that man was ready to burn down the building for you."

Della nodded. "It was super hot. Especially when he picked you up like it was nothing. Even when you were screaming the song at him."

"I'm never going to recover from this," I said, burying my face in my hands.

Della's voice was coy as she asked, "How are you going to recover from hot sex with the doctor?"

Thankfully, no one heard, because my cheeks were flaming even more. "It was so freaking good. He did things, said things, no man has ever done or said."

"Hot," Hen said with a smile.

We paused conversation while Agatha brought us our drinks and took our orders, then got back to talking.

"He's been so sweet, asking me on a date, going all in on our relationship. There's just one thing. I don't know if it's really a problem but..." I ripped my straw wrapper in half and then in half again.

Hen's voice was full of concern as she asked, "What is it?"

"Yeah," Della said, "do we need to beat him up?"

"He doesn't want to get married again. He said he's committed to me and wants to be with only me, but a wedding is off the table."

Hen frowned, but Della seemed more curious. "I think that's normal nowadays," Della said. "Especially for someone who's been married before."

Hen said, "I don't understand though. If he wants to be with you forever, isn't that what a marriage is?"

I shook my head. "I think being divorced did a number on him. His parents were so committed to each other, and his dad's never remarried..."

Della tilted her head, drinking from her Diet Coke. "It's still really soon to be talking about marriage."

"I agree," I said. "I love him so much already and we have so much fun together, both him and me, and us with Maya. I don't want to ruin it..."

Della nodded. "As long as he's showing you that he's all in, that's what matters."

We both paused, waiting for Henrietta to chime in. But her smile seemed forced when she said, "If you're happy, I'm happy."

50

FLETCHER

By Wednesday, my accountant, lawyer, and banker had signed off on my purchase of the practice. And when I drove toward Herbert Law Office on Thursday morning, I couldn't believe what I was doing.

I was just a kid who grew up in a modest country home, with three younger brothers who always wore my hand-me-downs. Now I was a doctor with letters after my name. I had a house bigger than I'd ever dreamed of. A daughter who'd never have to worry about student loans like I did. And soon, I'd have a practice in the town that raised me and welcomed me back with open arms.

I parked and walked down the sidewalk to go inside, but waiting by the door... were my dad and my brothers. Even Bryce, who must have taken time out of college to be in town.

"What are you all doing here?" I asked them incredulously.

Dad said, "Hayes told us when the sale was going down, and we wanted to be here for you."

We Madigan men... we didn't talk much about our feelings, but ever since we lost Mom, we were always there for each other. For the time Ford signed on to his professional football team, when Knox graduated the police academy, when Hayes had a ribbon cutting ceremony for his new shop but used caution tape instead and even when Bryce made the honor roll at college.

"Thanks for coming," I said, "but I'm afraid it's going to be boring. I'm just signing a few papers."

"Don't matter," Hayes said.

Knox nodded in agreement. "This is big, Fletch."

Ford said, "You're changing this town's history." Which was crazy since he was the first professional football player to ever come from Cottonwood Falls.

And then Bryce who was probably the most distant of all of us said, "You're showing us what's possible."

I put my arm around my youngest brother. "I love you guys," I said, my voice rough with emotion.

"We love you too," Dad said. He patted my back just as Doctor Deb came down the sidewalk.

"See you brought a crowd," she said with a smirk.

Dad lifted his chin. "More like a cheering section."

She smiled. "Shall we?"

We all walked inside, and after an hour, the documents were signed.

As we walked outside, Dad said, "Can I take you to the diner to celebrate?"

"I'll have to take a rain check—I have appointments to make," I said. "I wish I knew Bryce and Ford were coming to town. I would have cleared my schedule."

Ford spun his finger through the air. "Buys a clinic and thinks he's a big deal."

I rolled my eyes at him. "Careful, or I'll be booing you when the season starts."

"Won't be able to hear you over all the cheers," he replied, giving me a quick hug.

Knox shook my hand and Hayes gave me a nod of approval before we parted ways. Bryce promised to come see me over his winter break and Dad told me he'd be at the Griffens' house for dinner tonight.

When I got to the office, Brenda pulled out a confetti popper and shot it in the air. "Congratulations, boss!"

I chuckled, bending to pick up the streamers. "Thanks, Brenda."

When I dumped the confetti in the trash can, she held up a flyer for me.

"What is this?" I asked, glancing over the paper.

"Doctor Deb's retirement party is next weekend. But now I suppose it's also a party for the new owner of the practice."

I smiled, still in disbelief. It didn't quite feel real. "Do you need any help getting this ready?" I asked.

She shook her head. "I already have the decorations ordered, catering planned, and these flyers posted around town."

"First order of business?" I said. "You're getting a raise."

She winked. "Thanks, boss."

"But you don't have to call me boss," I said.

Laughing, she said, "It might grow on you."

"I promise, it won't," I teased. I walked back to my office and resumed work, because when all was said and done, I was still a doctor and my first priority was patient care.

At the end of the day, Brenda came and knocked softly on my door.

"Just finishing up some paperwork," I said, although I was tempted to take it home so I could spend more time with Liv and Maya.

"Um... you might want to check on your truck."

Drawing my eyebrows together, I looked up at her. "What do you mean?"

Color flooded her cheeks, even more so than the rouge she wore. "I'd rather not say..."

"I'll take a look." I got up, straightening my slacks, and walked past her. What could have happened to my truck?

I reached the front door and stood on the porch steps, seeing a massive, veiny, flesh-colored dildo suctioned to the hood of my truck like a damn unicorn horn.

Now my cheeks were feeling as hot as Brenda's looked as I ran to the truck, pulling the toy from the hood. I almost gagged when I realized how warm and heavy the silicone felt in my hands.

Now I noticed a piece of paper tied around the base of the penis and flipped it over, reading it.

Seven inches. Extra girthy. Just like you wanted.

I didn't even need to read the name to see who sent it.

Behind me, Brenda called, "Don't worry about it, boss. It was probably some teenager."

I gritted my teeth together. Some teenager indeed.

Standing in the parking lot, still holding the dildo, I sent a text to the culprit.

Fletcher: I hate you.

Seconds later, my phone chimed with his response.

Rhett: Told you I'd get you back.

So this was payback? Two could play that game.

Fletcher: Cool. Can't wait to use this on your sister.

Rhett: Okay, now it's really on.

Fletcher: That's what she said.

I laughed out loud at my joke.

Rhett: You're going to regret this.

Fletcher: Can't hear you over your sister.

Rhett: Watch your back.

I knew he meant it.

51

LIV

Fletcher asked me to be ready for our date at six Friday night and to wear a dress. Maya and I spent an hour after she got out of school going through Henrietta's closet and then Della's closet, looking for something to wear.

We decided to go with this pretty blue velvet wrap dress Della had ordered online but didn't fit her quite right. It fit me like a glove, and as I curled the last of my hair, I couldn't believe how beautiful I looked out of my regular jeans and T-shirt combo.

It was nice to get all dolled up from time to time. Especially when I knew exactly how beautiful Fletcher thought I was. I closed my eyes and tried not to think about how hot repeating my best qualities to him was while his daughter was in the room, putting hair clips on her scrappy puppy dog.

"Did I miss anything in the back?" I asked her.

She got up from the floor, looking at the back of my head. Then she picked up a section of hair and passed it to me.

"Thank you." I wrapped it around the barrel of the curling iron and held it for a moment. Once the curl held, I picked up the can of hair spray and doused my hair in the mist.

Maya waved her hand in front of her face. "*Why* do you use so much?"

I laughed, misting some on her hair. "Because my hair can't hold a curl to save its life. Are you excited to hang out with Grampy tonight?"

She nodded quickly. "He's coming over and we're watching *The Parent Trap* together."

"Again?" I remembered being a kid and watching movies over and over again.

"Yes! He's never seen it."

"He's in for a treat," I said with a smile. I brushed my hair over my shoulder and looked in the mirror. "How do I look?"

"So pretty," Maya said. "Like a princess."

I smiled. The highest compliment a little girl could give. "Thanks for helping me get ready."

From the direction of the living room, I heard Gray call, "Anyone home?"

Graham yapped and Maya groaned, mustering more exasperation than I knew an eight-year-old was capable of. "*Graham*, it's just Grampy." She scooped him into her arms, even though he'd already gained a good five pounds, according to our vet visit this week. "We're in here!"

We both walked out of the bathroom, and I felt my cheeks growing warmer. Gray knew I was going on a date with his son, and it was clear how much effort I'd put in with the dress, the hair, and all the makeup.

When we met him in the living room, his eyes fell over me, warmer than the chocolate chips in a cookie straight from the oven. "Well aren't you a sight for sore eyes."

His words echoed Fletcher's that first day in town, making me smile at the memory. "Thanks." I rubbed my hand over my arm. "I heard you and Maya are going to watch *The Parent Trap*."

"Can't wait," he replied with a wink.

Maya said, "Can you make popcorn for us?"

He nodded.

I gestured toward the door. "I'm going to wait for Fletcher outside."

Maya put Graham down and wrapped her arms around my waist. "See you later."

Feeling Gray's eyes on us, I hugged her back. "See you soon, baby girl."

I waved goodbye to Gray and then walked outside just in time to see Fletcher's truck coming down the dirt road, dust billowing and fading into the bright blue sky. A smile spread on my lips as the sunshine touched my skin and hope warmed me from the inside out.

It felt like everything I'd dreamed about was coming true. It just took a dozen years to come to fruition.

The pickup slowed to a stop in the driveway, and I swore the moment happened in slow motion. Fletcher stepped out of his freshly washed truck, wearing a tux with a lilac tie and pocket square. He carried a plastic case with flowers inside and walked to me like he'd been trained on a runway.

"What is this?" I asked, in almost disbelief.

His smile had so much light behind it. "I'm taking you to the prom. And this time, I'm doing it how I want to.

Not as your friend, but as so much more. Back then, Rhett told me I shouldn't date his sister, and I listened. I missed out on so much with you. Not anymore."

I pressed my hand to my chest. "Fletch..."

"You don't have to say anything; just let me put this corsage on your wrist."

I extended my hand, and his fingers were full of heat as they stretched the band and adorned the beautiful lilac flowers and baby's breath on my wrist. I lifted the flowers to my nose, inhaling the fresh scent, and the petals tickled my nose. "I love it."

"I hoped you would." He smiled. "And I think Maya and Dad approve."

I turned toward the window just in time to see the blinds close, and I laughed. "They're adorable. Now let me put that boutonniere on your handsome suit."

He passed the flower to me, and I carefully pinned it to his lapel. When I was done, I brushed my hand over his chest, remembering the last time we went to prom together. His mom hadn't been there, but my mom told him she would have been proud. I felt like someone needed to say it now too.

"Fletcher..." I looked up at him, catching his brown eyes. "Your mom would be so proud of the man you've become."

He didn't have words, only a trembling smile as he extended his arm for me and led me to his vehicle. He held the door open for me to get inside.

I looked around the interior and said, "This is nicer than the one you used to have. Remember that silver dollar you had glued over that crack in the dash?"

He chuckled. "We had to keep it from rattling somehow." Shaking his head, he added, "I can't believe you remember that."

"I remember everything from our first and only date, right down to what was playing on the radio."

"'Ten Thousand Hours' by Dan and Shay, featuring Justin Bieber?" he finished, glancing my way. "You sang so loudly I could barely hear the radio."

Half mortified, half impressed, my jaw fell open. "You remember that?"

"That night mattered to more than just you... In fact..." He tapped at the screen on his dash, and the opening lines of the song began playing.

I covered my mouth, taken back to our first date. The way he'd looked so handsome in his tux with the lilac tie. How good his cologne had smelled and when we spun around the dance floor, how much I wished the night would never end.

And this time, he sang along to the song as we drove into town, the notes like honey falling from his tongue.

I soaked in all of it, holding his hand in my lap, wondering how this fairy tale had somehow become mine.

We drove into town, and when he parked beside the school, I asked, "Here? They're letting us in the school?"

He winked, reminding me of his playful side that I loved. "I may have had a little help... Let me get your door."

As we walked toward the front door, it swung open, and Rhett stood in a suit, the same shit-eating grin on his face as always. "Welcome to the prom, *sir and madam*."

I punched him in the arm, my cheeks bright red. "Oh stop."

He pretended to be wounded, then said, "I'm under strict orders from the boss to behave tonight... Although, I do have something for him." He reached into his pocket and handed Fletcher a tube of cream. "Here's that jock itch cream you asked for." He raised his hand and pointed in Fletcher's direction. "Might want to stay away from him tonight."

Fletcher rolled his eyes. "I hate you."

Rhett only smirked before leading us the several feet to the gym door.

"Do you really have jock itch?" I whispered to Fletcher.

His neck got red as he said, "Absolutely not."

When Rhett held the door open, my jaw dropped, the ointment long forgotten.

This... was incredible.

52

FLETCHER

Liv spun in a slow circle, taking in the gym, from the vinyl covering the floor to the disco ball dangling from the ceiling. Della stood behind the speakers, playing a country song, and Henrietta and Tyler waited by the drink and snack table.

"No way," she breathed.

I put my arm around her, holding her close. "It's not a do-over if I don't do it right."

She shook her head, wiping moisture from her eyes, and Della began speaking over the microphone.

"Welcome to the prom!" Della said in a low DJ voice. "This year's theme is Second Chances and Fresh Starts. Let's kick it off right with a slow song. You crazy kids have a great time!"

Liv faced me. "Fletcher... This is all..." Her lips quivered, and she brushed at her eyes again. "It feels too good to be true."

I took her close, linking my hands behind her waist

and swaying to the music. "This is the truest thing I've ever felt, Liv."

She looked up at me, blue eyes searching my own. "Fletcher... you can't do this if you don't mean it, because..."

Her voice trailed off, and her eyes slid down.

I moved one hand to lift her chin. "Because...?"

"Because I'm falling for you all over again. I don't see how I could ever get back up if this goes wrong."

"You don't have to worry, because I've fallen for you, Liv. Then. Now. Forever."

She lifted her chin, searching for my lips, and I met her kiss. She felt like coming home.

We spun around the dance floor for what could have been hours or minutes, singing along to the songs, talking about life and Maya, her birthday party, that damn dog that preferred my shoelaces to any of the toys we bought.

Then the music changed to "Copperhead Road," and Liv tossed her head back, laughing. "We have to do this one!"

"On it!" Rhett said beside me, Maya holding his hand and Dad trailing behind them.

Liv's jaw dropped. "You're here?!" She picked my daughter up and held her tight, spinning her around. As they spun, she got a full view of everyone coming into the prom. My brothers, all her siblings and wives and even her nieces and nephews in their Sunday best. Then Liv looked at me. "You invited everyone here?"

"You didn't think we could have a prom with just us two, did you?" I asked her over the building music. "This... it's bigger than us."

She smiled back at me and held my hand. "Then dance with us."

We all danced to "Copperhead Road," then the "Chicken Dance" and even "Footloose." It was so fun watching Liv, Henrietta, and Della try to teach Maya all the moves.

Then Della took over the microphone again and said, "Now it's time for a father-daughter dance! Liv and Jack, Maya and Fletcher, enjoy a song together, just for you."

"My Little Girl" by Tim McGraw played over the speakers, and Maya came running up to me, her tulle dress flaring behind her with her speed. When she jumped in my arms, I almost fell over with the force, but then I held her, spinning in a circle as the music played.

"I'm so happy to have this dance with you," I said, holding her and swaying to the music.

"You too, Daddy. Prom is so fun. Can we do this next weekend too?"

I chuckled. "I already pulled in all my favors for tonight, but when you're in high school, you'll have all sorts of dances to go to, just like this."

"Will you come with me?" she asked.

I smiled, holding her just a little tighter. "I hope you'll still say that when you're older."

"I'll still be me," she said like I'd done something silly.

"You will be, and just like this song, you'll *always* be my little girl."

Dad and I watched Fletcher and Maya dancing together so sweetly. My dad was never a man of many words, but he was always there for me, whether it was my first time falling off a horse or those times in community college when he loaned me money because a roommate bailed on rent.

"Fletcher's a good man," Dad said.

I looked back up at my dad, just a few inches taller than me. "He is," I agreed.

"Someday, he'll be dancing with a room full of your children," Dad said.

My heart felt like it was splitting, because I'd always wanted to have a big family, just like mine. "Sounds like a dream," I said, but it wasn't in my cards. Not children, and not marriage. And the realization was wearing on me.

Because Fletcher was willing to do all of this for me, willing to tell me he loved me forever, but not make it official. I couldn't help feeling like I was getting everything I ever wanted, but in a shade of gray.

The music faded to a close, and Dad hugged me tight. "That's our cue to head home."

"Home?" I asked.

He smiled. "Midnight starts a little earlier when you get to be my age."

I shook my head at him—he may have been nearing sixty, but he worked as hard as any man my age. "Goodnight, Dad."

"Night, kiddo."

I waved goodbye and watched as everyone began leaving the prom, just Fletcher and me staying behind as music played softly over the speakers.

"What happens now?" I asked.

He had an evil glint in his eyes. "After-prom."

"I assume we're not watching a movie?"

He shook his head and took my hand. His lips were hot on my ear as he said, "I told you, tonight is my do-over. There's no way I'm letting you go home without you screaming my name tonight."

I shuddered against his words, my eyes drifting closed.

"Follow me," he ordered.

I nodded, letting him lead me outside to his truck. There was the same giddy feeling in my chest as all those years before. Back then, I'd been hoping he would take me home and kiss me on my doorstep. Now, I *knew* he was going to fuck me like his good girl. It was way better than any movie could be.

But there was still something tugging at the back of my mind as we pulled out of the parking lot. I bit my lip, wishing tonight could be perfect like he'd worked so hard to make it be.

He glanced over at me in the dark cab of his pickup. "What are you thinking?"

I freed my lip from my teeth. "You were so sweet with Maya tonight."

"I love her with all I have," he said earnestly.

"Have you ever thought about having more children someday?"

He slid his fingers through mine as he drove slowly down the empty city streets. "I want to have a million babies with you. A big family just like the ones we grew up in, with noisy dinners and rowdy birthdays and holidays with every seat in the house full of friends and family."

My heart melted at the picture he painted, but it broke too. "My endometriosis..."

"The surgery will help," Fletcher said, squeezing my hand. "And if we have trouble conceiving, I already have what I need in you and Maya. Besides, I don't mind trying with you every damn night if that's what it takes." He winked at me.

I laughed, so much weight off my chest.

The pickup slowed and then stopped as he parked in front of the practice.

"What are we doing here?" I asked.

"I wanted to show you something." He got out of the truck, coming to my side and letting me out, then walked down the sidewalk. "You know Doctor Deb owned this practice, right?"

"I didn't," I admitted. "I didn't know someone could own a doctor's office."

"Yeah, this one is a private practice. And she offered to sell it to me." He paused at the door with his keys. "Her party tomorrow isn't just to thank her for all she gave to this community. It's also a celebration of new ownership."

"You're kidding!" I said, in awe of all he'd accomplished. "You're only two years older than me, and you have a whole business, and I'm just—"

He kissed my lips, silencing me. "You're the woman who made me feel strong enough to chase this dream. Because I knew I'd have you by my side through it all."

I looked up at him, seeing nothing but the truth in his eyes.

He unlocked the door and walked me inside, toward the storage closet by his office. When he opened it, he pulled out a metal sign. I ran my hand over the letters...

Madigan Medical

The last name I would never have.

I shoved down the sad, worried feeling, putting on a smile. "Fletcher, this is amazing. Congratulations!" I looked around the place. "I wish I'd known. I would have done something for you..."

"Tonight is about us," he replied, heat in his eyes.

His gaze flicked to my lips, and I lifted my chin to meet his kiss. Our embrace quickly heated.

"Fletcher," I gasped. "Get me home. To a hotel. Your truck. I want you so bad."

He gripped my hands, dragging them to his hard cock. "Why do you think I brought you here?" Before I knew it, he was guiding me back into an exam room. My hips butted against the table. "Lie down," he ordered.

My eyes flared open at the demand. "Here?"

He nodded, reaching into the drawer and pulling out a stethoscope. "Now."

I lay back, my dress rippling over my body as I moved.

He paced beside the table, snapping out the stirrups. "Feet in."

Fire pounded through my veins as I followed his commands. Every last one.

His voice was silken lead, soft but hard, commanding. "Hands above your head."

My chest heaved with anticipation as I did, and he walked to the top of the exam table, his erection pressing against his pants. I licked my lips, wanting to taste him. To feel him on my tongue.

But he captured my wrists in one of his large hands and then tied the stethoscope around them.

"Holy shit," I breathed.

He tightened the restraint and took his time removing his jacket, unbuttoning his shirt as his eyes roved my body.

"Baby," I said. "Please." My nipples strained against the fabric of my dress, and I shifted to ease the need, pressing my toes into the stirrups.

He smiled, undoing the last button, and slid the shirt off his body. This was the prom fantasy I never knew I needed, having his abs, his cock at eye level.

"You want my dick in your mouth, don't you?" he said, his voice low, rough.

"Please," I whispered. I don't know what came over me with this man, but the noises he made when his dick was against my tongue made me want to please him even more.

He unzipped his dress pants, pulling them down and freeing his cock. It hung heavy, thick, hard between his legs. And as he got closer, I angled my mouth to take it in. Tightening my lips so he'd feel the pressure and then sucking until my lips popped around him.

"Fuck, Liv." He pulled back, undressing further, and walked to the foot of the exam table where my legs were spread, ready for him.

He pulled my dress up, revealing the silky underwear I'd bought. He ripped them down harshly, tossing them to the floor, and then looked at me.

Any ounce of self-consciousness I had dissolved at the way he took me in. He was so turned on by me.

Me.

He ran his hand over my seam, his eyes rolling back in his head when he felt how wet I was for him. "You're a fucking dream."

My lips curved into a smile, and I arched my head back against the table. "Then fuck me."

"In due time."

He drew his lips to my knee, then the other. Slowly, tantalizingly drawing his kisses closer to my center and farther away again.

"Fletcher," I begged.

He took two fingers, pressing them inside me, making me shake. "Is that what you want?"

"I want you. Inside me," I panted.

He curled his hand, keeping his fingers inside me but rubbing his thumb over my clit.

It caught me so off guard my moan was more of a scream.

His grin was salacious. "Good girl."

My chest heaved with my arms overhead, my legs shaking as he continued his assault, and I came on his hand so fucking hard I watched liquid splatter onto his bare stomach.

My jaw fell open. "Oh my god. Did I just..." I was gasping for air.

He rubbed his hand over his stomach. "You squirted, baby. You did so fucking good."

With my legs feeling like rubber, he angled himself between them, stepping closer until his tip teased my entrance. I moaned as he pressed all the way in until the front of his hips pressed against my ass. His cock was so big it stretched me tight. He gripped my thighs, holding on to me as he let me have it, all of him, hard and fast, and so fucking good.

I rolled my head back, overwhelmed by the sensation, but his voice was rough as he ordered, "Eyes on me."

I watched him, the clench of his jaw, his fingers pressed into my soft flesh, his ab muscles flexing as he fucked me.

The building friction pushed my sensitive pussy higher until I was shattering around him, crying out with ecstasy, and he finished inside of me, claiming me as his.

He leaned over me, kissing my stomach, then pulled out. Cleaning himself up and wiping me with a wet wipe from the drawer under the sink.

He slowly undid the stethoscope, pressing kisses against my wrists, and then helped me slide from the table. I landed on my feet, legs feeling weak until he held me up, kissing my lips, my cheeks, my forehead.

I'd been with guys before who were great in bed but

emotionally unavailable and guys who were kind but had no spark. How was it possible to feel so much heat and so much love for the same man? And why was I so afraid that even when he gave me so much... it wouldn't be enough?

54

FLETCHER

Since the first night Liv and I were together, my nightmares stopped. I felt at peace in a way I'd never been before. I loved waking up to see her in my home and enjoyed even more lying beside her until she fell asleep. Seeing her wake up.

After the prom, we decided to stay in the same room, and if it bothered Maya, she didn't say anything. The first couple weeks at school had gone great, even if she was grumpy right when she got home.

Life was good. The best it had ever been.

That was, until I saw Regina's name on my phone during my Saturday afternoon run. I stopped alongside the road, trying to catch my breath, and answered. "Hey, Regina, I was in the middle of a run."

"You always were a stickler for that morning workout," she said, a small smile in her voice.

"What's up?" I asked. "Everything okay?"

"I was calling about Maya's party."

My stomach dropped. "You're not backing out, are you? Because Maya really wants you there."

"No, I'm not backing out," she said, sounding a little frustrated. "I've really been trying here, Fletcher. I haven't missed an evening call since I saw Maya at Sugar Rush."

"I know," I said, not adding that it had only been a couple weeks since then. I didn't want to fight with Regina. Not anymore. Especially not today when I was feeling so good.

She took a breath, audible even over the phone. "Look, I'm coming to the party, and I wanted to know if... if I could bring my boyfriend."

My eyebrows rose, and I felt winded for another reason. "You want to bring a guy with you?" I knew she'd been with a little girl when Liv and Maya saw her at the ice cream shop, but I didn't realize it was serious enough for him to meet my daughter.

"I think it's time they met," Regina said.

I began pacing down the dirt road, gravel crunching under my tennis shoes. "At her birthday party?"

"We could always come the day before, so we don't take away from her big day. And since Maya's birthday is over Labor Day weekend, I wanted to know if she could come stay with me for the break before she has to go back to school on Tuesday."

My eyes practically bugged out and I began walking faster, not needing a run to get my heart pounding. "You treat our daughter like a burden when we're together, and then when we're apart, you barely call. And now you want to keep her with your new boyfriend out of the blue? What the fuck, Regina?" I knew I was coming across harsh, but I'd defend Maya to the grave.

"She's my daughter too, regardless of how I messed up, and I have a right to her. You may have full custody, but I'm guaranteed at least one weekend visit a month, unsupervised. Unless you want me to hire a lawyer and revisit the custody arrangement."

"You'd bring a lawyer into this?" I demanded, my chest so tight I could barely breathe. "Because I don't think a judge would understand your sudden change of heart. Is your boyfriend behind this?"

"I'm trying to start over, damn it." Her voice grew louder. "I wasted nine years of my life on you, hoping you'd love me, trying to get over how much it hurt to look at my daughter and only see you. I know I've been a shitty mom, but seeing the way Ben is with his daughter makes me want to be a better mom, okay?"

I raised my eyebrows. "Ben?"

"Ben Jordan," she said.

"*My old coworker*? The guy we had over to dinners when we were married? *That's* the person you're seeing?"

"You haven't called him since you left town, and we ran into each other at the store one night. I filled him in on the situation, and one thing led to another."

So she was dating my old colleague, and now she wanted to bring him to Maya's party? At least I knew he was a decent guy at work, but when it came to family... "How long have you been seeing each other?"

"Just about six months."

"It's serious?"

"We're living together."

I turned back toward the house, wanting to get closer to my home, closer to the place and people who made me feel safe. "If Maya wants to stay with you, it is fine with me."

"Good." She paused for a moment. "You know, someday you'll start seeing someone and you'll understand."

It struck me how little Regina and I really talked, and I felt guilty. Because she had been trying the last couple weeks, and I didn't want that to change, for Maya's sake. "Actually, Regina, I am seeing someone. Liv."

"The nanny?" Regina asked.

"She's more than that," I said.

"How so?"

"I love her," I answered simply.

Regina was quiet for a long moment. "I liked her when I thought she was just the nanny."

"She's still the same person."

"I want to be happy for you. It's just hard to know she is what I couldn't be for you..."

I felt bad for Regina, but we both needed to move on from the hurt of our relationship. "You don't have to be happy for me. I understand. But be happy for Maya, because she has someone who's there for her no matter what." I knew it came out harsh, but damn it, Maya had spent more time with Liv than Regina in the last year.

"Ask Maya about visiting and the party," Regina said, "and let me know what she says."

"I will," I replied and hung up.

For a moment, I just stood on the road, staring out at the countryside around me. This world was so big, so many people, and here I was in this life, with an ex-wife in Dallas, a daughter in Cottonwood Falls, and a nanny sleeping in my room.

Sometimes I wished I could go back and do things the "right" way. But that would mean life without Maya, and I wouldn't trade her for the world.

Taking a deep breath, I turned and started jogging home.

When I got back to the house, I found my girls in the living room as Liv curled Maya's hair at the coffee table. I'd asked them about it once but got a longwinded explanation about how doing hair in front of the TV is better. They both looked up at me, and Liv said, "Don't move, Maya! I'll burn you!"

Then Graham barked at Liv like he was yelling at her for yelling at Maya, and both the girls laughed.

"It's okay, Graham," Liv said.

I smiled at them, wishing it could always be like this, just the three of us. "Why don't you put that curling iron down? I have something to ask you about, Maya."

Liv set the iron aside, and Maya leaned back against Liv's legs, slinging her arms over Liv's knees. "What's up, Daddy-o?"

"Daddy-o?" I asked with a chuckle.

"That's what Lyssa calls her dad."

I shook my head as I went and sat on the chair to talk to her. "I just spoke with your mother, and she asked if it was okay that she bring her new boyfriend to your birthday party."

Maya got quiet, and I swore I could feel Liv holding her breath.

"What did you say?" Maya finally asked.

"I told her it was up to you."

Maya bit the side of her fingernail for a moment before finally saying, "That's okay. He can come."

"Are you sure?" I asked. "Because if you're uncomfortable at all, I will tell her no. You can meet him another time."

Maya shook her head. "If you tell her no, she might not come."

My heart wrenched in my chest. "She says she's trying to do better to be there for you, and she asked if you could go stay with her for a few days after your party. I said it was up to you if you wanted to go."

"I can go stay with Mommy?"

I nodded, surprised by how excited she was. Children forgave so quickly, especially the people they loved. We didn't deserve it.

"I want to go," she said quickly.

"We'll make it happen." I gave her a hug, then got up. "I'm going to take a shower before we go to the party."

As I walked toward the bedroom, Liv said, "Maya, why don't you take Graham out for a potty break?"

"Okay." Maya went to the door, her poufy puppy trailing behind her.

I continued to the bathroom, but Liv said, "Wait, Fletcher."

"What?" I asked, my nerves already strained.

She paused, her brow creasing. "I mean, are you really going to let Maya stay with her mom after everything?"

"What can I do?" I asked. "Tell her no? Wait for a lawyer to reopen our custody case?"

Liv worried her hands. "I didn't realize that was at risk..."

"No, because you're not her parent."

She recoiled, and I instantly felt guilty.

"Liv, I'm sorry, I just—"

"No, I get it. It's not my place. Enjoy your shower." She turned to walk away, but I caught her hand, drawing her close.

"I love that you look out for Maya, and honestly, I'm not thrilled about it either, but our agreement states Regina gets one visit a month. She just hasn't called it in until now."

Liv linked her arms around my waist. "Poor Maya."

"I know. I hate knowing she won't be here, but we'll send her with a phone, and she can call us any time she needs. With the way you drive, I know we'll be to the city in no time flat."

"Hey," she teased, a small smile on her face. "Thanks for explaining that, about the custody. I want to feel like I'm a..." She shook her head.

"What?" I asked.

"Like I'm your partner, not just a nanny."

I lifted her chin and kissed her. "You'll never be my partner. Because that implies we're equals."

Her lips pinched. "Excuse me?"

I tweaked her nose with a smile. "We both know you're far better than I'll ever be."

The door opened, Maya and Graham coming back in, and Liv said, "Go get naked, Fletch."

"I better hurry before you turn that curling iron on me," I teased.

She rolled her eyes and continued getting ready with my daughter.

55

LIV

Doctor Deb's retirement party was decorated so beautifully. There were twinkle lights out in the back garden area. The caterers brought a grill, and the smell of delicious food filled the air. Added with soft instrumental music playing, it was a beautiful way for the practice to turn over a new leaf.

My only complaint was that Maya was so busy playing with the other kids and Fletcher was getting reacquainted with so many people at the party that I didn't get to spend much time with either of them. Luckily, Mom, Henrietta and Della were all there.

We found ourselves a table and took our drinks, sitting around and chatting.

"This is a great party," Henrietta said.

Della nodded. "You know, it's hard to believe that Rhett's best friend is a doctor with his own practice."

Mom laughed. "We all know Fletcher was the one keeping Rhett out of trouble most of the time... Speaking of, where is Rhett?"

I nodded toward a corner of the yard where Rhett was chatting up Brenda's daughter. "Poor Morganne."

Mom swatted me, but she was still smiling.

Della said, "I never imagined you being with a doctor either, Liv. I always figured some farmer would sweep you off your feet."

Mom gave a dreamy smile. "They'll be married and having babies before you know it."

The table instantly tensed.

"What?" Mom asked. "You are thinking about marriage with him, right?"

That comment surprised me. Mom didn't seem like one to rush into things. She'd never pressured me about marriage before. "What do you mean?"

Henrietta said, "Just that you two seem so happy together, right, Deidre?"

Mom sipped from her drink. "That and... I mean..." She took a breath.

Della cringed.

"What, Mom?" I asked. "Why do I have the feeling you're going to say something I don't like?"

Mom laughed. "It's just an old woman's advice."

"Advice?"

She nodded. "Look, you're working for the man, you're raising his child, you're living in his house... It won't be long before you won't be taking a salary anymore, right?"

My heart stiffened. I really hadn't thought about my salary, but I didn't want to admit that she had a point.

She waved her hands. "All I'm saying is that marriage offers certain...protections. I'd hate to see you build a kingdom with a man and have no right to the castle in case, God forbid, you break up or something happens to him."

I looked at Della. "Tell them they're crazy. It's way too soon."

Della looked down at her drink. "She does have a point, Liv..."

Turning toward Henrietta, I raised my eyebrows.

"You never know," Henrietta said. "Freak accidents happen all the time..."

I frowned. "What happened to 'if you're happy, I'm happy?'"

"I want you to be happy," Hen said. "But I also want you to be smart."

Mom looked between us, her expression apologetic. "I didn't mean to upset you, honey."

Well it was too late for that. "I just need some air." Which was a stupid thing to say when we were outside, but I got up anyway and walked toward the practice so I could hide in the bathroom until I cleared my head.

Because my mom? She was right.

Even if I could get past the symbolism of a wedding and what it meant for a relationship... how could I get past having no protections, no security for my future if something happened to Fletcher?

When I got inside the bathroom, I locked the door behind me. On the verge of tears, I pressed my hand on the vanity and looked in the mirror.

Was this really what I wanted for myself? I loved Fletcher, but what if he got sick or passed away unexpectedly? I would be shut out of all decisions, be out of a home, out of a bank account I supported him in building, out of Maya's life unless Regina decided to count me in.

All because... he messed up with Regina in the midst of battling PTSD? He could make different vows to me, ones that stuck this time.

I blinked quickly, trying to hold back tears, wishing that my mom hadn't said anything and that I could be in a blissfully ignorant kind of love with Fletcher.

A knock sounded on the door, and I called back, "Just a minute."

Then came Fletcher's voice. "It's me. Can I come in?"

My heart somersaulted. And I hated that my first thought was *no*.

"Sure," I replied instead, unlocking the door and stepping back. I wrapped my arms around myself, attempting to keep it together.

Fletcher looked stunning in his dark-wash jeans and button-down with the sleeves rolled and the top button undone. "Hey." He leaned in and kissed me. "Della said I might want to check on you... What's going on?"

"We don't have to talk about it now." I tried to smile reassuringly but failed miserably.

"Liv, what's wrong?" he asked, studying me. "Did something happen?"

I bit my lip, shaking my head. "This really isn't the place or the time."

His eyebrows furrowed. "If you're upset, here and now is the place and time to talk about it. I can't enjoy the party knowing there's something wrong with the woman I love."

I let out a sigh. "I wish you would let it go."

A knock sounded on the door, and Fletcher's jaw ticked as he replied, "I'm going to be in here a while." He turned his gaze on me, and I knew he wouldn't let it go.

"It's about you not wanting to get married."

His lips parted like that was the last thing he expected me to say. "I thought you said it was too soon to talk about marriage..."

"I thought it was, until I realized what continuing a relationship without the possibility of marriage would mean."

He turned away from me, linking his hands behind his head. He was clearly frustrated.

I ground my teeth together, mad that he was upset with me. I wasn't the one asking him to forgo a dream he'd had for years. Being married, promising forever to someone in front of all my friends and family... that was sacred to me.

"Where is this coming from?" he asked, facing me again.

I folded my arms across my chest, feeling more vulnerable than ever. "I realized that if we never get married, all I'll ever be is a live-in nanny with benefits. I'll have no rights to this life that we built together."

He put his hands on my arms. "Liv, I'd never betray you like that. If we ever parted ways, I'd make sure that you were set with half of what we have."

"And my resume?" I asked. "What should I list? House not-wife?"

He pressed his lips together.

"And what if something happens to you, Fletch? You know it's a possibility with what happened to your mom, and I'd have no say in any of your care or rights to our home—"

"We could plan a will," he snapped, "and I hardly

think manipulating me by using my mother's death is a fair way to get what you want."

My jaw dropped. "You think I'm *manipulating* you?" I flattened my hand on my chest. "I'm trying to protect myself. Something you clearly don't care to do."

He frowned. "I'm sorry, manipulate wasn't the right word. I'm just caught off guard. But I meant what I said, Liv. I can work you into my will, I can add your name to ownership of the house and the practice, but I won't be getting married. Not when I've already promised forever and failed once before."

I looked at him, the depths of his brown eyes, and realized... "You're not over what happened."

He reached out and cupped my cheek with his hand. "I love you so much, Liv Griffen. You deserve everything you want in this life. But if marriage is one of those desires... I can't be the one to give it to you."

I looked up at him, my heart slowly breaking. I loved him, and he was willing to commit to me in so many ways, but he was still holding back. I could see that now. "I need to think about this."

"Of course." He kissed my forehead. "Take all the time you need."

56

FLETCHER

Dad had invited us all over to grill and hang out on Sunday. Ford couldn't come since he was busy in Dallas with football training, and Bryce was back at college, but the rest of my brothers were there, along with Maya. She and Hayes were in the yard, passing a football back and forth while Knox and I were getting food.

"Where's Liv?" Knox asked as he used a set of tongs to grab a burger.

"I fucked up," I muttered, admitting to the brick of lead that had been in my stomach since I told her I wouldn't get married. Liv and I hadn't gotten intimate last night for the first time since we'd been together, and today she said she wanted to hang out with her brother Gage and his family in the city instead of spending time with Maya and me.

Knox gave me a long look before focusing on the tray of grilled vegetables. "What happened?"

"I told her I couldn't get married after Regina." I stared out at Hayes and Maya playing catch as Graham pranced between the two of them. By the end of the night, Hayes would have her throwing a perfect spiral.

Knox was silent for way too long. "You're afraid?" he finally said.

"Not really."

He shook his head at me. "You want to be with Liv, don't you?"

"Yes," I replied. "Of course I do."

"Think there's anyone better out there?"

"Fuck no."

"Then what's holding you back?"

I set a burger on my plate. "It's complicated."

"For a guy who made it through med school, you can be a real dumbass sometimes."

I set my plate down, facing him. "You don't understand. I made those vows to Regina. How can I make the same vows to Liv and not look like a piece of shit to everyone involved? What kind of message does that send to Maya?"

"It sends the message that you know better now than you did back then," Knox said.

"Do I? Because I honestly thought I could provide for Regina and be a good husband, at least until Maya was out of the house. I was wrong."

"That's in the past," Knox argued.

"And five years from now, when I fuck up again, Liv will be hurt even worse because I made a promise I couldn't keep instead of being honest about the kind of man I am. And this time, Maya will be *watching* me say the vows I broke."

Knox shook his head at me. "You're just—"

"Just what?" Dad asked, coming up behind him with a plate of hot dogs from the grill.

Knox looked at me before smirking at Dad. "He's just a glorified pill pusher."

I rolled my eyes at Knox, and Dad chuckled. "Put him away with the rest of the drug dealers, will ya, Knox?"

Knox lifted an eyebrow thoughtfully. "It could be good to have a guy on the inside."

I scoffed. "On the inside at the city jail? When's the last time you even used a cell?"

"Oh hell. Guy got too drunk last night and needed a place to sleep it off."

With a chuckle, Dad returned to the grill, and Knox gave me a hard look. "I swear to god if you hurt her, we're all taking her side."

"Like I didn't already know."

57

LIV

I sat in the stands with my brother and sister-in-law, watching my nephew play in his summer baseball league. He was at shortstop, knees bent, bouncing lightly as he anticipated the pitch, where the bat would guide the ball.

"He reminds me so much of you," I told Gage while Farrah took the younger two kids to the concession stand. Even though Levi wasn't Gage's biological son, he had Gage's determination and athleticism.

Gage smiled at the comment. "He has a lot more raw talent. I can't wait to see what he does if he plays in college."

I loved the way Gage supported Levi like he was his own son. "Can I ask you something?"

He smirked. "If you ask me to burn that god-awful Ropers jersey you made me buy last year, then I'm happy to report it's already been done."

I rolled my eyes at him. "I'm serious."

"What is it?"

I bit my lip, needing to know the answer but having

trouble being vulnerable. Once I plucked up the courage, I asked, "What's it like being married to someone who's...already been married and had kids before?"

He was the only one of my siblings who would understand what I was going through.

"Is this about Fletcher?" he asked.

I nodded. "I'm sure Farrah told you about us."

"She tells me everything." His smile bordered on gooey, and it made me happy and jealous at the same time. "We both want you to be happy. But let me think about your question for a second." And by the thoughtful look on his face, he was going to give me a real answer, not just one to get my hopes up.

I bit my lip, waiting and hoping I could survive his truth.

Levi's team was jogging back to the dugout when Gage finally replied. "You know, when we were kids, everyone always told us that marriage is between two people, but that couldn't be further from the truth. When you marry someone, you're getting their family, their past. All those people affect the relationship. And if you marry someone who has an ex and children, you have to accept that the ex will always have a past with your partner you weren't a part of, and you're tied to that person just as much as the one you married. Because you can't love those kids without loving what brought them into the world."

I nodded, understanding him in a way I never would have before meeting Maya and falling in love with her and her father.

"Is Fletcher talking about marriage?" he asked.

I shook my head, taking a swig from my water bottle.

"He says he doesn't want to get married. He'll sign my name to his house and put me in his will, but he won't give me his last name."

Thankfully, Gage was less expressive than Rhett, but I still clocked his frown.

"You're going to tell me to break up with him," I said.

Gage shook his head. "I was thinking that marriage is about so much more than sharing a last name—it's about sharing a life."

Farrah came back to the stands with Cora and Andrew, sitting on the other side of Gage. Soon after, Levi walked out of the dugout to bat, and we all cheered for him.

He squared up at home plate, poised to swing. The pitch sailed toward the plate, and his bat cracked against the ball, sending it to deep center field, over the player's outstretched arm. Levi sprinted toward first base, then second and third as the outfielders scrambled for the ball, trying to stop him from stealing home.

But instead of playing it safe, Levi pushed toward home plate, running with his full force as the ball sailed toward the catcher. Ignoring the risk, he dove toward the plate in a cloud of dust.

It hadn't yet settled as the umpire yelled, "SAFE."

58

FLETCHER

I wanted to see Liv when we got home from Dad's house, but she wasn't there. I went about putting Maya to bed and even stayed up after, but Liv still wasn't home. I was starting to get worried about her, so I took out my phone and dialed her number.

After a few rings, she answered, the background noise telling me she was still in her truck. "Hello?"

"Hey," I said, breathing a sigh of relief. "I was just worried about you. I know last night was hard, and I thought..." My throat clogged with sudden emotion. "I didn't know if you were coming home."

There was a tenderness in her voice as she said, "I'm just a few minutes away. My nephew's game went to extra innings, and then we had to celebrate his win."

The tension in my chest eased slightly. "Do you want to come lie in my bed when you get here?"

"Why wouldn't I?" she said.

We both knew the answer. "I want to lie with you."

And I don't know how many nights I have left, I didn't say out loud.

"Okay," she said quietly.

If I listened closely, I could hear her engine as she came down the road. "I missed you today."

Her engine grew louder, closer, and then it turned off, echoing through her phone. "I missed you too."

She was quiet for a moment, and I heard her soft breath as she walked toward the house, then I heard her open the door, walk down the hallways, and slide into my bed. I put my phone on the nightstand and then curled around her, wrapping my arms around her soft middle.

She smelled like vanilla and sunshine. Her wavy hair fell over the white pillows illuminated by the dim light from the bathroom.

I kissed the back of her neck, ran my hands over her full hips.

She arched her back, grinding her backside against me and sending blood to my cock. I dragged my nose up the nape of her neck.

She moaned softly, reaching back and pressing her hand against my growing erection.

I moved my hands down her hips, sliding them into her leggings and rubbing slow circles around her clit as she moved against me until I couldn't take it anymore.

There were no words this time, no fun orders or sexy pleas.

Just Liv and me as I took off my pants and pressed into her, savoring every bit of her body, her soul.

And all I could think was... I'm going to lose her.

I'm going to lose the best thing that ever happened to me.

Fletcher had to work late often the week leading up to Maya's birthday. Purchasing the practice and switching everything over to Madigan Medical was a time-consuming process. I didn't mind so much because I didn't need to watch Maya while she was in school, and it gave us time to hang out in the afternoons.

Not to mention, I still hadn't made a decision when it came to Fletcher, and I knew I'd have to make it soon. I couldn't live in limbo like this. It was only hurting us both, me standing with one foot in and one foot out of the door.

The morning of Maya's birthday, I got up early and wrangled Fletcher into helping me blow up balloons. I'd seen this thing online where you could make a whole balloon cascade, so when Maya opened her bedroom door, she'd be covered in balloons—a great way to start her day.

The problem? It had been a hot minute since I'd

blown up so many balloons. My face was red and so was Fletcher's, which made us both laugh so hard we had to steal away to the bedroom to keep from waking Maya up before we could carry out our surprise.

Eventually we finished blowing up the balloons and taped a sheet to her door to hold them all in. Then we went to the kitchen, and he made coffee while I went about cooking her birthday breakfast—pancakes with her name spelled in chocolate chips.

"You make birthdays so special," Fletcher said with a smile as he sat at the island with his coffee cup. "Makes me excited for mine."

In that moment, I could see my future laid out before me. Waking up with him, sipping coffee as the sun came up, seeing the light shine in his eyes and the mess in his hair. Giggling about birthday shenanigans and enjoying our time together. But my heart broke because we'd be lacking the one thing that I'd always held sacred.

Marriage. The promise that we'd be together forever, through richer and poorer, in sickness and in health. That tradition that tied me to my parents and grandparents and so many generations before us. He'd shared that with Regina, and he shared a daughter with her. How much had he given to Regina that he would never have with me?

"What's going on in that pretty mind?" he asked, looking up at me.

I quickly cleared my expression. "Just wondering if we should apply sunscreen halfway through the float or if once at the beginning will be enough."

He seemed to hesitate like he knew that wasn't it, then

went along with the lie. "If I have it my way, Rhett will be wearing sunscreen on a necklace from now on, along with one of those dorky fishing hats."

I chuckled. "Rhett's worn that wire cross necklace as long as I've known him. Doubt sunscreen goes along with that."

Then we heard Maya's bedroom door open, and an eruption of barking ensued.

Fletch and I shared a smile before walking toward her bedroom, hearing Maya say, "It's okay, Graham. The balloons won't hurt you, see?"

The barking got even louder, and Maya laughed.

We reached her as she came out of the room, her dog writhing in her arms. "I think Graham's afraid of balloons," she said.

Fletcher half laughed. "Of course he can survive on the side of the road but can't handle a party balloon. Happy birthday, *nine*-year-old."

She hugged her dad, holding the puppy between them, then turned to me.

"Happy birthday, sweet girl! I'm so excited to celebrate with you!"

"Me too." She grinned and then passed Graham to Fletcher. Ever since the coyote scare, morning potty times were his responsibility, much to his chagrin.

The two of us went to the counter and I set out her plate, showing the pancake with a chocolate chip design.

"It's my name!" she said happily.

I kissed the top of her head, then said, "The best for the best."

She began pouring syrup on her plate, and then I

made my own plate with eggs and pancakes before sitting beside her.

A few minutes later, Fletcher returned from Graham's potty break and ate with us. Once we were done with our food, he said, "Why don't we open your presents here before we set up for the party?"

Maya grinned. "Yes! Yes! Yes!"

Maya and I got comfortable in the living room while Fletcher retrieved the stack of wrapped presents from his closet. She eagerly tore through the paper, getting a specially designed collar and leash for Graham, a few new outfits for school, and a smartwatch that would count her steps for the day and let Fletcher digitally assign and track her chores.

"Thank you, Daddy!" she said. "Everyone in my class has one of these watches!"

Fletcher and I exchanged a glance. Back when we were kids, Tamagotchis were the cool new tech. Life had changed so much since then.

"Let me get my gifts for you," I said, rising from the couch and walking to my room. I found the wrapped boxes in the back of my closet and brought them out.

She carefully peeled away the white bow and gold wrapping paper on the biggest box before opening it. When she pulled back the cardboard lid, she screamed. "The boots from the store!" She immediately put them on her bare feet.

I laughed, delighting in her joy, how she could so wholly love something so simple.

"They look great on you," Fletcher said.

"A true cowgirl," I added with a smile. "They should match that hat I gave you too."

She ran back to her bedroom, getting my old cowgirl hat, and walked out swinging her hips. She looked adorable in her nightgown and the cowgirl getup.

"I love it," I said. "Just one more gift." I grabbed the two small boxes from the top of the pile. "These technically are for you and your dad. I figured this is Maya's birthday, but it's also the day you became a dad."

Fletcher tilted his head, his brown eyes weighing on me as I handed both of them a box.

They peeled back the paper at the same time and opened the items. Maya got to her gift first. The silver necklace caught the light as she pulled the chain from dark blue velvet.

"A heart necklace," she said, staring at it.

"A locket," I replied. "Open it."

She studied it closer, finding the clasp, and then split it in two. On one side, a photo of her dad, the other a picture of her mom.

"Mommy and Daddy," she breathed. "But where are you?"

My throat felt tight with emotion. "I'm in the heart. Every time you look at it, I want you to remember that I'll always be here for you. No matter what."

Fletcher blinked quickly as he rubbed my back. "That's great of you, Liv." He opened his box next, taking out the silver bracelet matching the design on her locket.

"It's to match Maya's," I explained.

"I love it," he said. He put it on and then pulled me into a hug.

I leaned into his arms, letting him embrace me and trying to enjoy this moment with the man I adored and the girl we both loved so much. I knew, deep in my heart, it would be one of the last.

Hayes and Knox came over to pick up Maya and take her to the diner for milkshakes before her party. Liv left soon after to set up the food, drinks, and dessert where we'd be ending the float. And I stayed in Maya's room, packing her bag for a weekend with her mom and dreading the moment Regina would arrive with her boyfriend. My old friend.

Maya was going home with her after the party, and it would just be Liv and me and the chasm my past had created between us.

I carefully folded some of Maya's favorite dresses, setting them in the suitcase. Her clothes with the eight on the tag were just a reminder of her growth. I remembered packing up her infant clothes and wondering how so many of them still had brand-new tags. Then boxing up her toddler clothes and not believing that she'd ever been so small. Before I knew it, she'd be ten, then a teenager, and moving on to live a life of her own.

My little girl.

The doorbell echoed through the house, and Graham yapped loudly, his claws scrabbling over the hardwood toward the foyer.

"Oh hush," I told him, following him to the front door.

When I opened it, I saw Regina in a flowy white shirt and denim shorts beside my old colleague, Ben. He wore swim trunks and a T-shirt, different from the business clothing I'd always seen him in.

"Fletcher," he said, extending his hand.

I nodded, wishing I could say it was good to see him. "Come on in."

They followed me inside, and Regina said, "Wow, I didn't know they made houses like this in the boonies."

I tried to ignore the jab at small-town living and said, "It's a nice place for Maya and me to call home."

She didn't reply, looking around.

"Maya should be back soon," I said. "Why don't you two sit in the living room. Can I get you a drink?"

"I'd love a beer," Ben said.

You and me both, I thought.

"Just water," Regina replied, following Ben to the couch. "Where's Liv?"

Going to the fridge, I said, "She's prepping for the party. She's been so good to Maya today."

I'd brought them both drinks when my brother's loud truck came roaring into the driveway.

"Hayes?" Regina asked knowingly.

I chuckled. "Some things never change."

Soon, Maya came running into the house, a ring of chocolate around her lips. "MOMMY!" She ran to Regina, leaping into her arms.

To her credit, Regina didn't pull away from all the chocolate, instead circling her arms around our daughter. With Maya still on her lap, Regina said, "Maya, this is my boyfriend, Ben. Phoebe's dad."

"Hi," Maya said shyly.

"Nice to meet you," Ben said with a smile. "I heard you met Phoebe at Sugar Rush."

Maya nodded. "Did she come for the party?"

Ben shook his head. "She's with her mom this weekend."

Hayes and Knox came into the house in their swim trunks and cut-off T-shirts. They were nice enough to Regina and Ben, saying hi before Knox said, "Should we head out to the river, Fletch?"

I nodded. "It's about that time."

Maya asked, "Can I ride with Mommy and Ben?"

The fact that she didn't want to ride with me hit me in the gut. I knew I shouldn't be jealous, but some things didn't come so naturally. "If it's okay with your mom, it's okay with me," I finally said.

Regina smiled. "Of course it is. Ben, can you carry her bag to the trunk?"

"Sure thing," he said.

I turned to my brothers. "I'll ride with you two if that's okay."

Knox and Hayes said they'd wait in the truck, and I walked Ben back to Maya's room to get her bag. As we went, he said, "I really appreciate you letting me come to this party. I know it's awkward, but it means a lot to Regina. I think she was worried about being around all your family and friends after everything."

I held Maya's flower bag tightly in my hand, trying to

push back my frustration. My family had never been anything but kind to her. "I'm glad she started showing up for Maya."

Ben frowned. "Can I be straight with you?"

I lifted my chin, waiting for what he had to say.

"I've always respected you as a doctor, but what you did to Regina, it fucked her up pretty bad."

And there was the guilt. Heavy and pressing on my chest. I took deep breaths like I'd learned in therapy, remembering that breathing was one of the only ways to rid cortisol from my system. I didn't need to feel guilty for the past because I couldn't change it. I could only learn and grow from it. "She's still Maya's mom, regardless of what happened between us."

"But she's human too, and you of all people should know that means we make mistakes."

I passed him the bag, not wanting to have this conversation anymore. "Take care of my daughter while she's with you. She has a cell phone in this bag that can make calls to me or Liv. Have her call us if she needs anything. Nothing's too small."

"Got it," Ben said, taking the bag.

We walked out of the house, and when I got into the truck with my brothers, Hayes said, "He looks like a tool."

I chuckled, patting him on the back. "I love you too."

61

LIV

I was pretty sure the creek had never seen this many people on it at one time. Twelve out of twenty kids from Maya's class showed up with a parent, then my whole family was there and all the Madigan boys.

Hayes had found a waterproof speaker and was blasting Shania Twain. Fletcher was up toward the front of the group floating down the river, closer to Maya and her mom. Meanwhile, I brought up the back with my parents.

As Mom and I lagged behind, she put her hand on mine atop my tube and said, "I'm sorry about last weekend, honey. I didn't mean to put my nose where it didn't belong."

My throat felt tight because I'd been holding back tears all day. "You were right, Mom."

"What do you mean?" she asked.

I let out a heavy breath before lowering my voice and saying, "Fletcher doesn't want to get married."

"Like soon?" she asked.

I shook my head. "He never wants to get married."

She covered her mouth with her hands. "No, honey..."

I wiped at my face, but only accomplished rubbing some sunscreen in my eyes, making them sting even worse. "I thought we had something special, but he can't let go of his past enough to give us a future." Before Mom could say anything, I added, "Maya's going to be at her mom's for the long weekend, and I need to know if it's okay for me to move back into the house."

"You're moving out? Are you sure?" she asked. "Maybe he just needs more time to get used to the idea of marrying again. Lord knows men can be slow to come around sometimes."

"I don't want him to 'come around.' I want him to want to marry me." I half laughed through the tears. "Gosh, I shouldn't be crying at a little girl's birthday party. Sorry, let's just have a good time."

"You cry all you need," Mom said.

I shook my head. "It's not the time." That would come later.

When we reached the end of our float, the table was set up on the sandy bank. I had worked all morning to make it a cute space with a colorful tablecloth and tissue paper decorations hanging from the cottonwood trees.

While everyone sat around the card tables we'd hauled out here, I got out the cookie cake with the sparkler candles and lit them.

Fletcher helped me carry it toward Maya as more than thirty people sang "Happy Birthday" at the top of our lungs, making birds start and flutter from the trees.

When we reached my favorite little girl, I said, "Make a wish!"

She grinned at me and said, "I don't need to. I wished my dad would fall in love with you, and it already came true."

My heart ached as she blew out the candles.

For the next couple hours, the kids splashed in the slow-moving stream and the adults hung out, talked, drank beer from red coolers filled with melting ice. But eventually, the sun started to sink, and we had to call it a day.

My parents and brothers went about driving everyone back to their cars at the beginning of the river while Fletcher and I worked to clean up the party space.

We had to fold up all the tables and chairs, fill garbage bags with the disposable tablecloths, and toss out all the beer cans and paper plates. Fletcher and I didn't talk much, working silently side by side as the wind rustled through the trees and the river song played beside us.

But then new music began playing from Fletcher's phone.

I looked over, seeing him standing with his hand outstretched. "Dance with me?"

Glancing around, I said, "We still have some work to do..."

The opening lyrics to "Ten Thousand Hours" played from his phone. "Please?"

My heart ached as I slipped my hand in his. Because this didn't feel like a dance in the middle of the country.

It felt like goodbye.

WHEN WE GOT BACK to the house, I went to the bathroom and showered, rinsing the river water from my hair. But I was only putting off the inevitable.

I came out of the bathroom, wearing shorts and T-shirt, and found Fletcher waiting in his room, sitting on the end of the bed.

"You decided," he said. It wasn't a question.

I set my wet towel on the table by the door. "I did."

His features fell. "Can I talk you out of it?"

My chin trembled as I shook my head.

"Liv..." He got up, but I stepped back.

I needed to get this out. "I'm moving in with my parents. My mom and dad are going to look after me while I recover from the surgery next week. I'm sure your dad and brothers can be with Maya after school."

His lips parted. "You're quitting?"

"No. I told you I'd be here for Maya, and that isn't changing, but I can't live in this house with you. Not when it's a reminder that I almost had everything I've always wanted."

His brown eyes were full of pain, void of light. "But it's just a ceremony. We can still build a life together."

"If it was 'just a ceremony,' we wouldn't be having this conversation," I said. "We both know it's more than that. And I'm not going to stay here, hoping—" My voice broke, and I took a shuddering breath. "Hoping to convince you that life with me would be worth it."

His lips parted, and he held his hands out to me. "It's not a question if you're worth it, Liv. We both know you'd be the best wife in the world."

"Then it's your past," I said, tears sliding down my cheeks. "And even though you're not married to Regina, and you're not in love with her, you're not letting her go. You're not letting go of the person you were when you told her 'I do.'"

"I love you, Liv," he said, reaching for my hands.

This time, I let him take them.

"I love you, Fletcher. But I love myself too."

He held me close, cupping the back of my neck as he kissed my forehead. "I wish I could be what you deserved."

I stepped back, looking into his eyes. "You could be, Fletcher." I twisted my lips to the side. "I'll see you next Monday, when I've had a chance to recover from the surgery."

"You're leaving now?" he asked.

I looked around the room. "I'm out of reasons to stay."

62

LIV

I drove away from Fletcher, from *home*, tears streaming down my cheeks.

I barely registered the music on the radio or the countryside passing out the window until I reached the Griffen Farms sign. Just like the windmill tattoo on my arm reminded me, these would always be my people. This would always be home. No matter how far I went, no matter who came in and out of my life.

I pulled into the lot and got out of the truck, taking deep breaths and wiping my eyes as I walked down the sidewalk. The lights in the house were off, but the door was unlocked. I went inside, but I couldn't find it in myself to lie alone in my childhood bed. It would be just another reminder that I was right back where I started. No college degree. No life partner. No home. Nothing to show for thirty years of life.

So I walked to my parents' front door, left open as always. My dad's snores echoed through the room, familiar, soothing. And I went to my mom's side of the bed, kneeling beside her.

"Mom," I whispered, my voice breaking. "Mom."

Her eyes snapped open, and she took me in. "Liv?" Understanding registered on her face. "No..."

"I had to leave," I cried over the words. "I couldn't stay there, and I can't be alone. Not right now."

She scooted back and said, "Come here, honey." She lifted the blanket.

I curled under the covers as she wrapped her arm around my middle, and I cried until I couldn't keep my eyes open anymore.

It hurt like hell to leave that man with his big brown eyes begging me to stay. But I had to stand up for myself and what I wanted in life, even if it ripped my heart to shreds. This was the gift of growing older—perspective.

I'd been through heartbreak before.

I'd survived, even if it had never hurt this bad.

And I had to have faith that someday I would find a man who had the same dreams in life as I did and would give me all of himself. If not, it would be better to be alone than living with someone, knowing they didn't love me quite as much as I loved them.

63

FLETCHER

I sat on my couch, staring at the blank TV screen, and Graham pushed his head under my hand.

My heart broke further as I scratched his ears, remembering how he came to be ours. "She's gone," I whispered.

He let out a short whine.

"I know. Me too."

I looked around the house and saw Liv everywhere. At the counter, making pancakes in the morning. On the living room floor, wrapping Maya in her tortilla blanket. On the couch, laughing at a movie she'd seen a million times before.

If I got up and left the living room, I'd only see more of her.

Coming into my room during a nightmare to make sure I was okay.

Sitting with Maya at bedtime, singing "Red River Valley."

Lying with me in her room, curled together as her breaths slowed and evened.

With Maya in the bathroom, letting her experiment with makeup.

Stepping toward me on the front porch, wearing a stunning blue dress.

Telling me my mom would be proud of me.

She'd brought so much sunshine into my life, and now I felt caught in the dark.

So I got off the couch and took Graham with me to the truck. I started driving without knowing where I was going. I half expected to end up at the cemetery to see my mom. But instead, I parked in front of a white clapboard house, wild sunflowers waving from the flowerbeds, illuminated by the front porch light.

He was the first person I needed and the last one who'd want to see me.

But I couldn't stop myself as I walked to the front door, Graham trailing at my heels. I pushed the doorbell, and a few moments later, Rhett pulled back the wooden door, looking at me through the screen door. He wore sweats and no shirt and ran his hand over his hair.

"Don't you know it's late?" he asked, his voice scratchy.

"I know you're going to hate me. But Liv and I broke up, and I—" My voice broke. "I need you."

He stared at me for a long moment. I half expected him to slam the door in my face. To come out and punch me. Instead, he reached out, pushing the screen door open for me, then walked to his small kitchen table. The one that used to be in his grandpa's house.

"Sit," he told me, going to the freezer. As I did, I

watched him get a tube of cookie dough from the top shelf.

"I can't eat," I said, with my stomach still roiling.

"If my mom taught me anything, it's that nothing fixes things like a chocolate chip cookie. She just didn't know frozen dough is ten times easier and does the trick just fine." He pulled out a knife and sliced through the packaging in silence. I watched as he lined a baking sheet with parchment paper and rows of cookies.

"Why did you let me in?" I asked, still waiting for him to blow up at me.

When he had the pan in the oven, he poured Graham a bowl of water. He set it on the linoleum floor and said, "When your mom was really sick, near the end, she asked to talk to me alone."

My eyebrows rose. "What? You never told me about that."

"Seemed like it was between her and me," he said with a shrug, his back still to me, the scar still full of color. "She told me you would need a friend and asked me to be there for you, always. I promised her I would."

My heart wrenched. Maybe I had come to Mom tonight without even knowing it. Because even beyond the grave, she was still there for me. And so was Rhett.

He went back to his fridge and got out a gallon of milk, poured me a glass in a mason jar.

"I think I need something stronger," I muttered.

He shook his head. "Take it from someone who tried to drink away a girl. Some things are meant to be felt."

I stared at my glass, then took a sip. "Go ahead. Tell me how stupid I am."

"Seems like we both already know," he replied. "But I gotta ask... What happened?"

"She wants to get married someday, and I...can't. I just can't." I ran my hands over my face, wishing I could have stood up to Rhett in high school and dated Liv then, back when we didn't have baggage like we do now. The only thing I wouldn't change is Maya.

"Because of Regina?" Rhett asked.

"Because of me. You can't take marriage vows twice, Rhett. They mean something."

He drew his eyebrows together. "Didn't Regina leave you?"

"What does that have to do with it?" I asked. "We promised forever, and last I checked, that's a hell of a lot longer than eight years."

Rhett said, "Because you would have stood by her your whole damn life even though you *knew* she wasn't the one. I know everyone talks about storybook endings, but the wedding vows don't say you have to be madly, recklessly in love. Just that you're there for that person no matter what. As far as I'm concerned, you can still stand by the promises you made to Regina, look out for her in sickness and health, richer and poorer, because you have to for Maya. But what you have with Liv..." He shook his head, ran his thumb over his bottom lip. "That's fucking magic, Fletch. It's once-in-a-lifetime kind of love, and you can't make both of you lose out on it because of a mistake you made eight years ago. You have a chance to build a life, build a family with the best girl in the world. Are you really going to let it go because you can't forgive yourself and turn over a new leaf?"

My chest tightened, and Graham climbed up my leg. I

picked him up, holding him near because he was the closest thing I had to Liv and Maya right now. "What if it's too late?" I asked. "Liv moved out."

Rhett chuckled. "You're a doctor. Shouldn't you know it's only too late when your heart quits beating?"

64

MAYA

Mom's new house with Ben was nice. They even asked me what color I wanted to paint a wall in my bedroom there. I went to the store with Mom and picked my favorite shade of purple, and Mom and I painted the wall together.

I just liked spending time with her. I missed her, even though I liked living with Daddy and Livvy.

But while we painted the wall, Mom got a phone call. She smiled at me and said, "Don't get any paint on the carpet, okay? Be extra careful."

I nodded as she walked out, leaving me alone. I liked to paint flower shapes on the wall before covering it all the way with paint. Maybe I could talk Daddy into letting me paint flowers onto my wall at home. I betted Livvy would help me.

I could hear Mom talking on the phone in the hallway but couldn't quite tell what she was saying. Hopefully she didn't have to leave. I really did like spending time with her, even if we weren't painting. I would have watched her pay bills, and that was super boring.

Mom came back into the room and said, "Looks like we have some extra time together. Your daddy said he'd come and pick you up this afternoon instead of us driving back there."

Good thing he wasn't getting me early, because then I would have argued, and Daddy didn't like me arguing. "Why?" I asked anyways. "Is he bringing Graham?" Next time, I wouldn't leave my doggy at home. I'd sneak him in my suitcase, even though Ben was allergic to dogs.

"I didn't ask about Graham, but I can text him," Mom said. "And I'm sure he'll explain the change in plans when he gets here, but I think it's good news."

"How good?" I asked.

She smiled. "Really good."

I smiled, too, because I liked good surprises. "Can we finish painting first?"

"Absolutely," she said, picking up her brush again. "It's going to look so good."

I looked at the mostly-done wall. "I like it already."

"Good, because you're stuck with this color," she teased.

It took forever to finish up the room, but when we did, Mom peeled off all the tape and we stood back by my bed to look at the wall.

"What do you think?" she asked.

"I love it," I said. "Can I bring the extra paint back home?"

She laughed. "You need to take that up with your dad. Now go shower. Try to get that paint off your arm."

I liked the paint. It was almost like a tattoo like Liv

had. But I went to the shower and did what Mom asked because I wanted to hear Daddy's surprise.

When I got out of the shower and dressed in the bathroom, Daddy was with Mom, looking at my new room. It was nice that they were in the same room and not arguing anymore.

But they weren't fun together like Dad and Livvy or Mom and Ben. They always felt more like Daddy and Brenda together. Like they were doing a job.

Dad rubbed his hands together and said, "Ready, kiddo?"

"I'm ready for the surprise," I said. "But where's Graham?"

"Uncle Rhett's watching him for the day," Daddy said.

"I wanted to see him, but that's okay. Because Rhett is fun and Graham will have fun with him."

Daddy smiled and said, "Why don't you say bye to Mommy?"

I looked at my mom getting that hot spiky feeling in my chest. I didn't like saying goodbye to her. And now I thought I might cry when I was just so happy.

Mommy got on her knees in front of me and pulled me into a hug. "I promise you can come stay again next month, okay? And I will call you tonight."

I looked at her, not sure if she was telling the truth but hoping she was. "Do you promise?"

She nodded.

"Pinky promise? Tessa told me you can't break a pinky promise."

Mommy smiled and held up her pinky. I shook it extra hard so it would stick.

"I love you," she said. She said that a lot lately. It made me think she meant it.

"I love you too," I said, hugging her extra tight.

"Let's go," Daddy said.

We went out to his truck, and I climbed into the back seat, mostly because he said I couldn't sit in the front seat until I was at least twelve. Total bummer. He drove for a little while until we got to a park, and I said, "This isn't our house."

He laughed a little, like I said something funny. "I wanted to talk to you about something serious."

My face got all pinched because I was confused. "What is it?" I thought this was supposed to be a surprise.

He said, "Come on. Let's go to the swings."

We walked together to the swings, and I pulled my shorts down a little so the swing wouldn't burn the backs of my legs. Then I kicked off the ground to get started and asked again, "What's are we talking about?"

He used his legs to push himself back and forth and said, "It's about Liv. What do you think of her?"

"I love her," I said quickly. "She's totally fun." I stuck out my legs to show my cowboy boots. "And I *love* the boots she got me. Are you wearing your bracelet?"

He held out his arm showing me the bracelet on his wrist. I wondered if it made his hair itchy.

He asked, "What do you think about me dating her?"

"Well, kissing is totally gross."

He laughed again. But I still thought it was gross. "Do you have any worries about us being together?" he asked.

I thought about it for a second, which made me stop swinging as much. "I don't want you and Livvy to break up like you and Mommy did. That sucked."

His face confused me. He wasn't smiling, but he wasn't frowning either. "I agree; it sucked. And I don't want to break up with Livvy ever. That's why I got this." He moved his hips on the swing and pulled a box out of his pocket. He opened it, showing me a pretty ring with a sparkly diamond. "This was Grandma's ring. I want to give this to Liv and ask her to marry me, but only if you're okay with it, because we're all a family, and we all get a say."

I jumped out of the swing because I was just so dang happy! "Yes, Daddy! You need to ask her today!"

He smiled big, like he was hoping I'd say that. "I think it would mean more if we both asked her. Will you come with me?"

I nodded quickly. "But we need to get food on the way home because I'm hungry. Can we get ice cream?"

He laughed again. He seemed so happy now. "Okay, we'll get ice cream. You know, I missed you like crazy."

"I didn't miss you so much," I said. "Because I knew I'd see you in, like, two days."

Shaking his head, he said, "Come on, kiddo. Let's go see Liv."

65

LIV

I sat on the front porch swing, rocking back and forth in the hot sun, trying not to cry. Trying to think how I'd handle being back in Fletcher's home for work after my surgery. Seeing him, knowing he was my person, would feel like a knife to the heart. But I couldn't let Maya down either. I wished I'd listened to Farrah all those weeks ago, taken more caution. Because if Maya wasn't around, I'd get a job out of town for a couple of years to reset my heart, get Fletcher out of my system before moving back home.

Dad's truck came up the driveway from the pasture, and when he got out, he yelled over at me, "Go shower up, then come out. I need some help working on the windmill."

I let out a quiet groan. I didn't feel like doing anything other than sitting here and wallowing, but when Dad needed help, you just didn't say no. "Do I have to shower?"

"You've been moping around the house for two days.

You smell like shit," he said simply. The way only Dad could.

"Gee, thanks, Dad," I said sullenly.

"Nothing soap can't fix," he said.

I rolled my eyes, pushing up from the swing. "Be back in ten."

I went upstairs, took a quick shower and then pulled my wet hair into a twist atop my head. Since we'd be working, I changed into a pair of jeans, boots and a T-shirt. When I went back out, Dad was waiting in the truck, the window down and country music playing. Of course, it was another heartbreak song. I swore they'd followed me these last two days.

I walked down the driveway to him and said, "Are you sure you can't wait 'til Mom gets back from town to help?"

"Why would I wait when I have you?" He winked.

I got in the truck and sunk back in my seat. "I'm not going to be much fun to be around."

"And why's that?" He put the truck in gear before driving over the dirt path toward the pasture with the windmill.

I stared at him. "Did you fall off the windmill earlier or something?"

Dad shook his head. "Not that I remember."

My lips twitched at the joke. "You should get that checked out."

"I'm fine," he said.

"Are you sure?" I teased.

"Course I am."

"How do you know?"

"Because I'm old, and when you get to be my age, you

can sense things. Like when two people are meant to be together."

My eyes stung with tears. "I don't want to talk about it."

"I do," he said. "Humor me."

"What's the point?" I asked. Didn't you hear? This is the end of the road for Fletcher and me. He doesn't want marriage. Not ever again."

Dad looked over at me, catching my gaze. "I need you to hear this. Because I know I messed up a lot as a dad, but I've been with your mom thirty-six years now, so I know a thing or two about marriage."

I nodded, folding my arms tightly around my chest, because thinking about Fletcher, relationships, marriage, it hurt like hell.

"When two people love each other, you'll reach times when you feel like it's the end of the road. Most of the time, it's not a dead end; it's time to make a turn and get yourselves going in the right direction again."

"I'll happily use that advice someday," I said. "When there are two people in eternal love instead of just one."

"What about three?" he asked.

My eyebrows drew together, but I didn't have time to ask what he meant, because the windmill came into view as we crested the hill. And standing by the water tank was Fletcher and Maya.

"What's happening?" I asked, tears filling my eyes at the sight of them. I couldn't be imagining things, could I?

Dad reached over and rubbed my shoulder, continuing toward the two loves of my life. "You get to decide now if this is a dead end or time for a turn in the right direction. I'll support you either way." He stopped several yards away from Fletcher and Maya, and I stared at them through the windshield, not believing they were here.

Just the sight of Fletcher in his jeans and button-down shirt with the sleeves rolled was a balm to my heart. And Maya was so precious in her shorts and tank top and cowboy boots. I'd missed her so much, and it had only been a couple days.

"Go on," Dad said. "You at least need to hear him out."

My heart raced jauntily in my chest as I got out of the truck and walked toward them. "What are you doing here?" I asked.

Maya grinned at her dad. "We have a question for you, Livvy."

My lips parted as I stared from her to Fletcher. "What?"

Fletcher reached into his pocket, then knelt in the dirt. Maya got to her knees beside him, and she took the top off the box, revealing a ring I recognized.

I covered my mouth. "Your mother's ring?"

Fletcher said, "I know I've messed up a lot in my life, but letting another moment go without you isn't going to be one of my mistakes. Maya, me, you, we're a family, and I want to make the kind of family that never breaks up, the kind that's there for each other through it all." He looked at Maya and nodded.

Maya smiled up at me as she put her arm around her dad. "Will you marry my daddy?"

Tears flowed down my cheeks as I stared between the two of them. But I had to ask a question of Fletcher before I gave my answer. "Are you sure this is what you want?"

"I've never been surer of anything than I am of my feelings for you, Olivia Griffen. I've loved you since I was a kid, and I know that's never going to end. I'm sorry it took me a little while to realize that's exactly why we should get married. If that's still what you want."

Maya nodded quickly at me, mouthing, *Say yes.*

I let out a tearful laugh. "Of course I'll marry you." I went to hug them both, holding them tight and knowing I had more than a family. I had a home.

66

FLETCHER

Liv's dad got out of the truck, whooping and cheering for us.

As we broke apart from our hug, Maya said, "Does that mean I get to call you Grandpa Jack now?"

Jack picked her up and said, "Of course it does, kiddo."

She hugged his neck, grinning, and I swore I'd never felt happier than I did right now.

"Let's go back to the house," Jack said. "I'll put some steaks on the grill, and we'll celebrate."

Liv and I agreed that sounded like a great plan. We rode back with him, and while Jack had Maya help him get the food ready, Liv and I went up to the bedroom to call everyone to tell them our good news.

Della screamed so loudly, I thought my eardrums might break.

I swore Tyler and Henrietta were both crying for us from the amount of sniffles coming through the phone.

Gage immediately offered to pay for our honeymoon

as a wedding gift.

My dad said, "It's about damn time."

Rhett whooped and hollered for us.

Knox said, "How's it feel to know I dated your girl?"

Liv popped off, "Better than knowing my future brother-in-law bailed on our date."

"Water under the bridge," Knox returned.

Hayes laughed, saying, "If you have to get married, I guess Liv's a good one to do it with."

Ford wanted us to get married in the off season, and Bryce made us promise to check with his class schedule before setting an official date.

But then we saw Liv's mom's car pull up in the driveway, and she ran downstairs, hugging her mom and telling her the good news.

Tears shined in Deidre's eyes as she looked between the two of us for confirmation. "I'm so excited for you both!"

As I looked between my future wife and her mother, embracing with tears in their eyes, it all felt real.

We were getting married.

"Have you decided on a date yet?" Deidre asked, pulling back and holding Liv's hands.

Liv and I exchanged a glance. "We haven't discussed dates. Yet," Liv said, sending me a cheeky grin. "How's tomorrow, Fletch?"

I smiled at her, imagining having her as my wife right away, but I realized that I wanted more. I put my hand on Liv's back and said, "If you don't mind, I want to do this right. My last wedding was rushed because we had Maya on the way. With you, I want it to be perfect. I want to send the invitations in the mail to everyone in town, I want to taste test cakes with you and pick out flowers and get fitted for tuxes with my brothers and hire the expensive photographer and make it the best day of your life. And most of all, I want time to write our own vows, so I can tell everyone we know how much I want to spend the rest of my life with you."

Liv's mom held her hands to her chest, crying even more now, but Liv came to me. "Are you sure? I know it's a lot with your new practice and Maya and..."

I silenced her with a kiss. "I will never ask you to sacrifice because I'm busy. You are my priority."

"You mean it?" Liv asked.

I nodded. "Absolutely."

Liv glanced back toward her mom and grinned. "Mom, you ready to plan a wedding?"

Her mom was smiling so big her cheeks must hurt. "Thank God you're not springing a wedding on me like Tyler and Henrietta."

Liv laughed, holding her mom's hand and mine. "Their wedding was perfect, and ours will be too."

Her mom's voice cracked. "I'm just so happy for you."

I held Liv close to my side, never wanting to let her go. "Is it okay if we have it at your family's ranch?"

Liv nodded. "I'd love that."

"Of course," Diedre said. "Nothing would make me happier."

For the rest of the night, as Liv's family and friends showed up to celebrate. The food, beer, and tears flowed freely late into the evening. Even though our wedding wouldn't be for a while, I already felt like we were living happily ever after.

67

LIV

Six months later

I drove to the Cottonwood Falls Cemetery and got out of my truck, carrying a bouquet of flowers to my future mother-in-law's grave. With mine and Fletcher's wedding the next day, I knew he was feeling her absence more than ever. So was I.

Maya's namesake was an amazing friend to my mom, but also to me. She made sure the boys looked after me and always helped me feel included, even though I was younger. She told me I was the daughter she never had, and I couldn't help but wish she could be my mother-in-law in person instead of in spirit. I knew she would have been an amazing Grandma to Maya and cheerleader to me.

I reached her headstone and ran my hand over the rough marble at the top. "Fletcher and I are getting married tomorrow." I smiled tearfully. "I always thought of you as a second mom, and now you really are." The spring wind cooled the tears falling down my cheeks, and I wiped them away. "You raised an amazing man. He's not perfect, but he has your heart, always there for other people and trying so hard to do the right thing. He's the best dad to Maya, and I want you to know I'll always love them both with my whole heart."

I looked at the bouquet in my hand and said, "I asked our florist to make an extra bouquet for you, because I knew if you were here, you'd be walking him down the aisle and dancing with him in the backyard." My smile shook as I laid the flowers among all the other gifts her family had left. "Thank you, for raising my future husband."

I kissed my hand and dropped it atop the stone, feeling so much love for this woman, and when the wind stilled for a moment with the sun shining down, I swore it was her, loving me right back.

I left the cemetery and drove back to my parents' house, where all the girls and I were having a sleepover before the big day.

Mom, Maya, and my niece, Cora, were in the kitchen making cookies while Della, Henrietta, and Farrah were in the living room picking a movie for us to watch. As I took it in, it struck me that I was already living my dream.

I had a big family full of love, regardless of whether I had biological children or not. The surgery to remove extra tissue because of endometriosis had gone well, and my gynecologist was hopeful for my fertility, but conceiving would still be a miracle.

"Need any help?" I asked Mom and the girls as I took off my jacket.

Maya looked up and said, "Can you make some of that homemade frosting so we can decorate the cookies?"

"Sure thing," I replied, going to the fridge for the cream cheese. I worked for the next half hour, making frosting in multiple colors and separating them into Ziplock bags with a corner cut off.

We took the bags of icing and the cookies to the living room, vegging out and watching Maya's favorite movie, *The Parent Trap*.

When we finished with the movie, Mom said, "We did something before my wedding to Liv's dad that I thought was so special. We went around the room, and everyone gave me advice for my future. I'll go first." Mom scooted closer to me across the floor littered with pillows and put her hand on my cheek. "This is something Fletcher's mom told me before the wedding. Lead with love, always. It was the best advice I ever got."

I smiled, holding her hand to my cheek. "Thanks, Mom."

Farrah smiled, saying, "I've made a lot of mistakes in marriage, but I think the best thing you can do is make sure you're marrying a man with a good heart. Because even if he makes mistakes, he'll do all he can to heal them. Your brother is one of the best there is."

I grinned at my sister-in-law, reaching toward the couch to squeeze her hand. I loved knowing that at least two of my brothers had found their happily ever after.

Della said, "I'm not married yet, but I'll give you a piece of selfish advice. You might be Mrs. Madigan, but you're still Liv. Don't forget us while you're living your happily ever after."

I hugged my friend tightly. "I could never forget you, Della. You're still my soulmate."

Della wiped at her eyes, making moisture form in my own.

Mom brushed back Cora's hair. "What about you, honey?"

Cora tapped her chin thoughtfully. "Gage always picks Mommy dandelions from the yard. Tell Fletcher he should do that too."

I giggled at her sweetness, and Farrah sent me a wink. "I'll tell him that," I said.

Maya said, "I think you should make Daddy the pancakes with his name in chocolate chips. That always makes me really happy."

"Sweet girl," I said, kissing the top of her head. "Of course I will."

Henrietta was last. She smiled at me as she said, "Before I married Tyler, my dad told me to see disagreements as opportunities to come back stronger than ever. It's been huge in helping us have a marriage and a business together."

"It's good advice," I agreed. I took in the room at these women who were here to celebrate Fletcher and me. They'd been with us every messy step, always looking out for me, even when it meant having hard conversations. "I want to thank you all for being here with me. I know it hasn't been easy, and it might seem fast, but when it comes to Fletcher, I feel like I've been waiting all my life."

68

FLETCHER

All the guys were dressing at my dad's house while the bridal party got ready at the Griffens'. I never thought I'd be having another wedding, but today felt so different than the first time.

Instead of marrying out of a sense of obligation, I was marrying Liv because I couldn't imagine living my life without her. These past six months had been the best of my life, and even though I knew troubles were sure to come, so would endless amounts of love and happiness.

I thought back to what Doctor Deb told me about finding something that fills my soul, and Liv was it. She made me gentler with Maya, more fun around the house, open to new adventures like having a roadside puppy (who Maya insisted on being a flower dog today) and even planting roots in a small town like generations of Madigans before me.

Hayes came behind me in the mirror and said, "Let me help you with your tie. It's crooked as shit."

I laughed. "Thank you."

Hayes adjusted the knot, and from the desk chair Knox, said, "Looking good, brother. Especially now that your head's out of your ass."

I rolled my eyes at him, but then said, "Thank you for your help with that extrication, by the way."

The door to the room opened, and I heard Rhett say, "I have something for you, Fletch."

I turned, looking at my friend in a suit. I'd expected him to look out of place when not wearing jeans and boots, but he cleaned up well. "What is it?"

He passed me an envelope, and I drew my eyebrows together, peeling back the flap and seeing a letter from Liv.

DEAR FLETCHER MADIGAN,

I'd like to formally submit my resignation from my duties as your nanny, effective immediately. I'm eager to assume my new role as your wife.

Love,

Liv

I CHUCKLED, scrubbing my hand over my face and held up the paper. "Her letter of resignation."

The guys around me laughed, and Rhett said, "Better than a bucket load of shit."

"Or a dick on the hood of my truck." I teased.

Dad shook his head like he didn't want to know.

Rhett put his hand on my shoulder. "I never told you how excited I am to have you as my brother."

I shook my head, hugging him. "You've always been

my brother, Rhett." My throat got tight as he clapped my back.

"Then let's make it official."

I stood in front of the floor length mirror in my room wearing my mother's wedding dress.

My wedding dress.

My hair was curled into an up-do with a veil tucked into the bun. A necklace with Maya's birthstone, a sapphire, hung around my neck for something blue. My engagement ring was old and my dress borrowed.

"Shit," I muttered.

Farrah came closer, wielding the tide pen she kept on her person at all times. "Did you spill some mimosa on your dress?"

I shook my head. "I forgot 'something new.'"

Rhett's voice came through the door. "I think I've got something for that."

I turned, seeing him coming into the room with all my bridesmaids. He tilted his head, putting his hand over his mouth. "Sis... you look."

My eyes stung. "Don't you make me cry, Rhett Griffen."

He shook his head, coming to hug me. "That song is bullshit. Cowboys cry when their sister's getting married."

I hugged him back and when he pulled back, I said, "Does it count as new if I borrowed it from you?"

He reached into his pocket and got out his wallet.

I said, "I swear if you give me a condom."

He tossed his head back, laughing as he took out a condom with a pink, shiny wrapper from his wallet. "I just got it from the store this morning. I usually use one with one of the bridesmaids, but I know all of them at this wedding, so..."

I hit his shoulder. "Are you ever going to grow up?"

He shrugged. "Where's the fun in that?"

"What's a condom?" Maya asked.

"Party balloon," Rhett said quickly.

"Can I have one?" she asked, coming closer.

"When you're thirty," he replied, handing me the condom.

Laughing, I took it from him and bent down, lifting the layers of mom's dress so I could tuck the condom in my boot. For something new, it would certainly do.

"It's time," Mom said.

Rhett excused himself, and I glanced around the room at my friends Della and Henrietta in lilac bridesmaids' dresses and Maya in her poufy flower girl dress, and I said, "Can I have a second alone with Maya?"

Everyone wished me luck before shuffling out of the room, leaving just Maya and me behind. Her dress was white with a lilac band around her waist. She held her cowboy hat with flower petals inside, ready for the ceremony.

I took the hat, putting it aside, and sat down on the bed. "Sit with me?" I asked.

"Okay." She slid into my lap, a layer of tulle spread around us.

I gave her a hug and said, "I just want you to know that your daddy and I are getting married, but you always come first, okay? We both love you like crazy."

"I know that," she said. "Can I put Graham's leash on?"

I laughed. I'd been worried about her and how she'd feel with her dad remarrying so soon, but she was all on board. "Sure you can," I said, smiling. She went to the spot where he lay on his dog bed like a little prince, clipping on his leash. Then we went to the door to see Dad waiting for me. His hazel eyes filled with tears, and he covered his mouth with his hand. "You are a beautiful bride, Olivia Griffen."

"Dad." My voice cracked.

I hugged him tight, and Maya rushed by saying to Graham, "Come on, good boy! You're going to be the best flower dog there ever was!"

Dad chuckled and said, "Are you ready?"

I nodded. I'd never been more ready for anything.

Mom led Maya out of the room and then Dad held my hand as we walked downstairs so I wouldn't fall over. As we crossed the living room of the home I grew up in, I couldn't help but feel that everything was changing.

I would still be my parents' daughter, but more than that, I would be someone's wife. Someone's stepmom.

I stopped at the patio door, and Dad looked over at me. "I love Fletcher, but if you gotta run, now's the time."

Letting out a tearful laugh, I shook my head. "I'm just realizing how much everything will change."

His smile was tender. "Sweetheart, everything's already changed. Just gotta make it official."

I nodded, studying my dad's face. He looked the same as always, even if he'd gotten signs of age over the years. Same smile. Same hazel eyes. Same hats he got free from the co-op every year.

"Dad!" I hissed, staring at him. "You were gonna wear your hat to walk me down the aisle!"

He felt at his head like he had to check it was there. "Well shit. Where's my cowboy hat?"

"You're hopeless," I said with a laugh as I looked around the living room for his hat. I found it hanging from a hook by the front door and passed it to him. "Now you're ready to walk me down the aisle."

He smiled as he swapped his ball cap for the black cowboy hat he only wore for special occasions. "I might be ready to walk you down the aisle, darling, but I'll never be ready to give you away."

"Dad..." My voice broke.

But he hugged me tight and said, "You be here on Wednesday nights or a take my blessing back."

"Yes sir," I said with a smile.

"Now." He held out his elbow for me, and I looped my arm through his.

He opened the curtain, showing our wedding out back, everyone sitting on haybales covered with flannel. At the end of the makeshift aisle, stood all the brides-maids, the groomsmen, and Maya and Graham were reaching the end of the aisle where my future husband stood.

Dad slid the door open, and we stepped onto the patio. Everyone stood and turned to face us, but all I had eyes for was the man at the end of the aisle.

Fletcher wore a suit with a lilac tie and pocket square. His hands were folded in front of him, and his smile shook as I walked toward him.

Tears fell down my cheek as I realized that this was my person, and I was getting to spend forever by his side.

Suddenly, this aisle was too long. My dad was walking too slow.

I wanted forever to start right now.

Graham let out a yip when he saw me, making me and everyone around me laugh.

Then Fletcher started walking toward me.

Dad said, "Looks like you're not the only eager one."

Fletcher met us at the middle of the aisle and took my face in his hands, kissing me as I hugged him back.

When we pulled apart, Fletcher said, "Standing there seemed stupid when I wanted to kiss you so damn bad."

I let out a laugh. "Dad wouldn't let me run to you."

From up front, Rhett called, "Too early, Fletch! But I'm sure that's nothing new."

Fletcher rolled his eyes at my brother, and I laughed.

"Are you ready?" Fletcher asked me.

I nodded.

"Good. Wait here." He walked back to the front of the aisle, and then Dad and I resumed our walk toward my new life as Mrs. Madigan.

70

FLETCHER

The preacher greeted everyone and spoke about marriage, but I had a hard time hearing any of it with Liv standing across from me. She was the most beautiful woman I'd ever seen, with her brown curls framing her face, dimples dotting her cheeks with her smile. And the way the afternoon sun caught her blue eyes, it was like the sun existed only to be reflected in her gaze.

Liv squeezed my hands, and I squeezed back. It was like I needed to feel her to know this was reality and not some fantasy I was dreaming.

But then I heard the word vows and knew I needed to focus on marrying this woman in front of me.

Liv glanced back at Della, and Della handed her a slip of paper. As Liv unfolded it, I saw her neat handwriting across the lines.

But instead of reading from it, she glanced to the front row where Maya and Graham sat with my Dad.

"Maya, sweetie, can you come up here?" Liv asked.

Maya nodded, standing up and bringing Graham to

the altar. He tried to jump, and I moved to pull him away, but Liv bent down and scratched his ears.

Maya knelt beside him, taking him in her lap to sooth him, and Liv. My future wife. She sat down in her wedding dress on the wooden platform. My throat already feeling tight, I knelt beside Maya, a hand on her shoulder.

The preacher handed Liv a microphone, and she thanked him softly before turning to face my daughter and me. But then she only had eyes for Maya, and I had to sniff back tears.

"Your daddy and I are getting married today. Pretty crazy huh?" I heard a soft chuckle go through our family and friends, but Maya only nodded. "Marriage is a big deal for your Daddy and me, but also for you, and I want you both to know, that I understand you two are a package deal. So Maya, I promise you that I will always be there for you, on good days and bad days, when a random coyote shows up in the yard, when you're accidentally putting gum in my hair, and when we're pulling pranks on your dad. When you're sick, hurt, sad... I'll be there. I promise to always support your relationship with your mom and never come between you. And I promise, if your dad and I ever have a baby together that you will be loved every bit as much as that baby and treated just the same. Deal?"

She nodded. "Graham too?"

I let out a tearful laugh. Of course, she'd want the damn dog to be a part of the deal. He was her best friend in the world.

Liv smiled and aimed her gaze at the dog in Maya's

lap. "Graham, you'll always be our special road dog. We love you to bits and pieces."

Maya smiled, satisfied, and I wiped at my eyes again.

"You can go sit with Grampy, sweetie," Liv told Maya.

As she and Graham went back to my sniffling dad, I stood and helped Liv up too.

Thank you, I mouthed. What she did meant more to me than she'd ever know.

71

LIV

I tilted my head with a smile, glancing at my paper so I wouldn't miss a part of what I had to say. "Fletcher Madigan. You have been my brother's best friend. My prom date. The guy I crushed on from afar and the one who made me wonder what might have been. You've been my friend. My boss. My inspiration. The love of my life. And I'm so glad you'll soon become my husband." I choked on my words, overcome with emotion. Taking a deep breath, I wiped at my eyes and smiled across the aisle at him. "I promise, I will always be there for you. I'll be your best friend when you get home from work, your partner in crime when the kids are asleep, your girlfriend on date nights, a soft place to land when you've had a hard day, a kick in the ass when you need it, because we all know you'll need it." He let out a tearful laugh, and I reached up, cupping his cheek, "And I promise, for as long as I live, I'll be your wife every moment in between."

He held my hand and kissed it.

I smiled up at him before passing him the microphone.

Fletcher reached into his pocket, taking out a notebook. He flipped over the cover and held it as he spoke, his thick, dark, contrasting his skin.

"Olivia Griffen, when you walked into the doctor's office, I was lost as sea doing my best not to drown under the weight of it all. Not just my responsibilities, but the guilt of my past. I asked you to be my nanny, not knowing you'd quickly become my everything. A smile I looked forward to seeing in the morning, a laugh I wanted to hear at every turn, a shoulder to lean on and above all else, the life raft I desperately needed.

"Over the years, you and I have lived parallel lives because of timing, distance, family loyalties, our careers, and sometimes my inability to realize when I have a good thing in front of me and shouldn't let go. I promise you, in front of all our family and friends, I will always remember that *we*, us together, are a blessing. I promise I will never take for granted the support you give me, or the invincible way you make me feel, like I can take on the world with you by my side. I'll always remind you exactly how beautiful and loved you are. And whether we have only Maya or a hundred babies, I promise, you'll live a life surrounded by family, friendship, and most of all, love."

He looked up at me, and I could see it in his eyes. *Forever.*

The preacher announced us man and wife, and Fletcher took me in his arms, kissing me until I forgot everyone around us. When he let go, I opened my eyes and saw him.

My husband.
My happily ever after.

EPILOGUE
RHETT

THREE MONTHS LATER

Hard to believe a few months ago, we'd celebrated Liv and Fletcher's wedding in this very backyard. Now, the grass was turning green and summer was finally coming back as we had another Wednesday night dinner. Fletcher and Maya had been a part of every last one for the last several months, and Grayson even came over most weeks.

It felt like our family was growing all the time, and even though they joked about me being a perpetual bachelor, I couldn't help feeling a little left out with everyone having their spouses and children around.

There'd only ever been one woman I loved that way, and I'd fucked it up so colossally it was better not to look back.

So instead, I sat at the table with everyone, drinking

my beer and eating my steak Dad refused to cook any way but medium rare.

Toward the end of the table, Liv stood up and said, "Can y'all be quiet for a sec?" When we only got marginally quieter, she said, "I know it's hard, but give me a few!"

The talking slowly died down and Liv grinned, reaching down to touch Fletcher's shoulder. "We have some news. We just found out Baby Madigan is on the way! Maya's going to be a big sister!"

If she thought we were loud before, she was in for it now because no one was louder or more excited than a group of Griffens finding out another baby was on the way.

Everyone got up, going to hug and congratulate them. I clapped Fletcher's hand and gave him a hug. "Congratulations. I'll try to forget this means you slept with my sister."

He nearly choked on his beer. Just made me laugh more.

I gave Liv a big hug and then put my hands on her shoulders. "Looks like you didn't use that condom." She hit my shoulder, but I only smiled. "I'm happy for you, sis. You got everything you always wanted."

She grinned, touching her stomach. "I'm happy... Are you?"

I looked her over. "What do you mean?"

She twisted her lips to the side, hesitating. "I just mean... you don't smile as much as you used to. Everything okay? No new diagnoses you're hiding from us?"

I took a drink of my beer, hating how she always saw

right through me. "Just realizing all my siblings are falling in love and leaving little ol' me behind."

She smiled slightly but then looked down.

"What?" I asked.

"Nothing," she said too quickly.

"Liv, come on."

"I just... heard something at the salon this morning while getting a haircut," she said, toying with the freshly trimmed ends of her hair.

"You know the technical term is *hairs* cut, right?" I teased.

She rolled her eyes at me. "I guess you don't really want to know."

I arched a brow. "Out with it."

She patted my arm. "Mags is moving back to Cottonwood Falls."

♡

Read Rhett's story in *Hello Heartbreaker!*

Find out where Liv, Fletcher, and Maya are nine years later in *Worth It, a FREE bonus story.*

Get the free bonus story today!

Start reading Hello Heartbreaker today!

AUTHOR'S NOTE

I grew up in a small town in western Kansas, and the community had very traditional values. Children were to be seen and not heard, you didn't talk back to your parents or any other adult for that matter, and you better clear your plate at the end of the meal if someone gave you food. Many adults expect children to be disciplined, you know, the whole "spare the rod, spoil the child" thing.

I had my own opinions on what I experienced growing up, but a lot of my views of the world were shaped by that upbringing... until I thought about becoming a parent.

I always knew, even as young as seventeen or eighteen, that if I were to have children, I wanted to adopt them. I personally didn't want to birth a child when there were so many children out there waiting for a family to step up and love them the way they deserved.

That dream stayed in the back of my mind until my husband and I bought our first home with an extra bedroom. We both had graduated college, had good jobs, and that dream of fostering a child came back stronger than ever.

My husband, in all his infinite wisdom, said we should volunteer with foster children first and find out if we were truly ready and had the skills we needed.

By fate, I believe, we landed at HALO in Oklahoma City, an organization that provides therapy and also training to foster and adoptive families all over the world. They're truly the best at what they do, and we were lucky enough to help with their main program.

In the program, we learned the basics of TBRI, trust based relational intervention, something that had been shown to really help children from hard places. We learned things like "all behavior is communication" and that trauma changes the way our brains work. It flipped everything we both knew about parenting on its head.

Instead of "punishing" to get compliance, we learned to teach skills over time that would help the child throughout their lives. We learned that often the worst behavior is the biggest cry for love and connection. And we learned how to build relationships with children who had been shown that adults hurt you and then leave or show up and take you away from the home you love.

When our boys were first placed in our care, our parenting looked really strange compared to how we were raised. We messed up and fumbled from time to time. But the most amazing things started to happen.

Our boys came to trust us as their safe adults. They began to play the way children should. They went to bed after thirty minutes of laying down instead of two hours.

It was the hardest, but most transformative experience, and I knew I had to share some of what I learned in this book.

Ever since I introduced Liv in Confessions of the Funny Fat Friend, I've been dying to write her story. When I began writing, I knew she was older and had been single for a while, but I also knew she wouldn't settle for just any guy. She needed someone mature, who'd built up grit and strength and patience and had a heart ready for all of life's good and bad times. I knew someone special would need her in their life.

Maya wasn't an easy little girl to handle, but when Liv saw through her behavior and loved her through it, amazing things happened. But the funny thing about TBRI, is that it works on adults too.

After learning TBRI, my husband and I started using it on each other as well. Suddenly, in the challenges of new parenthood, we were building more connection with each other despite being stressed, overwhelmed, and exhausted in a way we'd never been before. It was healing to experience love in this new way.

In this story, Liv's kind of love helped Fletcher heal. He carried around so much guilt and shame for the way he responded to his trauma and for his struggles with Maya. But as much as Maya deserved love and understanding, Fletcher deserved the same.

If I could do one thing for every person in this world, it would be for them to learn TBRI and experience HALO the way we did. It's truly changed our lives and helped us be better parents, friends, partners, and people. If you want to take the course, you can do it online through TCU. I highly recommend it!

Even if you don't take the course, I want you to know

that you are loved and valued beyond measure. You deserve to know that you are worthy of all good things that come your way, and strong enough to handle any struggle you experience. And most of all, you are never alone. I hope these books can give you comfort on dark days and smiles on happy days, and a soft place to land no matter where you are. <3

Sending you so much love,

Kelsie

ACKNOWLEDGMENTS

Writing this book was a complete whirlwind, and I'm so thankful for everyone who came together to help me bring it to you!

My husband and children are always there for me, and having them support my writing journey is one of my life's greatest blessings.

My team, Sally and Annie, supported me by helping in the business and giving me more time to write! That extra headspace for creativity and depth helped make this story what it is. Sally also read an early draft of this book, and we have her to thank for encouraging me to make those spicy scenes last! Annie's daughter also read a chapter for the audio book and it was so fun making it a family affair!

Tricia Harden is an amazing editor and working with her is of my favorite parts of this process! I'm so thankful we met and consider her a colleague and an amazing friend.

Christina Herrera is an amazing author of sweet YA

romance, and has been an online friend for years! It was fun to work with her as she proofed this book to make it as clean as possible!

Luke Welland and Allyson Voller are a joy to work with on these audiobooks. I love knowing that my characters are in good hands for those who prefer to read an audiobook instead of digital or print versions. Dakota Hoss edits my author's note so you can hear my voice, and I'm so glad he uses his time and talents to help me in this way.

Najla Qamber designed the covers for this book, and I can't tell you how fun it is to work with her and her team! I'm in love with the covers and they're so inspiring to me as I write the story.

To the lovely souls in Hoss's Hussies, thank you for making the Facebook Group such a fun place to hang out online. I love sharing laughs, inspiration, and life with each and every one of you.

To the person reading this book, already know I love you extra because you're the kind of person who reads author's notes and acknowledgements. Thank you so much for reading Liv, Fletcher, and Maya's story. I can't wait to share the next one with you.

ALSO BY KELSIE HOSS

The Confessions Series

Confessions of a High School Guidance Counselor

Confessions of a Smutty Romance Author

Confessions of the Funny Fat Friend

The Hello Series

Hello Billionaire

Hello Doctor

Hello Heartbreaker

JOIN THE PARTY

Want to talk about Hello Billionaire with Kelsie and other readers? Join Hoss's Hussies today!

Join here: https://www.facebook.com/groups/hossshussies

ABOUT THE AUTHOR

Kelsie Hoss writes sexy romantic comedies with plus size leads. Her favorite dessert is ice cream, her favorite food is chocolate chip pancakes, and... now she's hungry.

You can find her enjoying one of the aforementioned treats, soaking up some sunshine like an emotional house plant, or loving on her three sweet boys.

You can learn more (and even grab some special merch) at kelsiehoss.com.

facebook.com/authorkelsiehoss

instagram.com/kelsiehoss

Printed in the USA
CPSIA information can be obtained
at www.ICGtesting.com
LVHW051231020824
786833LV00003B/3

VPT0000106944